Merlot in Maine

Jan Romes

WINE AND SWEAT PANTS SERIES BOOK 3

To my husband, children, grandchildren, siblings, extended family, and friends – you're a constant source of joy and I'm forever grateful to have you in my life!

Also, a big thank-you to my readers! Your feedback and words of encouragement warms my heart!

Dear Readers,

It was a leap of faith to temporarily switch from writing romance to writing women's fiction. I'm glad I jumped out of my comfort zone to create Elaina Samuels' character and those of her unruly band of cohorts – Tawny Westerfield, Stephanie Mathews, and Grace Cordray. It's been an indescribable joy. I knew I wanted to write about four quirky personalities who could laugh at themselves and make others laugh as well, but I didn't know where their stories would lead. These women had me in stitches a lot of the time, but I'll admit to a few tears too. While the humor was plentiful the message I wanted to convey through them was that life will always be unpredictable but when you surround yourself with positive energy you can survive just about anything. Elaina, Tawny, Steph, and Grace found themselves single at a time when they should've weathered most of life's storms. But there they were, in their forties, with no clear plan for their future. Fate stepped in and put them together at a cash-for-gold event. Their destinies began at that moment. They formed the No Sweat Pants Allowed – Wine Club in book one. In Sipping Sangria, book two, they affectionately referred to themselves as the 4 Hussy Homestead. I'm sure they'll come up with something even more unique in this book.

I hope you'll read on and cheer for these women as they find imaginative ways to outwit their insecurities, idiosyncrasies, mistakes of their pasts, and fears, when they start over in Portland, Maine.

Thank you for following their journeys and mine!

Much love to all of you,
Jan

'A friend is a gift you give yourself.'
~ Robert Louis Stevenson

Merlot in Maine

Chapter One

~ *Off to the rocks!* ~

"What are those?" Elaina eyed the bundle tucked under Tawny's arm.

"What do you think they are?"

Elaina did a half-eye roll. "Newspapers."

"Ding. Ding. Ding. You are correct, madam." Tawny dropped the rolled up newspapers onto an already wobbly heap in the recycle bin.

Stony, their adorable and nosy Husky, sniffed the papers, knocking some to the garage floor.

Elaina picked them up and rearranged the stack so they wouldn't fall again. Hauling the recycle bins to the curb was one of the last things she'd do before they left the house for good.

Grace came into the garage with a shoebox labeled, *Special Things.* Her gaze skimmed over Elaina and Tawny before lowering her eyes to the bin. She jerked her thumb to Tawny. "It wasn't me. It was her."

"Said every guilty person who was in on shenanigans."

Elaina snickered. "You yahoos did the opposite of what I asked you not to do."

Grace and Tawny fist-bumped.

Elaina struggled to keep a straight face. "I was the only one privy to Arden's 6:00 AM meltdowns when his newspaper wasn't on the front porch. He's going to make me wish we'd left for Maine yesterday." She glanced at the dozen or so papers still encased in plastic sleeves. "None of you get up early enough to pull off the heists. You had help."

The responsible parties mimicked locking their lips and throwing away the keys.

Steph joined them with Lula cradled in her arms. "I have an inkling what the discussion is about, but tell me anyway."

Elaina baited her hook. "*Sweat Revenge* sticking it to Arden."

Steph's eyes laughed before her mouth did. "We had to do one more job. For you. The louse had it coming. Rachel was more than happy to snatch the papers for us." She chuckled again. "Good to hear you've accepted the name of our revenge-for-hire enterprise."

"Stephhhh." Tawny gave Steph the stink eye.

"Whaaat?"

"We weren't going to nark out Rachel."

"Oops." Steph pressed her lips together but her eyes still gleamed with mirth and conspiracy.

"I'll oops-you." Tawny advanced on Steph.

Lula batted her away.

"Good cat." Steph stroked Lula's fur.

The smile Elaina tried to hold off twitched at the corners of her mouth until she had a full-face grin. Rachel from the winery always seemed to enjoy their antics. In no way did Elaina foresee her joining their chaos. Although, when they shared their tales of mischief, she'd give high-fives. "You drew her to the dark side."

"It didn't take a phenomenal amount of coaxing."

Rachel was in her twenties but had the wisdom of someone much older. When they were undecided about moving to Maine, she'd said they could be happy anywhere as long as they were together. Deep down, Rachel was one of them; an unofficial member of the No Sweat Pants Allowed – Wine Club and The 4 Hussy Homestead, which needed to be amended to five. "If Arden would've caught her in the act..." Elaina threw a hand to her forehead. "I don't even want to think about what might've happened." She huffed out a long sigh to make her point. "I can guarantee before we leave today he'll show up and browbeat me for my...your... bad behavior." Given the amount of newspapers they'd nabbed, she was surprised he didn't show up days ago to accuse her of pilfering the papers.

Tawny's mouth twitched with amusement. "You're not afraid of him."

"Not even a little." The angry confrontation Elaina had with her ex over the stalking incidents he'd staged was the first time she'd really taken him to task for being a pain. It hadn't been easy. When it was over, she was sweating profusely and her legs were shaking so hard she could barely walk away. The verbal smack-down happened two weeks ago. Since then she'd recovered and her backbone was once again rod-strong and ready to hold her up in case she needed to rip into him a second time. "It's just that I don't want anything to muck up our departure." Elaina thwarted the melancholy of leaving Cherry Ridge by changing the subject. "What's in the box, Grace?"

"You noticed the label."

"Hard not to. It's in giant letters."

Steph slung an arm around Grace's waist. "It's stuff that belonged to Brince. I'll bet there are some of Cody's things in there, too."

"It's a shoe box, not a packing crate." Grace's light blue eyes were glittered with mischief.

Tawny took a guess. "Breakable stuff?"

"Nope."

The movers emptied the house last night and now the bulk of their belongings were on the way to the northern most state in New England. Since there was no longer any furniture in the house, Elaina and crew spent the night in a hotel. They returned this morning to give their empty home one more walk-through and to retrieve the few things they left on the counter to personally tote to Maine, including Grace's mystery box.

Elaina lifted her wrist to check the time. "If we're going to make it to Albany by dark we have to get on the road."

Steph sucked in a sharp breath of air.

Elaina noted Steph's fair complexion was a lighter shade of pale; a hint she might not be dealing well with the move. Truth be told, she wasn't having an easy time of it either. Tears misted her eyes.

Grace apparently had been watching their reactions. "No blubbering babies in my car." She poked Tawny with her elbow. "You're riding with me."

Tawny sniffed.

"Okay you guys, stop it. We're starting a new life. In Maine. We agreed this was good for us, so shelve the freaking tears." Grace's voice cracked.

Elaina drew Tawny, Steph, and Grace into a quick group hug. "I'm on board with launching a new beginning but it's damn hard to drive away from our pasts."

The slam of a car door jerked them apart.

Stony barked and tried to break loose of Tawny's tight hold.

Elaina winced. "Tall, dark, and grumpy has arrived, as predicted." She squared her shoulders.

"We'll stand sentry," Tawny quipped.

"My own personal security-detail."

"You know it." Tawny hit Arden with a hard frown when he strutted into the garage with an I-own-this-place swagger.

He did own the place. Their lawyer was scheduled to hand him the keys at noon.

Arden brushed Elaina with a fierce look and then swept his critical gaze over the others. "Can Elaina and I have a minute alone?"

"For fifty bucks." Steph juggled Lula to stretch out a hand. At Elaina's raised eyebrows, she explained, "For all the grief he's put us through, the least he can do is buy our breakfast."

Arden narrowed his eyes until they were frosty blue slits.

Steph's hand remained in front of him. Tawny coughed like she had a chicken bone caught in her throat. Grace glared.

Arden's temper escalated in a blink and was hot enough it could've caused third-degree burns. "This is absurd!" He shoved a hand in his jeans pocket to get a gold money clip. Unfurling a few bills from the wad of greenbacks, he slapped them on Steph's open palm.

Lula hissed.

Stony bared his teeth with a low, threatening growl.

Arden sneered like someone held a smelly gym sock under his nose. "I hate pets."

"The price just increased."

Elaina was amazed at Steph's fearlessness. Her red-haired friend had a well-known penchant for letting men rule her world. Not this morning, however. Steph was being gritty and aggressive, and it was fun to watch.

"There's at least seventy bucks there."

"Pony up a hundred, mister."

Arden's scowl was so stiff a mere flick would've cracked his face. He pulled his anger from Steph and landed it on Elaina. "You allow this kind of behavior?"

"Yours? Or theirs?"

His protest was indecipherable as he smacked three more bills into Steph's waiting mitt. "Now leave!"

Grace scoffed and accidentally on purpose pushed against him as she sauntered off.

Arden didn't like being touched and only allowed certain people to breach his personal space, so the invasion was hilarious. Elaina pressed her lips together to stifle a laugh.

Tawny followed Grace's lead, but instead of using her body to make contact she guided Stony into him.

Arden flinched and went into a heated rant about dog hair and threatened to call the dog warden.

"Dog wardens make great lovers."

Arden chuffed out an annoyed breath at the silly, off-the-cuff remark. "There's something wrong with her, Elaina."

Tawny fired back. "There are a lot of somethings wrong with you."

Elaina lowered her lashes in a harsh squint, remembering the many times Arden had called the dog warden. If a dog barked for what he considered an inordinate amount of time, he made a call. If a dog owner walked his or her dog down their sidewalk and the dog hiked its leg on the flowering trees in front of the house, he made a call. "Still have the dog warden's number on speed-dial?"

Arden ignored the question and continued to drill Tawny with a disgusted expression.

Tawny called him a homely mongoose and walked away.

Steph fanned the loot to heckle and pranced off with Lula.

Elaina was happy to see Steph was no longer pale, and tickled that she'd one-upped Arden. He needed to be one-upped, daily.

The trio of trouble relocated to the sidewalk in front of the house.

"You didn't have to pay her." Elaina took a subtle step back so she wouldn't inhale his yummy cologne.

"They're just as stubborn as..."

"Me?" Elaina put plenty of wicked into her smile. "Yes, they certainly are." Over Arden's shoulder, she watched the three women who made life more than interesting; the women who wanted to call themselves *Sweat Revenge* – an adaptation and expanded version of *No Sweat Pants Allowed – Wine Club*. Yeah, she didn't foresee them becoming sweaty anything. Although, she was starting to perspire in Arden's presence – the way she always did when he got in her face.

Arden closed the gap between them. "I came to..." He started again. "I came to tell you..."

"I don't want to rush you, but we have to be going. What is it you want to say?"

Arden took her hand and brought it to his lips. "I'm sorry I hoodwinked you out of the house." He expelled a heavy pant of peppermint.

Elaina silently gasped. His touch still made her tremble. She connected their gazes and almost gasped again, this time out loud. Arden Wellby Samuels was as handsome as ever. His sexy blue eyes were arched by dark, bushy brows – an allure that would forever mess with the strength in her knees. His cologne was an enticement in itself. And he'd taken care of his breath with mint. Arden was one of those mouthwatering temptations that made a woman lose her inhibitions the second he smiled. Of course, once you got to know him you wanted to glue your eyes shut and seal your nostrils so his handsomeness and great smell didn't override your brain and delude you into thinking he was a catch. Elaina's strong inner-protector flashed a mental exit sign to snap her out of his pull and to replace the heady feeling with a prickle of irritation. "You didn't hoodwink me out of anything. You tried but failed miserably." She glanced at the two-story dwelling that had once been their home. "The only reason you now have the deed to the house is…" She was going to say 'because I allowed it to happen'. At that precise second the full impact of a new beginning hit her full force. "Because I decided Cherry Ridge is your town. Portland will be mine." She and her friends were the proud owners of a bed and breakfast, and the sooner they got to it the better. Excitement zapped every cell in her body. "What's the real reason for the visit?" She expected him to harangue her for the missing newspapers.

"Val quit the gym. So did Nora. I haven't heard from Brynn but with the other two gone, I'm sure she will be as well. You need to call Val and get her to reconsider. After all, it was your business. You can't leave the members high and dry."

Elaina swallowed hard. Over the course of their membership, most members had become her friends and she couldn't allow the heinous new owner to disrupt their exercise regimen or determination to get fit. "I'll make the call but I can't guarantee you'll have your employees back." From the pocket of her fleece jacket, she removed her phone and palmed it instead of scrolling the contact list. "Before I beg Val to return, I need you to swear you won't renege on the things I'm about to promise her."

The featherlike crinkles at the corners of Arden's eyes deepened. "You're going to make me regret this, aren't you?"

Elaina clicked her tongue. "Oh yeah." She moved to the far side of the garage to hold a hushed conversation with Val.

Arden struck a defensive stance with his arms crossed and feet shoulder-width apart.

A few minutes later, with monumental reluctance, she came back. "Val's in your employ once again and she'll get the others to come back, providing you accept their conditions. They want fifteen dollars an hour and a five-hundred dollar bonus at Christmas."

Arden scoffed. "Fifteen bucks an hour? It isn't factory work. It's a gym. All they have to do is watch so no one gets hurt and clean the equipment at the end of the day."

"Boy have you got a lot to learn. Owning a gym isn't babysitting and disinfecting equipment. Not by a long shot. You, of all people, should know that." The suspicions she had regarding him wanting the gym only to resell it for a much higher price raced across her mind. It was moments like these that made her hedge on leaving Cherry Ridge. "Don't make me wish I'd never sold it to you. If you run it into the ground I swear I'll come back to Ohio and beat the snot out of you."

Arden drew back at the increase in her voice and a muscle ticked at his jaw. "I'm not paying fifteen bucks an hour."

"You don't agree with the conditions?" Elaina moved her phone back and forth, inches from his face.

"Everything's negotiable." His tone was tight and the blue eyes she considered sexy, hardened.

"Wanna bet?" Elaina flicked her phone across his chin. "One last chance. Is it a yes? Or does it remain a no?"

Arden grabbed the phone from Elaina's hand and spoke in a tone equal to having his tongue dabbed with vinegar. "Val, get your butt back to work. You and the others will get fifteen bucks an hour and a Christmas bonus." He disconnected the call and handed back the phone. "I don't like being strong-armed."

"You strong-arm people all the time. What you can't handle is being on the receiving end for once."

"Once? Once?" He repeated in a shout. "You're..."

Elaina displayed the phone like it was a hand grenade and she was ready to pull the pin. "Keep it up and Val walks."

Arden scaled back his anger but the criticism continued. "You hornswaggled me out of an SUV for Landyn Macintosh."

"The SUV was part of a deal you made with Landyn. He was to give the appearance I had a stalker. He did your dirty work and you tried to welch on a promise. I made you keep your word to him."

Arden started to speak but Elaina shut him down. "He wasn't supposed to get caught. Blah. Blah. Blah."

Arden bit down on his bottom lip so hard Elaina expected it to spurt blood.

"You're not the woman I married."

"Thank the Lord!" Elaina ran a hand across the top of her head. "I still have thumbprints on my scalp from you holding me down."

"If your intention was to be funny, you botched it. Keep your day job, lady."

"I will, once I get there." Elaina jingled her car keys. "I'm off to Portland."

Arden inhaled and exhaled loudly. "You won't be happy there. They get a ton of snow."

"Seventy inches on average. I foresee skiing and snowboarding in my future."

"You're a loon."

Elaina was no longer intimidated by the financial barracuda that used to own her heart. "It takes one to know one." She stepped on her tiptoes and planted a kiss on his temple. "We weren't a good fit, Arden. I want you to know I don't harbor any ill feelings for what happened and didn't happen between us. Someday you'll find the one person who will set your soul on fire. Until then, be happy, play fair, and turn the world of finance upside down. If you're ever in Maine, stop by for a cup of coffee." She pealed with laughter when she realized what had been in Grace's shoebox. Her three besties were wearing the eye patches Grace had saved from her son's wedding. That wedding had rocked. "Speaking of rocks, it's time to head to the rocky shoreline of the Atlantic."

"We weren't talking about rocks."

Elaina laughed her way to her friends and donned an eye patch.

Chapter Two

- Delays and displays! -

Grace's blinker went on to signal another pit stop. They hadn't even crossed into Pennsylvania and this was the third rest area visit. Elaina shook her head. "We have to clear their vehicle of any and all liquids."

Steph was still wearing the eye patch. "I don't get it. I've finished two bottles of water since we left home and haven't had to go once. My stomach feels weird though."

"Are you getting car sick?"

"I don't get car sick."

"Then why are you clutching your belly?"

Steph shrugged. "I'm not sure."

The second Elaina threw the SUV into park, Steph hurried out. She dashed to the grassy area and bent at the waist.

Grace met Elaina on the sidewalk. "What's up with her?"

"Her stomach feels weird but she says she isn't sick." They watched Steph make a beeline to the restroom.

"Maybe she's got herself all worked up about the move and her body is fighting back."

Grace patted the cat carrier in an attempt to soothe Lula who was hell-bent on escaping the contraption. "Steph admitted to being scared."

"I'm scared, too. I'd be lying if I said I wasn't." Elaina was a mix of scared and excited. Both sentiments were equally hard on the nerves.

Tawny moseyed up and commented as though she'd been part of the discussion all along. "I'm not."

"Ert!" Grace took a drag off a pretend cigarette. "For the last fifty miles you've twisted my ear about how badly you need to burn one."

Over the last couple of months Tawny tried to quit smoking. She wasn't able to stop but she'd cut back. "I do need to burn one. It has nothing to do with pulling up stakes." At Elaina's raised eyebrows, she backpedaled. "Okay, maybe it's partly to blame. The bigger issue for me is Quentin and Bo. I've sent them a half-dozen text messages and got zilch in reply."

"Send a text every fifteen minutes. Sooner or later they'll get the hint that you want to talk." Elaina knew squat about kids but the bugging technique should work on just about anyone. Hopefully the Westerfield sons would have the decency to get fed up with the nonstop pings of incoming messages and reply to their mother.

"I try to give them space, but geez, how much do they need? It's been almost a month. I'm at my wits end. Your plan can't hurt." Tawny handed Stony's leash to Elaina. "First, I have to hit the Ladies room or my bladder's going to explode." She did a funky waddle-run up the sidewalk with her thighs scrunched together.

Grace chuckled. "Are we there yet?" She placed the cat carrier on the ground and untwisted the lanyard from around the handle. "Lula wasn't thrilled to be restrained in the carrier. She's really going to hate me now." Inching open the door, Grace held onto the wily cat while she snapped on a lanyard-type leash.

Lula took off on a sprint but stopped dead in her tracks when the retractable device only gave her so much leeway. She fought being limited with a series of meows and tried to bite through the polyester cord. After some unsuccessful gnawing, she turned and blinked up at Grace.

"She's cussing me out with those green eyes."

"No doubt." Elaina led Stony to the area reserved for pets.

Grace followed. "Stone-man and Lula, time to stretch your legs."

Stony galloped from tree to tree, sprinkling liquid DNA on each one.

Lula wasted most of her time trying to get free.

Stony chased a leaf that blew past him, chomped on a stick, and stared at a poodle that yipped from her master's arms.

Tawny burst onto the scene, frantic. "Steph's really not feeling good."

Elaina stretched her mouth wide with a wince. "Is she throwing up?"

"Not that I know of, but she's making a lot of racket."

"Did you tell her to stick her finger down her throat to get it over with?" Grace crouched to see what Lula was batting around. "Eww! A dead mouse."

"I banged on the stall door and asked what was wrong. She told me to go away. I think she might have cramps."

"Stone-man, I'm turning you over to the boss. Tawn', he's watered everything in sight. He has yet to do his real business."

Elaina made haste to the brick building and called out to Steph when she entered the Ladies room. "Where are you?"

An elderly woman washing her hands provided the answer. "Hon, she's in the last stall. It sounds like she's wrestling a bobcat in there." There was a glimmer of concern in her eyes. "How well can you do the limbo?"

Elaina tried not to appear baffled by the inquiry, but it wasn't a question generally asked in a public restroom. "At sixteen, I could get down low. At forty-three, who knows?"

"I saw a janitor go in the men's restroom. I could have someone get him."

"That won't be necessary. I'll do the limbo even if I need a chiropractor when I'm done."

A weak groan curbed the chitchat. "I'm coming, Steph." Elaina gave the woman a weak smile and headed to the farthest stall. "If you could open the door you would've already done so. Don't freak out, but I'm about to join you." She dropped to her knees and noted Steph's jeans pooled around her sneakers. Elaina peered under the door. "Are you stuck?"

Tears clouded Steph's eyes. "No. I'm bleeding."

"Do you need a pad or tampon?"

"That's not it." Steph's face contorted with what could only be construed as pain. "My pee is brown."

"Ohhhh." Now it made sense. Steph didn't have a stomach ache and she definitely wasn't car sick. "You might have a urinary tract infection."

"A UTI?"

"I'm guessing you've never had one."

"I have not."

"Well, you've just joined the millions of men and women who have. We'll need to get you on antibiotics ASAP. For the sake of modesty, I'm going to let you get your pants up. When you're ready I'll help you back to Grace's vehicle and we'll search my phone for the nearest ER or clinic."

"I'm sorry, Elaina. I didn't mean to make a scene."

"You didn't make a scene."

Steph whimpered. "There's so much pressure."

"Been there. Take a deep breath and blow it out. That probably won't help but it'll take your mind off it for a second or two."

Grace walked into the restroom just as Steph slid open the lock. "You're looking mighty pale there, Stephy-girl."

Elaina instructed her to take one of Steph's arms. "I'll take the other."

Steph threw up a hand seconds before they latched onto her. "Stop. I don't have a broken leg, I have a UTI."

Grace asked for Elaina's opinion. "Is this a sign of bad things to come?"

"No. It's a sign she needs a good flushing."

Grace stretched to get a look around Steph.

"Not that kind of flushing."

Steph's knees buckled.

* * *

Elaina and Grace took turns relieving Tawny from pet duty while they waited for Steph to be seen by the doctor. The clinic was small and there were enough patients in the lobby to fill all the chairs.

"We're not going to make Albany by dark." Steph hugged herself as if trying to control the pain.

Elaina knew what her friend was going through. It had been a long time since she'd had a UTI but it was hard to forget the discomfort they brought. "No worries. Really. It doesn't have to be Albany. Although, if everything goes smoothly from here on out we'll make it." She uncapped the bottle of water she'd gotten from the gas station across the street and handed it to Steph. "Drink up."

Steph waved it away. "You're a masochist."

"I don't mean to be. It's going to hurt to go to the bathroom." Elaina held out the bottle again. "The doc is going to tell you to drink water. You might as well get a head start."

Steph grumbled "masochist" again and grabbed the bottle in a pretend huff. Barely wetting her lips with a sip, she set the bottle aside.

Tawny drooped into the empty seat beside Elaina.

"Stony's being a bear."

The eyes of the little girl sitting across from them doubled in size. Kids were known to take things literally, forcing a clarification from Tawny. "He's a big, hairy dog who's as grouchy as a bear."

The blonde tyke giggled and the woman next to her mouthed the words, "Thank you." Perhaps in appreciation for the distraction?

They all seemed to notice the bandage wrapped around the child's hand at the same time. Tawny nudged Elaina with the side of her knee as if prompting her to say something profound. Instead, Steph jumped in with both feet - figuratively. "Oh my. What happened?" She must've realized the error and overcorrected. "I mean with Stony, not your hand." At Tawny's pointed look Steph picked up a magazine and thumbed through it.

Elaina covered Steph's snafu with some playful imagery. "Our cat, Lula, thinks she's a tiger. You should see her chase Stony. He runs but he isn't scared. When he's had enough he puts a paw on her to hold her down. Did I mention my roommates are monkeys? It's like living with a circus." She snickered quietly remembering the oath she'd spouted the day they met – 'Not my circus, not my monkeys'. Thank goodness the vow had been short-lived.

Again, the wee one giggled. "I love monkeys."

"You never know what they're going to do." Elaina jabbed Tawny with her elbow. "Especially this one."

A nurse stepped to the middle of the room. "Stephanie Mathews."

Steph walked hunched over and conversed with the nurse.

The nurse went back to the desk and flipped through charts.

Steph returned to her perch and whispered from the side of her mouth, "I just threw another wrench in the plan to get to Albany."

The nurse announced the next patient, which happened to be the little girl.

"That's me, Mommy."

On the way to the examination room, the mother thanked Steph and told her she was awesome. Then she gave Elaina a high-five. "What an incredible group of monkeys."

"They'll do in a pinch."

Tawny also picked up a magazine and buried her face in one of the articles. "You willingly joined the circus."

"I blame wine. It distorted my judgment." Elaina's cell phone plinked with a text message from Grace. She read it for Tawny and Steph to hear. "Lula threw up." She grabbed her purse. "My guess is she ate too much grass or she's upchucking hairballs – Lula, not Grace."

"A little grass never hurt anyone." Tawny made big eyes at the old guy who sat across the aisle and two seats over. He'd homed in on them the second they sat down.

"Not everyone gets your sense of humor." They didn't actually smoke weed. Tawny liked to give the impression they did. Sometimes her silly remarks drew a laugh. Now that they were out of state, Elaina didn't want the good-humored fib to rally the attention of Pennsylvania's men in blue. The last thing they needed was to be tailed and nailed by an unmarked police car as they made their way toward New York. "Behave, Tawn'." Elaina headed outside to assist Grace with the heaving feline.

"Take her." Grace shoved the cat at Elaina and then displayed nasty scratch marks on the side of her hand. "She peeled out when she got sick." Stony's leash was wrapped around her other wrist. "Ever try to chase a cat with a dog in tow? Not fun."

"They're a handful." Elaina held Lula away from her to check her eyes. You could tell if a human was sick by their eyes. Why not a cat? "She doesn't look sick-sick. Her nose is cold and wet. I'm going to give her an antacid."

"Can cats have antacids?"

"The unflavored ones. I'll only give her half. She'll never know."

"Let's fix you up." Elaina opened the hatch of the Escalade and rummaged through the tote filled with items from the medicine cabinet. She tossed Grace an alcohol swab to dab on the scratches and continued to search for the antacids. "They have to be in here."

"Looking for these?" Grace held up a plastic bottle with a red cap. "Tawny had them stuffed in the door compartment and hidden under a pair of gloves."

Elaina snickered. "Gotta watch her like a hawk." Opening a can of moist cat food, she stirred in crushed antacid, and hooked the much-hated leash to Lula's collar. "It's time to chow down, my furry friend."

Stony tried to block the cat from the food.

"Stone-man, back up."

The command was obeyed right away. Elaina slipped him a treat.

"Are you sure you didn't have pets growing up? You seem to have a special touch."

"My parents weren't fond of pets and neither was Arden. He'd be happy if they all became extinct." Elaina tweaked the softness of Lula's ears. "I had to love animals from afar. That's no longer the case." She never thought she'd get so attached to a dog and cat, but Stony and Lula were a big part of her life now.

"You should become a veterinarian."

"Wow. I can see it now. A bed-and-breakfast slash winery slash veterinary clinic. That's a lot of hats to wear." She poured water for Stony and Lula from a plastic jug they'd brought along.

"Did you just say..."

Elaina finished the thought. "Wow? Yes. I said wow." She bounced with a laugh.

"Brat."

"Definitely a brat."

"Are you seriously considering a winery?"

"According to Steph we have grapes. Why not put them to good use? It'll be a while before we can turn them into wine though."

"A very long time. If I remember correctly she said it was a spindly arbor."

"She also said it needs some tender loving care. Who better to give some TLC than the 4 Hussy Homesteaders?"

"That should be our brand. The 4 Hussies."

Elaina mulled over the name. It fit on so many levels.

"Not bad but it needs something else. Maybe by the time we get to Maine we'll know."

Grace leaned against the SUV with a reflective look. "I have to tell you something."

"Shoot."

Grace took a deep breath and let it out as a lengthy exhale. "I almost backed out of leaving Cherry Ridge."

"Really?"

Grace turned to fully face Elaina. "I hate change. I fight that sucker hard. The bank was forever changing things to stay current. Anytime they updated their systems I went into a mild state of panic. I was able to fake my way through until I caught on to the latest and greatest way of doing business. Quitting my job and moving to Maine are two radical changes for me. I'm ready to embrace my future but first I had to talk myself down from a mental ledge."

"I didn't know you felt this way. You should've said something."

"You're a fixer, Elaina. That's what you do. I had to fix this myself. I had to do some fancy talking in my head to calm down. The farther we got from home the more I accepted my decision to start over. Silly, huh?"

"It isn't silly. This all happened so fast that it's a bit overwhelming, even for me. When you think about it, in six short months our worlds have been turned upside down. In a good way, but still, who wouldn't freak out a little?" Elaina smiled. "Are you seriously on board with going to Maine? Because if you're not, I'll turn this wagon train around and we'll head back to Ohio."

"I'm on board. I talked to Brince about it while you three were lollygagging inside the clinic." Grace lifted her shoulders in a shrug at Elaina's surprised look. "I'm not daffy. I said I talked to him. I didn't say he answered. Although, after discussing it with him, a sweet peace came over me. I'm taking it as his nod of approval."

Elaina thought it perfectly normal for Grace to consult her late husband. She did the same thing, only with her parents. In fact, before she ever put it out there to the others about the opportunity in Maine, she had a lengthy chat with her folks. It had been a one-sided conversation but afterward she felt even more confident that The Pine Tree state was where she'd soon call home. "He answered, Grace. That's why you're here." She looked around. "In Erie, Pennsylvania; waiting for Steph to get checked out so we can continue on."

Grace enveloped her in a hug. "I think Brince also had a hand in me being at that cash-for-gold event so you and I would meet."

Elaina was thrilled that she and her friends didn't hold back when they were genuinely moved to show they cared. Happiness coated her words. "Brince definitely put you in that jewelry store, as well as helped you climb down from that mental ledge today."

Over Grace's shoulder, Elaina spied the other half of the wine club coming toward them. Tawny had hold of Steph's arm. She smiled. They were four goofballs. Four sassy women meant to partner up and seize the day in whatever way possible – even if they raised an eyebrow or two with their antics and affection.

Chapter Three

~ Guard me! ~

At first, it was just a few drops. Now rain was coming down so hard it was like driving through a never-ending car wash. Sheets of water cascaded across the windshield, making it difficult for the wipers to keep up and hard to see.

Elaina's phone rang. In that split-second before she could say if it wasn't Grace they weren't going to answer, Steph pushed the button on the navigation screen to take the call.

"Hey, Rachel, how are you?" Steph said, not sensing it wasn't a good time to chat. The death grip Elaina had on the steering wheel and her constant grumbling about the deteriorating weather should've been giant clues. Then again, Steph still wasn't feeling up to par and had been in her own little world, playing games on her phone.

"Good. Good," Rachel repeated. "How's the trek east?"

"We've had a couple of bumps in the road but the

wheels are still turning." The figure of speech should've prompted the question 'what kind of bumps'. It didn't – at least not directly.

"So y'all are doing okay?"

There was an odd nuance to Rachel's voice. Steph must've completely snapped out of whatever things were going on in her head and away from the phone games that had held her mesmerized. She gave Elaina a puzzled look.

Elaina could only spare a quick glance at Steph since cars were cutting in front of her in an attempt to get off the interstate. Cars and trucks now lined the berm of the road to wait out the deluge of water that was making it increasingly dangerous to be on the highway. "Other than Steph having a UTI and driving in torrential rain, things are peachy."

"I'm a bit nauseous, too." Steph went back to holding her stomach.

"What? Why didn't you say something?" Elaina inquired at the same time a semi-truck barreled by going faster than the normal speed, seemingly unaffected by the rainstorm. The water kicked up by the truck sloshed hard against the SUV. It felt like a giant push to the right. Elaina did some swift maneuvering to avoid sideswiping a wide-load truck that had pulled over and was hogging all of the berm and a small part of the lane.

"I didn't want to cause another delay."

"Are the meds they prescribed messing with you?"

Steph pinched her nose. "It's not the meds. It's the lingering smell of garlic."

"Ooooo. I love garlic." Rachel went on to say she used a lot of minced garlic tonight when she made mango salsa.

"I'm a big fan of garlic. In a confined space it's overpowering. We ate dinner at one of those Italian fast food places where you get unlimited garlic bread sticks with your meal." Steph scoffed. "I loaded up on those things, now I'm paying the price. I'm surprised Elaina hasn't complained."

"Garlic's supposed to be good for you and keep away evil spirits." Rachel sounded more like the fun-loving, easy-going woman they'd met at the winery, instead of someone who might possibly be holding something back.

"Can it stop this ridiculous rain?" Steph asked with a laugh.

"Not sure a stinky herb can influence the weather."

Steph was quick to inform Rachel that garlic wasn't an herb. "It's considered a vegetable and I believe it's from the lily family."

Elaina was tense and had heard enough about garlic. She flicked on her turn signal to warn Grace she was taking the next exit. "Rach', are you at work?"

Rachel hem-hawed, stirring even more curiosity. "It's my day off. I'm vegging out on the couch – all by myself – with a bottle of Dom Perignon."

Elaina noted the emphasis on 'all by myself.' She also thought it was peculiar for a person alone to open an expensive bottle of champagne. "What are you celebrating?"

"What do you mean?"

"You're drinking Dom."

"Umm..."

There was a muffled voice in the background. Yeah, Rachel wasn't by herself. Why go to lengths to convince them otherwise?

Steph came up with a viable reason. "You got a pay raise."

Rachel's small laugh barely qualified as mirth. "You might say that."

Elaina waited for more information; none was offered. In fact, the conversation came to an awkward halt.

Steph tapped Elaina's arm and dipped her brows with question.

Elaina bunched her shoulders in a shrug. "Sweet about the pay raise. Steph and I just lifted pretend glasses to join in your party. Clink." She drove into the parking lot of a motel. "Thanks for checking on us. The rain isn't letting up and I've been afraid to blink for the past hour for fear of not being able to react in time. My eyes are dry and Steph's going to have to pry my fingers off the steering wheel. We're calling it a night. Tomorrow we plan to check out Vermont and New Hampshire. Wednesday we should arrive in Maine. We'll call you to let you know we made it. Until then, party on. One more thing – a while back when we were at the winery we invited you to join us in the hot tub at my house. You couldn't make it because you had to put in a few more hours at work. We no longer own the house or the hot tub. Arden hated the hot tub. I'll bet he'd give it to you if you asked. He'd probably even have it delivered to your place to make sure it's gone."

There was another stretch of inaudible conversation on Rachel's end. Elaina surmised that whoever was with her, liked the idea of a hot tub. "We've got to go. Tawny and Grace are now standing under the covered entrance of the motel motioning for us to hurry up. Give the hot tub some serious thought."

"I will. Thank you. Tell Tawny and Grace I said hello. Y'all have fun."

"You, too." Elaina almost added, "With whomever you're trying to hide." She didn't want to make things uncomfortable between them so she kept it as a thought only.

Steph unlatched her seatbelt. "Miss Rachel Bigelow wasn't being entirely straightforward. Question is, why?"

"She might not want us to know she has an overnight visitor of the male persuasion." Elaina looked at the clock on the dash. It was almost midnight.

"Who are we to judge?"

"Exactly." Elaina tossed her key fob into the bottom of her purse to keep it from getting wet. "We're old enough to be her mom. She probably thinks we would frown on her having..."

"Don't say sex. My hormones are bouncing all over the place these days. I might attack the first guy I see."

"You might want to wait for your UTI to clear up."

Steph snorted a laugh. "Right."

* * *

"We'd like two rooms with two double beds." Droplets of water rolled from Grace's hair and onto the counter.

Steph shifted restlessly from foot to foot. With every movement there was a squishing sound. On the way into the motel she'd tried to avoid a huge puddle by doing an ungainly leap which landed her smack dab in the middle of the water.

Elaina blotted moisture from her face with a tissue.

"Sorry, ma'am, we only have one room left. Due to the horrendous weather, we've had an influx of guests."

Grace turned to get their opinions. "Do you want to double-up in double beds?"

Tawny yawned. "At this point, I'd double-up on a single bed." Her shoulders sagged and there were dark circles beneath her eyes. "I hope you're pet-friendly."

The guy's mustache twitched. "Again, sorry." He stretched an arm toward the sign at the end of the counter that stated in bold letters NO ANIMALS ALLOWED. In fine print below, there was an exception: Service animals permitted.

In principle, Stony was an emotional support animal. He did good things for Elaina's mood and he definitely kept Tawny on an even keel...until he was in the mood to harass the cat. And Lula? She was her own cat; in service to no one.

"Can you bend the rules for tonight?" Tawny sounded as exhausted as she looked.

The authority in the clerk's voice escalated. "The owners would fire me on the spot!"

Tawny's sluggish gaze coasted to Elaina. "Now what?"

"Not to worry. I'll sleep in the Escalade with Stony and Lula. The front seats recline and I can lower the backseat to give them more room."

"I can't let you do that."

"I'm too tired to argue and so are you. I'm bunking with Stone-man and our crafty cat. End of discussion." Elaina smiled at the clerk. "Would I be able to borrow or buy or rent a pillow and blanket?"

"Certainly. You can borrow them." He smiled and then winked. "And for the inconvenience of sleeping in your vehicle, I'll give you a voucher for a free stack of pancakes. You can redeem it at the restaurant across the street." He disappeared behind the door in back of the desk and returned with a clear drawstring bag stuffed with bedding.

Elaina thanked the man and hefted the bag over her shoulder. "Ladies, I'll see you early in the morning."

"Is it safe for you to sleep outside?" Grace asked.

The clerk advised them they had a security guard who patrolled the parking lot all night long.

All night long? Was it a high crime area? Elaina wouldn't dwell on the questions. "Get some shut-eye, peeps." Proceeding outside, she was happy to find the gusher of rain had diminished to sprinkles. When she got to her vehicle, she set Lula free of the carrier and clamped on the lanyard. "It's time to stroll, girl." Stony flattened his nose against the passenger-side window. "You're next, buddy."

Walking Lula back and forth under the amber lights of the parking lot, Elaina waved at the gawking security guard as he passed by. "Of course I look ridiculous," she mumbled through a smile, "not many people walk cats."

The second time the security guard drove by she was lugging Stony away from the puddles he wanted to play in. Too bad she didn't have a parrot to parade around to blow the guards' mind on his next pass through. Dang. Fatigue was making her goofy.

Elaina was loading Stony back in the vehicle when her peripheral caught movement by a large bush. Alarm prickled its way up her spine and the hair on her neck stood on end. "Come on, you ferocious dog, let's walk for another five minutes." She said it loud enough to dissuade anyone with ill intentions. In truth, all Stony would do was lather the person with dog spit but at least he looked the part of a threatening mongrel.

The person stepped into the beam cast by the parking lot light. She couldn't make out a face. All Elaina could see was a not-so-tall figure wearing a grey hoodie. Where was the security guard?

Stony wagged his tail.

"That's it," she garbled with sarcasm, "make friends with the bad guy."

The hooded individual striding toward her, spoke baby talk. "Who's a good dog?"

Elaina breathed a sigh of relief. "You scared the crap out of me." The tension that tightened her shoulders, let loose. "I was about to tell Stone-man to sink his teeth into you."

Tucked under Tawny's arm were a pillow and blanket. "He wouldn't hurt his master." She bent to kiss his head.

"Right, Stony?" Straightening, she met Elaina's lifted eyebrows with a toothy grin. "I couldn't let you sleep out here while I snooze away in a warm motel room. It wouldn't be right."

"Translation: Steph's snoring so loud she's rattling the windows."

"She's not asleep. She's in the bathroom, repeatedly saying "Oww." Tawny opened the passenger door and lowered the seat to a reclining position. "That's not why I came to join you. I don't care if they do have a security guard. A woman alone in a car, in the dark, isn't safe. So there will be two women. We'll guard each other."

"I'm happy to have you," Elaina admitted.

The security guard pulled his Jeep beside them with his windshield wipers going full blast. There wasn't enough rain to warrant full blast so the wipers scraped the glass. He lowered the window and roved his curiosity over them. "Randall tells me you'll be staying in your car tonight."

Tawny glanced at Elaina first and then gave the man a stern look. "That wouldn't be the case if our pets were allowed inside the motel. It's probably good that they aren't, because they're fiercely protective. If one of your other guests, or anyone for that matter, made a wrong move, Stonewall Jackson Westerfield would be all over them. And Lula is one testy cat. Those claws can do a lot of damage. Our friend Grace held onto her too long today and she's now sporting some ugly marks on her wrist."

Elaina bit the inside of her cheek to thwart the laugh

that wanted out. Tawny was giving the guy fair warning not to mess with them.

The guard had the nerve to ask, "Where do they get their bad tempers?"

Tawny pointed to Elaina. She cupped her mouth with her other hand like she was sharing a secret. "She can be a real..."

Elaina tugged Tawny's hair to reinforce the idea she was a badass.

The guy looked skeptical.

Bright headlights sliced into the semi-darkness, signaling the arrival of another guest.

"Rest assured I'll keep an eye on things, ladies."

Tawny did a half-turn and muttered just loud enough for Elaina to hear. "Who's going to keep an eye on him?"

"Thanks. We appreciate you and the motel for considering our wellbeing. Have a good evening." Elaina waited until the Jeep was well away before she released the pent-up guffaw. "Okay then. That was interesting."

"He's probably a great guy. In case he isn't, I had to let him know we have wild animals at our disposal."

"He totally bought it, Tawn'. Not."

* * *

"Rough night?" Steph poured maple syrup in the shape of a heart on her French toast.

"It was fine until I was jerked awake by a clap of thunder so loud it shook the Escalade. The wind kicked up and it felt like we were going to tip over any minute.

To add to the fun, there was a spectacular lightning extravaganza that I could see even with my eyes closed." Tawny stabbed a sausage link like it was the guilty party instead of the weather.

Steph licked her sticky thumb and handed the syrup dispenser to Elaina. "I didn't hear a thing."

"Lucky you. Stony was terrified. He panted hard and tried to climb in front with me and Tawny. Lula meowed through the entire storm. I never realized how confining a vehicle could be until I couldn't see out the windows because it was raining so hard. Good thing I'm not claustrophobic."

"Raining *cats* and *dogs*, was it?" Steph teased between chews.

Elaina studied the impish redhead. "You must be feeling better."

"It's amazing what a good night's sleep will do."

"The powerful dose of antibiotics might've had something to do with it, too."

"True. If you hadn't insisted we stop at that clinic I'd still be crying the blues."

"You needed care. We got you care."

"It's what we do." Tawny raised her coffee cup. "To Steph surviving a UTI, and to me and Elaina not waking up with a horrendous stiff neck."

Grace wanted in on the action. "What about me?"

"To Grace not throttling me for stealing her bacon."

"You didn't steal my..."

Tawny swiped all three strips of bacon from Grace's plate.

Grace narrowed her eyes. She refrained from reading Tawny the riot act since the waitress showed up at that exact moment with a fresh pot of coffee.

"Where are you gals from?"

"Elaina, Steph, and I are from Ohio. The bacon thief," Grace jerked her thumb to Tawny, "is from there too, but we don't claim her."

"Sure you do." Tawny dramatically chomped one of the crispy strips.

The grill cook dinged the bell from the kitchen. His loud voice boomed through the dining area. "Order up."

"I'm being summoned." The waitress grinned at Grace. "I'll bring you more bacon."

Tawny and Steph slid out of the booth and took off for the Ladies room.

Elaina watched them leave. "Clowns."

Grace pasted on a scowl. "I can't believe she took my food."

"She knows what buttons to push."

"Well, I know her triggers too."

Grace would retaliate. It might take a day or a week but she'd get even. However she chose to seek revenge would be hilarious. "Yes you do." Elaina shifted to get comfortable. "Have you heard from Cody? Are the newlyweds and Karina still coming for Christmas?"

Grace's face brightened. "I had a text message waiting for me when I woke this morning." She smiled. "My wandering nomad of a son has found his happy place in Italy with Isabella and Karina. They booked their vacation flights to Maine yesterday. They'll be here on

December twenty-third. He mentioned a while back that his in-laws would be coming along. It seems they've changed their minds. He didn't say why." She left her side of the table to cloak Elaina with a swift hug. "I can't believe I have a daughter-in-law and granddaughter."

"They took to you like they've known you forever."

"Thanks for letting them visit."

"Grace, you don't need my permission for anyone to visit. You're part owner of the bed and breakfast."

"It hasn't sunk in."

"Same here. It feels like a dream, but it isn't. We actually own a bed and breakfast." Elaina searched her purse for her iPad and tapped the app containing her eBooks." She slid the tablet across the table. "I've been reading how to run a successful B & B. The book is filled with valuable information. When I'm done I'll pass it on to you."

"You swept over the fact we'll be spending the holidays with my son and his family, while we also tend to our other guests. Hopefully the place will be full which means things might get a little crazy."

"There are four of us. We'll manage. It's important for you to spend time with family."

Tawny and Steph returned.

Tawny smoothed her napkin across her lap. "You won't want to hear this, but all that rain we got last night and the stuff beating down on us now, is supposed to change to snow the closer it gets to the New England states."

"You came out of the restroom with a weather update?"

Grace had taken a drink of orange juice and choked on a laugh.

Tawny whacked her on the back. "It's the happening place to get the low-down on just about everything. Belinda loves Robbie. For a good time call Jazzy. Snow flurries in the northeast."

"Bwahaha. You're a constant riot of wit." Grace wrinkled her nose to drive home the light-hearted sarcasm.

"You don't appreciate comedic talent."

"I do when I hear it."

They'd had a sampling of snow and cold in Ohio but Elaina wasn't in the frame of mind to tackle the serious stuff. She'd rather Old Man Winter held off until they were safely tucked into the bed and breakfast. "We'll be driving into snow?"

Tawny burst into song to the tune of country superstar, Lorrie Morgan's classic hit *What Part of No Don't You Understand*. She cleverly switched up the lyrics. "What part of snow don't you understand?"

Grace apparently wasn't ready for the fluffy white stuff either. She curled her upper lip in a sneer. "Snow? Really?"

"Would I lie?"

Steph shook her head no but she said "yes".

Tawny slid a hand under her placemat to give Steph an inconspicuous middle finger.

Their waitress returned with a plate of bacon and another pot of coffee. She sat the bacon in front of Grace.

"You're awesome." Grace moved the plate to the

farthest side of the table, out of Tawny's reach.

Elaina noted the waitress's name tag and held out her cup. "Norma, today is one of those days where I need all the caffeine I can get."

"I hear ya. Most days are like that for me. I sneak into the kitchen every chance I get and gulp down a few swallows. I'm an insomniac who usually doesn't fall asleep until it's time to get up in the morning. Then I rely on coffee to get me through my shift."

Tawny dared to go for the bacon and stretched an arm across Grace. "I used to be an insomniac. These days I sleep like a baby. Last night was the exception. That was some storm."

Grace chopped Tawny's arm to discourage bacon thievery.

"How did you stop being an insomniac?"

"I moved in with Elaina."

Norma's interest toggled back and forth between Elaina and Tawny. "I don't understand the cure."

"She's better than any sleeping pill could ever be."

Elaina twirled a finger by her ear to indicate Tawny was loco.

Grace piped up with the short version of how they became friends and then added, "What Tawny is trying to say is that Elaina took in three strays, five if you count Stony and Lula."

"I'm still not getting a clear picture."

"We were misfits who were forced to start over." Grace lowered her voice. "I'm a widow. When Elaina found me, I was falling apart. Tawny had recently divorced Grady and was fraught with the knowledge he would soon dump her beloved Stonewall Jackson and she wouldn't be able to take him." Before Norma could ask who Stonewall Jackson was, Grace provided a clarification. "He's the most lovable Husky you'll ever meet. I digress. Steph had been tossed aside by her fiancé. Elaina's hubby chipped away at their happiness once he made his first million, then he let a midlife crisis finish them off. There we were – four oddballs who didn't have a clue how to start over. Elaina offered a plan that involved wine, sweat pants, and a place to stay. Essentially she saved our miserable butts. As a result, we all sleep better."

"Wow!" Norma appeared impressed.

Elaina snickered. "It was the other way around. They rescued me. Without them I'd still be shuffling around in that big house in Ohio, alone and ignorant to the fact there was joy to be had even when I didn't think there was."

"She's so profound." Tawny bumped Elaina's shin with her shoe. "And modest. Without her help, who knows where I'd be." She displayed her hand. "Look. I have fingernails. When I was married to Grady I bit those suckers until my fingers bled." She pulled an opened pack of cigarettes from the side pocket of her purse. "I used to burn two packs a day. Because of blondie here, I've almost kicked the habit. These days I might have one cigarette; two at the most. That's quite an accomplishment for someone who enjoys smoking but knows the tar in my lungs isn't healthy. Elaina's been a godsend." Tawny was on a roll. "Did I mention she makes me eat salad and asparagus? But she's no saint. The witch made me sleep outside last night. That's a whole other story."

Norma's forehead creased as though she was trying to determine if the tale was true or a steaming pile of B.S.

"She's such a drama queen," Elaina stated matter-of-factly.

"Damn skippy, she is. The fact remains we all sleep better because our lives are on track, thanks to you." Steph leaned against Elaina for a second.

Norma's smile was weak. "Where were you a year ago when Jethro decided the grass was greener in someone else's yard? Don't get me wrong, I have friends. However, they weren't comfortable with me being single while they were tied down. Instead of rediscovering the freedom of being on my own, I jumped into a rebound relationship with Maury."

Elaina kept her voice warm with understanding. "Many of us have gone down that same road, even with the support of good friends. It's almost as if we have to prove to ourselves we're not used up. Does that make sense?"

"It makes perfect sense."

Elaina bared her soul. "I jumped into a relationship with Michael, even though I swore to stay away from men for a year or two. He was a great guy. My heart just wasn't ready. He wasn't ready either. It took us a while to figure it out."

Steph was quick to offer a motive. "I blame hormones."

Tawny, always the nurse and wealth of biological facts, spouted hormones did what they were supposed to do. Normally. She expanded on the thought. "Sometimes though, those wily secretions undermine common sense. Instead of urging caution where the opposite sex is concerned, they toss us right into the lion's den. All logic flees and we try to entice the first lion who smiles at us."

"Secretions sounds disgusting. And lions don't smile," Steph corrected, "they roar."

"Roar. Smile. Whatever. My point being that thanks to hormones we don't always make the best choices."

Grace made an off-the-wall remark. "Do you know what they call a cross between a male lion and a tigress? A liger."

Tawny's eyebrows bumped together. "Talk about random. Where did that come from?"

Grace raised her hands, palm-side-up. "What can I say? You said lion and tigress. My mind came up with liger."

Norma giggled. "No one can accuse you ladies of being stuffy. You're hilarious."

"Not on purpose," Elaina suggested.

"Whether it's deliberate or not, this thing you've got going on between you, works. I'd love to be part of it."

Elaina searched her purse for a pen and scribbled down their new address on a napkin. "When you're ready to get away from it all for a while, stop by for a visit. We'd love to have you." She also wrote down her cell phone number and handed the napkin to Norma. "And for those times when you need someone to listen, give me a call."

"I'm just a waitress you met in a restaurant in eastern Pennsylvania."

Elaina gestured around the table. "Grace wasn't stretching the truth when she said we met at a cash-for-gold event. It goes to show you friendship can be found anywhere. Even in a restaurant in eastern P.A." She stuck out her hand. "I'm Elaina."

Grace, Tawny, and Steph also introduced themselves.

"You're taking a risk by putting yourselves out there for every Tom, Dick, and Harry." A smile crimped the corners of Norma's mouth and she modified the cliché. "I mean for every Norma, Evelyn, and Rita."

Rita. The name stirred the memory of one of Elaina's former gym members who'd sold wreaths to raise funds for a needy family. To help out, Elaina purchased twelve. Rita had seemed overwhelmed by the kindness and doled out two hugs. She also offered to cover her in prayer and asked what she could specifically pray for. Elaina had responded, "For me to make good choices." Some of her choices since then hadn't been well thought out, but things turned out okay. *Thank you, Rita, for intervening on my behalf. Thank you, Lord, for placing Rita in my path; also for doing the same with Tawny, Grace, and Steph.* She smiled up at Norma. *And for Norma. You put her in our paths for a reason. To cover her in prayer? Or to let her know that if she surrounds herself with good friends who have her back and occasionally make her laugh, the pain of heartache will pass?*

Steph broke into Elaina's introspection with something so deep it prompted a larger-than-life smile from everyone. "Living safely under a rock isn't living. It's simply existing." She toyed with her silverware. "We've learned to trust our instincts. There's a story about Elaina having a stalker."

Elaina subtly shook her head. The stalker bit wasn't worth repeating.

"Yes. I'm going to tell it. I want to make a point about how you went with your gut." Steph propped her elbows on the table. "Long story short – Elaina had a suspicion who was stalking and why. She's one intuitive woman, let me tell ya. The guy lurking in the shadows turned out to be exactly who she thought he was – a pawn of her ex-husband."

"Moving along." Elaina wasn't comfortable with anyone singing her praises. "I could go for a glass of wine and a pair of comfy sweat pants right now. I'll do the next best thing and order a tall coffee to go."

"You're not seriously considering driving in this nonsense, are you?" Norma directed their attention to the window where rivulets of rain ran down the glass. "It's supposed to storm all day, with heavy rain, high winds, and possibly hail."

"We don't have much choice. The motel across the street isn't pet-friendly, hence why Tawny and I slept in my SUV." Elaina used her right hand to massage the knotted muscles in her left shoulder. "It was a one-time deal. No more sleeping in vehicles."

"Hold on. I have an idea but Sammy's giving me the evil eye. He's the owner and cook. Be back in a bit." Norma shuffled off.

Grace confessed the thought of driving in the rain again made her anxious, especially in the hills.

"It's nerve-wracking but we aren't making progress by staying here. Let's tick off a few more miles. Who knows? We might run across a motel or hotel that accepts pets. But it's up to you guys. Majority rules."

Grace rubbed her forehead.

Tawny tapped the handle of her coffee cup.

Steph gave the window her full focus.

Norma delivered plates of eggs and sausage to a nearby table. She winked at Elaina and went back to the kitchen for more.

Tawny finally said, "We should keep going."

Steph sifted air through her teeth. "It has to stop raining sometime."

Grace wasn't afraid to object. "It'll stop when it turns to snow."

Tawny reminded them where they were headed. "Snow will be part of our world for at least six months; maybe seven. We're from Ohio. We got snow too. Granted we didn't get as much as Maine, but we'll adjust."

Elaina swallowed past a clog of indecision. They were placing their trust in her. She thought about the good choice thing. Proceeding in foul weather wasn't the best option.

Norma returned with their bill. "My brother and sister-in-law operate a bed and breakfast a mile off the beaten path. They designate one room as pet-friendly." She cleared Elaina and Tawny's plates from the table. "They sanitize it to the hilt after their guests check out. There's no lingering pet dander or pesky fleas left behind. I made a call from the kitchen. They're full except for that one room. Actually, it's a suite with two king-size beds. It's yours if you want it."

Elaina sat up from a slouch. "We'll take it.

"One small catch. It's a bit pricey."

"I'm sure it's worth every penny. Thank you, Norma. We owe you."

Norma scoffed at the notion. "My kin are the ones who owe me for sending business their way." Her gaze jetted to the window again. "It's dumping so much rain there won't be any leaves left on the trees. Once the leaves are gone, tourist season is over. Kaput. Their business practically dries up until spring. Unlike the east and west coasts we don't have a lot to draw those seeking adventure year round. When cold and snow arrives all we have is an inland lake that freezes over for ice fishing. The locals are the only ones who enjoy it."

"But you have a restaurant that serves great food." Steph shrugged. "Did that sound as lame to you as it did to me?"

Grace raised her eyebrows animatedly.

Elaina pondered the information. They were embarking on an enterprise too that was seasonal and depended wholly on tourism. Sure the northeast was known for some excellent skiing and snowboarding, but if Mother Nature was stingy with the frozen flakes few customers would come. The ski resorts were able to make powder, although many skiers preferred the real stuff. Buying the bed and breakfast had been a hasty decision fueled by emotion, but Elaina didn't regret it. To make it a lucrative investment though, they'd have to do some careful and creative management. "We're thrilled to stay another day. Maybe the rain will stop long enough for us to get a good look around."

Norma explained that there were some remarkable antique stores on the main street in town.

"Speaking of antiques," Steph squinted at Tawny, "is that a grey hair?"

Chapter Four

- *Quite the pickle!* -

The rain weakened to a mist although there were plenty of dark, heavy clouds above to warn the madness was far from over. Any second now Elaina expected those clouds to bump together and spill their contents. According to the local television station, flash flooding was taking place in low-lying areas along the route they'd planned to take. Elaina didn't relish the thought of their vehicles getting swept away by rushing water so staying put made even more sense.

Stony ambled to the door and whimpered.

"I took you out a half hour ago. You can't possibly have to go again." Tawny remained in the recliner with her nose buried in one of the tabloid magazines she'd picked up in town.

Unable to check into the bed and breakfast until three, they followed Norma's advice and got to know the little town surrounded by hills. Between downpours they darted in and out of antique shops, five and dime stores, an old-time ice cream parlor, and a bookstore where Tawny bought a stack of gossip magazines. Elaina ribbed her about them but Tawny defended the purchase. 'How else will I find out which famous celebrity gave birth to a two-headed toad?'

Stony thrashed his tail and went down on his belly with his bottom in the air.

Still, Tawny read on.

Getting nowhere, Stony plodded over to her and stared until she paid attention.

"I'm not taking you outside to play in the puddles."

Elaina stirred sweetener into her cup of orange tea and watched the exchange between two strong-willed creatures.

Tawny playfully pushed him away with her toes. Stony jumped but resumed his doggie stare.

"Go away, furball."

"She's afraid she'll melt, Stone-man." Elaina pulled at Tawny's sock to tease as she passed by on her way to grab her fluorescent green parka from a hook by the door where it was drying. "Let's go nose around."

Stony ran to the door and glanced back at Tawny. Elaina determined the look to be his version of a gloat.

The second they stepped outside they were met by a blustery wind and a gloomy drizzle. Something caught Stony's eye and he took off at breakneck speed toward the pine tree forest east of the guest house, yanking Elaina along with him. "Stop! We're not going into the woods!"

Stony disobeyed the order. He arched to put his full weight behind the effort.

Elaina didn't want to be slammed into trees in the dogs' attempt to catch a squirrel. Nor did she want to encounter a raccoon or possum who'd take on Stony to protect their territory. She pressed the button on the retractable leash.

Stony skidded to a halt.

"When I say no, I mean no."

Stony wouldn't give up without vocalizing his disappointment. He complained with a howl.

"Sass all you want, the woods are off limits." Despite being full grown, Stony was a puppy at heart. "This way." Elaina guided him to the wide open spaces.

As predicted, he headed straight for the puddles. Stony bounded into the water, lapped up a few drinks with his tongue, and splashed around some more. He was an energetic fur kid who was now dripping wet. Elaina prepared to be given the what-were-you-thinking expression when she took him back to the suite. Letting Stone-man frolic in the water wasn't the most intelligent thing she could've done. Now the question stood – how would she dry him off? Jeff and Beth, owners of the inn, were two of the sweetest, most laid-back people Elaina had ever met but she doubted they'd appreciate dog hair all over their plush, monogrammed bath towels. To stay in their good graces she had to use something else. The only other things available were the clothes in her suitcase. Elaina grinned at the thought of dressing Stone-man in her thirsty terry cloth bath robe.

Stony tugged hard to check out the top of a hill. Elaina resisted. He kept pulling. "All right all ready. We'll go. It's not like staying out a little while longer is going to get you wetter." She glanced at the sky, noting the ominous low-hanging clouds were still parked above them. "We'll go up, have a look around, and then it's back down. Okay?" She scoffed. "I'm trying to negotiate with a pooch who doesn't understand, and if he did understand, he'd use those blue eyes to plead for a longer stay...and he'd win." She was a pushover and he was well aware.

At the top of the hill, Elaina took in the valley below. The lake Norma talked about lay at the bottom. She was sure under sunshiny conditions it was a breathtaking view.

Stony spotted a gaggle of geese near the far end of the lake. He went down on his hunches and studied them. A goose flapped its wings and squawked. Another followed suit. In a flash, Stony was up on all fours. Just as quickly, he was at the very edge of the hill. The rough pads of his feet and toenails weren't enough to keep him from losing his footing. Almost in slow motion, Stony toppled over the side. Elaina was quick to react but powerless to stop the tragedy unfolding before her eyes. Digging in her heels didn't work. Thanks to the abundant rain, the grassy knoll had turned into a slip and slide. Elaina fought the momentum of the sixty-two pound dog. Gravity won. A panicked scream strained her throat and fear seized every cell in her body as she went over the side of the hill along with him. Holding onto the leash as tightly as possible, she let out another shriek when pain shot up her arm and into her shoulder. The burning discomfort was temporarily forgotten when Stony's head came dangerously close to striking a series of sharp rocks. "Dear God, please, don't let anything happen to him!" In that moment of pure dread she realized just how much she loved that dog. Hot, salty tears blurred her vision. Faced with the possibility of broken bones or worse, Elaina said a swift prayer for mental strength as well as physical. She'd gotten a second chance at happiness when Tawny, Grace, Steph, Stony, and Lula came into her life, and dammit, she wouldn't let any of it literally slide away.

The scrawny tree coming up to her left was their only hope. Elaina had the span of a blink to decide to move into its path. She whispered for divine help one more time. With an awkward, calculated swing, she closed her eyes, ducked her head, and crashed into the tree. She and Stony jerked to a jarring halt.

Elaina's heart thumped hard against her ribs and her breaths came in broken gulps as she tried to come to grips with the reality they were dangling from a tree. With gnarled limbs poking all her body parts, she let her eyelids drift open. Blood, warm and red, rolled past the corner of her eye and down her cheek. Somewhere on her head or face she had a gouge or laceration. There was fire in her muscles from having been stretched to their limits. She moaned hard from pain and from the severity of their circumstances. She was on the side of a hill with cold drizzle seeping through her clothes and darkness looming ever closer. "S-s-stony, are y-you, okay?" She was afraid to move, assuming the slightest shift would fast track them to disaster.

Stony didn't respond.

Elaina used her elbow to ease away the branch that lay against her face so she could see him. The poor dog just hung there, suspended in air, secured only by the retractable leash and the heavy-duty, padded harness-type collar she'd bought a few weeks ago. The day she brought the collar home, Tawny poked fun, saying it looked dorky and Stony would hate to be seen in it. She also said it would impede his movements. Contrary to Tawny's theory, it didn't hinder Stony in any way...until now, thank goodness. Had he been wearing the regular collar around his neck, there was a strong possibility he'd be struggling for air.

Stony blinked up at her with fear etched in his eyes.

"I'll get us out of this mess. I promise."

Elaina carefully leaned forward to look past Stony to gauge the distance to safety. Panic tried to override what little calm she had left when she discovered another hundred feet separated them from the ground. The optimist inside of her tried to scale back her anxiety with the rationale that things could be worse. Instead of a hundred feet it could be two hundred. One hundred. Two hundred. The result would be the same should they barrel end over end down the slick, rocky slope. A sob of distress gurgled from her chest as that scenario played out in her head.

"I'm sorry, buddy." Soaked to the skin, with her nerve endings now sending pulses to her brain that she'd put her body through a significant ordeal, Elaina tried to comprehend how this happened. The root cause wasn't

Stony's curiosity. It was her need for quiet time. As much as she cared for her friends and two pets, the events of the last couple of days had been overload times five. She volunteered for dog duty to get out of the suite for some breathing room. At the moment, she had more than enough breathing room and longed for the comfort and protection of her friends.

"Help!" Elaina shouted the plea several times. She waited a few minutes and tried again. "Help!" After loudly requesting assistance for what seemed like an hour, she tried to formulate an alternative plan. Normally, she had a plan for just about everything. That clearly wasn't the case when it came to risky circumstances. She had nothing. Surveying the scene, she noticed the string of her parka was wedged between two branches. The brutal truth that she'd have to unzip the jacket, remove her arms from the sleeves, and once again become a human toboggan made her adamantly shake her head. "I'm a strong person but I can't do that. It's insane." She had to do something and quick because it would soon be too dark for anyone to find them, except for maybe an owl. She'd never heard of a person being attacked by an owl. There was always a first time. Coyotes couldn't be ruled out either. They preyed on smaller animals. A defenseless dog, however, would be as good as handing them dinner. "Think!"

Stony emitted a shallow cry.

"I know, boy." If she could pull him up, she'd cradle him until someone came. Her arms would threaten to give out but she'd hold onto him for dear life.

Minutes ticked by and Elaina considered going with the human toboggan idea. It would mean plummeting a hundred feet, and subsequent full body casts if they survived. The thought made her shiver and the air in her lungs unexpectedly constricted. *Breathe. Just breathe.* She refused to be in the clutches of impending doom. "I'm not going to panic but I'm not sure what to do. Please, Lord, help me make the right choice. Please. I'm begging you."

The pressure of holding the leash made her hand quiver. She tried to coax away the trembling. "I'm not letting go. I'm not letting go. My hand might be rendered useless after this is over but I'm not letting go."

A few more minutes came and went. The sky grew even more ominous as dusk settled in. Hope dwindled. If a creature didn't get them, hypothermia would. Elaina's nose ran, tears gushed from her eyes, and she whispered into the twilight, "Take me if you must, but spare Stony."

Maybe if she closed her eyes, the madness would go away. Everything would be fine and she'd be safe and warm in her bed.

The strain on the leash increased. Elaina's eyes snapped open to find Stony going crazy trying to free himself. "No, Stone-man. Stop. We'll be okay. You have to stay still." She heard the words and took them as guidance from up above. They weren't to give up.

To make a bleak situation even more distressing though, the drizzle turned into humongous splats before changing over to ice cold buckets of water falling from the dreary sky. "We cannot get a break." The creak of a branch said otherwise. "That's not the kind of break I meant." Elaina said another prayer and glanced toward the heavens. "I know you're listening. Am I not asking the right questions?" Tears flowed from her eyes and rolled down her cheeks. "It would devastate Tawny to lose Stony." Elaina dropped her head back and sealed her eyes shut again. "This is a test of faith. I know you're with me. You're always with me. I also know my parents are right beside you in the kingdom. Hi, Mom. Hi, Dad." She choked on a sob. "I really need for you to get Stony..." A violent stabbing pain in her shoulder made the desperate plea fall away.

"Who ya talking to?"

Elaina startled. At the same time, a flood of relief washed over her. "Steph! Oh God! Steph!" Unable to use her hands, she made a mental Sign of the Cross. "Thank you, Lord, for answered prayers." She also thanked her parents for their part in bringing Steph to that hill.

"You've got yourself in quite the pickle."

Elaina could barely squeak out, "I'm glad you're here."

"Me too. When it started to rain hard again and you weren't back, we got worried."

Elaina braved a stretch to look up through the branches. Steph was on her hands and knees, peering down.

Tawny came to kneel beside Steph. "What have you done?" She palmed her face in alarm.

Elaina's arm was about to snap off from holding the leash and one wrong move could end it all for her and Stony, and Tawny tossed out an indictment of blame?

The tears that tried to dry up came back in an instant. "He doesn't appear to be hurt, but he's plenty scared."

"How did this happen? There's a huge, flat yard."

Tawny's angry tone hurt. Elaina wouldn't let on how much it wounded her, nor would she waste time explaining how their situation came to be, at this critical juncture. "Give us a hand up. Please?"

"Grace went to get Jeff and Beth. We need to use their truck as an anchor. There's just no way to lift you without us falling too." Tawny's harshness didn't ease even a little.

Elaina felt disheartened and crushed.

Jeff and Beth arrived dressed in yellow ponchos and rubber boots. Jeff shined a spotlight on Elaina and spoke in a soothing voice. "Everything's going to be okay. You'll be standing beside us in no time."

Elaina couldn't stop her vocal chords from trembling when she responded. "The s-string to my parka is s-stuck."

"That presents a problem." Jeff rubbed his chin. "There's only one solution. You're not going to like it."

Cold to the bone, Elaina sneezed and shivered. "Remove the parka."

Jeff nodded. "We'll get you up with a tow strap. One end is tied to the front bumper of my truck. I'll lower the other end to you. This is where things will get tricky. You'll need to tie the strap around your waist without letting go of the leash. It won't be easy given the strap is bulky. It will take a cool head and a steady hand. I know you can do it, Elaina."

"I have the cool head. In fact, it's freezing. My hand is anything but steady."

"The only way you'll be able to do this, is a mind over matter frame of mind. Go to that dark place of fear and tell it to kiss your..." Jeff stopped when Beth gave him a firm look.

"At times like this, I wish I was ambidextrous." Elaina expected her friends to zing her with wisecracks over the lame comment. When they remained quiet, it confirmed the severity of the 'pickle'.

Jeff offered reassurance. "We have to use what God has given us."

"I can do it."

"Atta girl. Now make sure the strap is snug around you. Then remove your jacket. When you're ready I'll back my truck up a little at a time. The force will hoist you. You'll feel a quick jerk. Don't let it frighten you. It's just the strap adjusting. One more thing – you're surrounded by limbs that will have to be kicked out of the way. If we're lucky they'll break so the dog won't get stuck on his way up."

Elaina fumbled with the strap. Just when she had it in place, it slackened, although it didn't fully untie. She repeated the process at least a dozen times. It seemed like wasted effort.

Grace demanded she not give up. "You saved us. So dammit, let us save you. Give it all you've got."

Fighting another round of doubt, Elaina changed tactics. Instead of tying the strap in a clumsy knot, she banded her entire midsection with it and wove the long end through the layers. She gave Beth the thumbs-up. "If this thing hugs me any tighter I won't be able to breathe."

Three sets of worried eyes stared down at her, none that belonged to Tawny. Stony's owner had backed away from the edge.

Elaina tried to act brave. Inside though, she'd maxed out on courage. She felt queasy and bile inched up her throat.

Beth asked if she had a solid grip on the dog leash.

"I've got him."

"It's go-time."

Elaina said a silent prayer, swallowed the bile, and nodded.

Even though she was prepared for a jerk, it still was a shock when it happened. Miraculously, it was enough of a tug to free her from the tree. The higher she was raised, the tension on the strap increased.

Grace, Steph, Beth...and at the last minute, Tawny... guided her to the top and onto solid ground. They made sure she was well away from the edge before they continued the hard work of getting Stony up as well.

Elaina crumpled into a heap. When Stony came into view a minute or two later, she shattered. "I'm so sorry, Stony; so very sorry." Still clutching the leash, she hugged him to her. Stony leaned into her like he needed to hug her back. "I was so scared for you." A tremble from being cold and wet coursed through her. Stony trembled at the same time.

Someone slipped their arms under Elaina and brought her to a stand.

In the semi-darkness, Elaina was eye-to-eye with Tawny. She stiffened, waiting for the most intense verbal thrashing of her life.

"Don't ever put me through that again." Tawny's voice bordered on hysteria. "It's selfish to say, but you put my happiness in jeopardy."

Awash with guilt, Elaina struggled to speak. "It was a... new place. I should've checked the area first. It shouldn't have happened. I know how much he...means to you."

Tawny grabbed Elaina roughly by the shoulders and wrapped her in an embrace. "This isn't just about Stony. You're the reason I'm so freaking happy these days and when I saw you about to die, I lost it."

Shaken, Elaina tried to form a coherent sentence. "I wasn't... I..."

Steph interrupted. "She wasn't about to die. Don't even talk like that. Knowing Elaina, she had a plan."

Elaina's nose ran from all the tears and from being cold. She sniffed hard and used the back of her hand since there were no tissues readily available. "The only plan was to keep Stony..." Her words fell away again when she was squeezed in a group hug. Even Jeff and Beth got in on the act.

"Don't let go" had been something she'd whispered in the throes of fear. Now she said the words out loud in the throes of joy.

* * *

"Just gulp it." Grace held out a jigger of whiskey. "It'll warm you in an instant and kill any cold germs trying to mess with your immune system."

Elaina eyed the fiery brew. Some folks considered it bliss in a glass. She never actually snubbed her nose at it, but she hadn't acquired a taste for it either. Usually her indulgences included wine, daiquiris, and margaritas. "Wouldn't chicken soup be better?"

"Jeff and Beth didn't have any chicken soup on hand. They had hooch." Grace mimicked bringing the shot glass to her mouth. "Throw the whiskey to the back of your throat and get it over with."

Stony lay at Elaina's feet. From the time they got back to the suite, he wouldn't let her out of his sight. When she went to the bathroom, he whined until she let him come in. The to-do about the whiskey made him raise his head. "Should I set my taste buds on fire, Stony?" Elaina chuckled for the first time in a handful of hours. "One blink for yes. Two blinks for pour it in the ficus when no one is looking."

Tawny came into the bedroom with a velvety blanket and a plastic grocery bag. Placing the bag on the nightstand, she tucked the blanket around Elaina. "There. How does that feel?"

"I'm starting to warm up."

From the plastic bag, Tawny produced a bottle of peroxide and a box of cotton balls. She wet a cotton ball with peroxide and gently dabbed the scratch above Elaina's eyebrow and the one at her temple.

Elaina wasn't used to people fussing over her. "Thank you for taking care of me, but I'm fine. Really."

"Zip it. Tomorrow we're going to give Mother Nature the bird and be on our way. No more dinking around.

It's Maine or bust. We need you to be healthy." Tawny took the shot glass from Grace. Instead of handing it to Elaina she guzzled the drink and winced from the burn. An impish expression flashed across her face. "Nerve medicine." She held out the glass. "Fill 'er up. It's Elaina's turn. Then yours. Then Steph's." She looked around. "Where is Steph?"

"I saw her curled up in a recliner in the common area. She had a notebook. My guess is she's working on her cookbook." Grace's eyebrows furrowed to form a small V. "Just between the three of us, I think there's something other than recipes going on with her. Her phone's been at her fingertips and she keeps checking it every few seconds."

Tawny drooped onto the bed and propped against the headboard next to Elaina. "This may or may not be relevant. I saw her in the hallway earlier talking on the phone. I heard her say Corbett's name."

"That can't be good." Grace helped herself to a shot of whiskey. "Do you think the snake is trying to get her back?"

"Normally I would say no. As soon as she saw me she flinched, so I'm going with yes."

Grace scrunched her face into a frown. "Has she forgotten how that slimy, slithering reptile mistreated her? Maybe we should jog her memory."

"If her heart's yearning for him, there's nothing we can say or do to change her mind." Elaina understood how easy it was to backslide. She'd done it. Tawny had done it. And now there was a good chance Steph was about to do it.

"We have to let this run its course?"

"Think about it. When someone tells you not to do something, the natural reaction is to want to do it all the more." Elaina grabbed the box of cotton balls for emphasis. "She'll shove these in her ears."

"It's hard to sit back and let her make a huge mistake." Tawny fisted her hands. "That slime-ball will sink his pointy fangs into Steph."

"Snakes usually do. We should buy a snake bite kit." Grace filled the shot glass with more whiskey. "While we're at it, we'll have to get Jeff and Beth a new bottle of whiskey because we're going to kill this one."

"No snake bite kit needed. We just have to be there for Steph, like you were there for me tonight."

Grace capped the bottle. "Can you feel the love?"

"Well yeahhhh," Tawny jokingly quipped. In the same breath she growled that Corbett the snake had better keep his venomous keister in Ohio.

Grace refilled the shot glass and held it out.

A chill followed by a sneeze made Elaina snatch the glass and pour the contents down the hatch. Liquid fire singed her throat and burned its way through her veins. It had been a hell of a day. It also had been a time filled with insight. The tiny part of her that fought change had been silenced. She couldn't wait to start this new chapter in her life with three amazing women who spoke their minds, made her laugh, and cared deeply.

Chapter Five

- Just get there already! -

Grace rubbed her hands together. "New day. New focus."

"When you get that twinkle in your eye, I get scared." Tawny slathered apple butter on an English muffin and chomped into it with gusto.

"What's the new focus?" Elaina held off a sneeze and gently stretched her neck from side to side in an attempt to work out the soreness from what could only be described as whiplash.

Beth came into the dining room carrying two ceramic platters. "Mini quiches." She raised one platter higher than the other. "Cheese and mushroom for those who prefer vegetarian fare." She held up the second plate. "For those who favor a little meat with each bite, these have bacon. Both recipes are gluten-free."

Everyone seemed excited by the arrival of yet another breakfast item.

Elaina smiled but she wasn't hungry. She wanted to go back to bed and sleep for a week. The after-effects of the hillside debacle left her exhausted, like she'd run a marathon and instead of an adrenaline rush from having crossed the finish line she shivered until her body lost its ability to tremor. When the clock-radio alarm had the audacity to ring close to her ear at 6:00 AM, she was immediately greeted by a resurgence of shudders so strong they wracked her from forehead to toe. Since then, every couple of minutes, she experienced a full-body quake despite having taken a shower with water so hot it should've melted the shower curtain. Because going back to sleep wasn't an option, she was tempted to forgo coffee and orange juice and head to the liquor store for more whiskey.

"I've got to try one of those bad boys." Grace followed Beth to the counter.

The sneeze Elaina tried to deny burst forth with enough strength to rattle her ribs.

A fervent round of bless-you's came not only from her friends but the other guests as well.

Elaina offered thanks and inadvertently touched the scratch above her eye. *Get past it, Samuels.* The thing about trauma, it embedded itself in a person's psyche. Her divorce had been mental trauma. Falling over a hill was a combination of mental and physical. If she was honest with herself, she hadn't fully gotten over the trauma of her crumbled marriage and yesterday she managed to add more psychological distress, with a few bruises and superficial lacerations to go with it. Her subconscious poked her with a candid reflection – she wasn't taking care of herself. Damn inner voice sounded remarkably like Arden Wellby Samuels. 'You've got to look good, feel good, and act the part of a fitness trainer'. Whatever. Blah. Blah. Blah. She tried to quiet the subliminal heckler with another sip of steaming hot coffee which resulted in burnt taste buds, followed by another powerful sneeze.

Grace snatched a bacon quiche, took a nibble, and offered a review. "To die for!"

Beth appeared humbled by the compliment. "We want happy guests."

"As soon as I try one of the mushroom ones, I'll be extraordinarily happy."

Tawny elbowed Elaina. "Have you ever met a bigger drama queen?"

Elaina didn't agree or disagree. She simply bared her teeth in a toothy grin.

"Mmm. Mmm. Mmm. Mmm. Mmm. Delish'. Tell me how you made them."

"I used cheese, mushroom, and a secret spice."

Grace licked her lips. "Would that secret spice be thyme?"

"Very good." Beth's face beamed with pride. "I was playing around with the recipe. I take it the thyme is a hit?"

"Absolutely. Steph, you've got to try these."

Steph sluggishly popped open a mini-container of French vanilla creamer and poured it into her coffee cup. "I'd better try one before I taste my coffee. Flavors sometimes fight each other. I don't want the French vanilla to battle it out with thyme."

"Or with red pepper flakes." Beth gestured to the

plate of bacon quiches. "Grace didn't mention that these are packing some heat."

Tawny was also no slouch when it came to being a drama queen. "We're used to heat. Right, ladies? Woo-wee that whiskey was strong stuff. It knocked my lights out around ten. In hindsight we should've mixed it with cola." She targeted Steph with a grin. "From the dark circles under your eyes, it looks as though you only got ten winks instead of forty. You should've come back to the room sooner. There would've been some whiskey left."

Elaina knew where Tawny was headed with the comment. She flicked her on the wrist in warning and received a goofy smirk in return.

Steph wouldn't meet their eyes.

Tawny wouldn't let it alone. "Is snake the other white meat?"

Elaina had just taken a sip of coffee. She spit, sputtered, and coughed until the coffee was everywhere except down her throat.

Steph ignored the question and informed them she'd made progress with her cookbook. "I have a whole section for appetizers and one for entrees."

"Do you have a recipe for snake tar-tar?"

Steph's eyes glazed over.

Elaina kicked Tawny under the table.

Beth had been in conversation with another table of ladies but she stopped long enough to shoot Tawny a puzzled look.

Grace pointed to Tawny. "We blame her weirdness on lack of tobacco."

Beth chuckled. "I get it. Jeff recently quit smoking." She didn't expand further on the topic and returned to the discussion with her other guests.

Elaina brought them back to Grace's initial thought. "You have a new focus for us."

"Does it involve snakeskin boots?" Tawny wrinkled her nose in amusement. No one paid any attention.

Grace squirted a glob of ketchup onto her heap of scrambled eggs. "Actually, it's not a new focus per se. We need to regain our focus. Let's proceed to Maine. No more stopping along the way for anything, other than bathroom breaks. Our future is waiting and I'm ready for carpe diem."

"I agree. I can't wait for the giant whoosh of relief when I step out of my vehicle onto the paver-brick driveway of our new home." Elaina cut her sausage link into a dozen pieces but pushed them around on the plate with her fork. She didn't want to eat. She wanted to grab her overnight bag from the suite and leave behind the dreadful near-death experience.

Steph seemed to have tuned them out.

Grace let the silence hang for a few seconds. "You in, Steph?"

Steph raised her head at the question.

Tawny slapped Steph on the back. "She's in."

"Remove your mitt from my person."

Ouch. Double ouch. Steph had either picked up on all the snake references and was put out by them or she had a serious Corbett-itch she needed to scratch.

Tawny removed her hand and shoved away from the

table. "We can't get to Maine soon enough. I'm taking Stony out to do his business, then Lula." Elaina started to get up to help. "Finish your breakfast. When you're done, you'll find me sitting in Grace's Equinox. I'm ready to hit the road."

Steph put out her forearm to keep Tawny from leaving. "I didn't mean to take my crappy mood out on you."

Tawny dropped back into the chair. "We're all on edge for one reason or another."

Steph blew out a breath. "I'm more than a little on edge. I have a serious issue that's making me nuts."

"Is the UTI still messing with you?"

Pressing her lips together, Steph shook her head.

"Does it involve a different body part?"

Steph's green eyes opened wide.

"Do that again."

"Do what again?"

"Flash your sclera."

Steph's annoyed gaze traveled to Elaina. "What's she talking about?"

"Sclera is the white of your eye."

"Sweet. Anatomy 101 at seven in the morning."

"I was trying to lighten things up." Tawny tucked a wispy strand of hair behind her ear.

Steph shifted in her chair. "My life is what it is – a mess. And it has to stay that way until it isn't. So let it be."

The information was sketchy but the logic made sense. Elaina could apply it to her own messed up state of mind.

"You've heard this a bazillion times, but I'm going to say it again. When you're ready to talk about whatever *it* is, we're here for you."

"I'm grateful for that, Tawn'. I have to work things out in my head before I open myself up to your opinion." Steph rushed to add more. "Not that you'd be critical. It's just that I'm not sure..." She left the thought unfinished.

"We won't hound you. Wrestle the dragon or..." Tawny met Elaina's gaze.

Elaina knew Tawny was going to say snake, again. She advised her not to with a steadfast look of no.

"You get what I'm trying to say. There's always an ear when you need it. Actually make it ten ears."

"Ten?"

Tawny gently jested, "Me, Elaina, Grace, Stony, and Lula. Two ears each, times five. Ten. Hellooo."

Steph squeezed Tawny's hand. "Thanks."

"All this touchy-feely crap is for the birds."

Elaina doled out another pointed look, this one to Grace.

"Mother Hen just gave me a visual smack-down. Let the touchy-feely crap continue. So Tawn', you said we're all on edge. Why are you?"

"There's not enough time or words to describe why I've been biting my nails to the quick again and wanting to rip open a pack of smokes every five minutes."

"Yeah? Well you better start yapping or Elaina will think I've thrown a pipe cutter in the touchy-feely process."

"It's a wrench, Grace. She'll think you've thrown a

wrench, not a pipe cutter." Tawny raised her cheeks in a high smile, although the mirth vanished as quickly as it had come. "My boys' lack of concern for me is what has taken me to the edge. They could care less that I've picked up stakes and am moving to the far side of the country. I've tried to get a conversation going with them. When I call Bo, I get his answering machine. It's the same with Quentin. The whiskey lulled me to sleep but I woke up around three. I stared into the darkness until I thought I'd go insane. I took my phone into the bathroom and followed Elaina's suggestion to repeatedly send text messages until they answered."

"You remembered that?"

"What can I say? A squirrel stores a lot of nuts. Shortly after four, which is one o'clock their time, I got 'Trying to sleep but you keep texting me' from Bo. I have yet to hear from Quentin. I know they're adults with lives of their own, but come on. I carried them in this temple for nine long months and put Grady through hours of nonstop cussing as I tried to squeeze them out. The least they can do is pretend to care."

"Temple?"

Given Steph's frame of mind, Elaina was surprised at the good-natured poke.

Tawny narrowed her eyelids to a thin slit. "Don't make fun of my Taj Mahal." She sighed. "I don't know how to get through to the fruits of my loins. Why are they rejecting me?"

"They're not rejecting you," Elaina said delicately, although she was becoming increasingly upset with

Tawny's boys too. It was one thing to get busy and forget to reply to a text. It was quite another to completely disregard their mother. If she was Tawny, she'd pay them an unexpected visit and get to the bottom of why they put her forty-ninth on their list of important people. Tawny was a feisty gal who normally wouldn't have a problem doing exactly that...to someone else. When it came to her boys though, she kept her temper in check. Maybe she felt guilty for divorcing their dad. Or maybe Bo and Quentin were clueless and didn't realize how much she missed them. Whatever the case, Tawny was depressed. It wasn't Elaina's place to interfere. If they didn't get their acts together though, they'd get an earful from her. She'd tell them in no uncertain terms that they'd better show their mom some love.

"It hurts like rejection." Tawny folded and unfolded her cloth napkin.

Grace offered her thoughts. "Speaking from experience, I wouldn't allow the gap between you to widen. Sons have to be hit upside the head every now and then. Figuratively, not a real smack." She paused. "I shouldn't throw all sons into one bin. Let me rephrase my point. Some sons need a good whack aside of the head because the part of their brains responsible for checking on the parentals, as they call us, is stuffed with circus peanuts. And it doesn't bother them to let two or three months pass without so much as a call, text, or email. They don't mean to be little shits. It's just a weird chromosome they inherited somewhere along the line."

"That's exactly what I'm trying to prevent. I don't

want to go months without hearing their voices."

Elaina made a mental note to do something drastic if they continued to hurt her friend.

* * *

"Earth to Mars. Come in, Mars."

Tawny snorted. "What's that about?"

"I haven't the foggiest idea." Elaina tried not to get drawn into the claptrap of dialogue going on between Tawny and Steph. She was trying to concentrate on the navigation screen and keep her bearings while they crossed into New Hampshire from Vermont.

"Are you talking about the time it takes for us to get to Mars? Or to Maine? Because it feels like equal distance to both."

"Maine. Mars. Whatever." Steph had said little at the breakfast table. Once she got in Grace's vehicle her lips hadn't stopped moving. They'd made the passenger-switch a few hours ago after eating a late lunch at a mom and pop diner. "I said it to get your attention, and quick like."

Elaina heard a strange noise coming through Grace's phone, which Steph was using because she'd forgotten to charge hers. "What's going on?"

"Grace has been whining for the last fifteen minutes about her foot cramping. Do you think she'll pull over and let me drive? Nope. She's being pigheaded."

Some barely intelligible chatter followed. Elaina strained to listen. It sounded as though Steph was scolding Grace for crossing the center line. Elaina and Tawny looked at each other when Steph raised her voice in a yell. "NOW you're riding the berm."

Steph grumbled. "She's being reckless. Do something."

"You want us to stage an intervention?"

"Must you joke about everything, Tawn'? Seriously. It gets old."

Elaina knew Grace's motivation for keeping Steph from behind the wheel. She was a terrible driver. Elaina found out firsthand just how bad Steph's driving skills were a while back. On the way home from the grocery one afternoon, she ran a red light, blew through a stop sign, and almost annihilated a cat.

Tawny tucked away the funny and the nurse in her took over. "She's dehydrated."

"Duh. I'm holding an uncapped bottle of water an inch from her hand. She doesn't want to drink anything because she doesn't want to make another pit stop. She was unaffected when I told her not only would her foot continue to cramp but her pee would turn brown."

"Put me on speaker."

"You're in trouble now, Grace. Tawny's going to read you the riot act and list all the things that are going haywire inside you because you're too stubborn to take a sip."

"She's not being stubborn, Steph. Her blood pressure is elevated because she's riding with you."

"Heyyyy. This isn't about me. It's about her."

"Right. I forgot. Grace, your blood pressure is elevated because you're dehydrated and because you have Mathews riding your butt about drinking water. I wouldn't drink it either if she was on my case. I'd let my whole body cramp before I'd drink. And even though the fluid sack that my brain sits in to keep it from bumping against my skull will get depleted, I wouldn't give in to someone insisting I drink H20."

Elaina covered her mouth to smother a laugh. Between her fingers she said, "Clever."

Tawny cupped her mouth to whisper. "Sometimes you have to paint a grisly picture."

Grace bellowed with another cramp.

"Did I mention dehydration can lead to blood clots and seizures?"

"Now she's glaring at me. Does that mean her brain sack is dry?"

Tawny roared with laughter. Every time she tried to talk she started laughing again. "Not her brain sack. The fluid sack that cradles her brain."

The only way to fix Grace's cramping issue and to prevent her brain from bumping against her skull, was to force water down her throat. Elaina spotted a sign for a rest area two miles ahead. "Time to restore our fluid sacks. Hashtag: weird things women in their forties say."

"Uh oh."

"What uh oh?"

"In hindsight an earlier intervention would've been a good thing. There are red and blue flashing lights in our rearview mirror. Grace is going to get reamed by a state trooper."

Excellent. Another obstacle. What next? A flat tire? A

hole in their radiator? A deer standing in the middle of the road? An airplane using the highway for a runway? Elaina dug her fingernails into the steering wheel. She was torn between complaining and wanting to click her heels three times.

Chapter Six

~ Silly name for a dog! ~

Steph took a huge bite of buttery lobster roll and moaned with delight. "If I had to choose between this and sex, lobster would win hands down."

"Then you're doing it wrong." Grace chomped the end of a ketchup-laden French fry.

"Okay then," Tawny teased.

"Whaaat?" Grace's knack for playing innocent after poking a sleeping 'liger', was amusing.

"Are you saying what I think you're saying?"

A real and unexpected tinge of pink coated Grace's cheeks.

"On multiple occasions you've said you're no vamp, yet the things that come out of your mouth say otherwise." Tawny stole a fry from Grace's plate to up the mischief.

"Trust me, I'm no sex kitten." The blush in Grace's cheeks heightened. "I just think sex done right is better than a lobster roll any day of the week."

Steph licked butter from her lips. "I don't know." She

held up her sandwich. "This is hard to top."

"How does one do sex right?" Tawny's brown eyes sparkled with possibly more monkey business than real interest in the subject.

Grace crammed a handful of fries into her mouth.

Tawny leaned back, crossed her arms, and waited Grace out.

Grace pulverized those poor fries, trying to stall until they grew bored and changed the conversation.

They'd been together long enough to know Grace was kidding herself if she thought Tawny would skip the line of questioning.

Grace washed down the fries with a slurp of unsweetened iced tea. "By discovering every inch of one another. No stone left unturned, so to speak." She fanned her face with a napkin. "Wayyyy better than lobster. Just my personal opinion."

Tawny tipped her head down but raised her eyebrows. "This coming from a woman who all but shelved men for eternity a few weeks ago?"

Elaina remained mum to see where this would lead.

Steph grinned over the bun that held so much lobster it was falling out the ends. "You should've seen her in action with that cop earlier. I swear they were having mind sex. She'd sweep her lashes over her eyes and he'd smile. That happened a half-dozen times. I might've imagined it, but I swear she ran her tongue suggestively over her lips too. I was tempted to say 'Don't mind me I'll just blend into the seat. You'll never know I'm here.'"

"I did not." Grace swatted Steph on the arm. Chunks

of succulent lobster went flying.

"Yes you did."

Elaina was happy to note that whatever had been bugging Steph was no longer front and center. Things were looking up.

"I was being friendly."

"When our waiter comes back, be friendly to him the way you were with Officer J. Chapman."

Elaina made big eyes. "You flirted with Johnny Appleseed?" She laughed and almost knocked over her water glass.

Three sets of eyes stared at her like she'd lost her marbles.

Grace ripped open a packet of sweetener and dumped it in her tea. "Lame."

"Your tea? Or Elaina's failed stab at humor?" Tawny pulled the tail off a deep-fried shrimp.

"This tea is funnier than that Johnny Appleseed joke."

Elaina squinted to act as though their toying with her, bothered her. Inside she was enjoying every minute of it.

Steph's gaze whizzed around the table. "I thought it was funny."

"Then why didn't you laugh?"

"It wasn't ha-ha funny, just mildly humorous."

No one paid any attention to Elaina's phony reaction.

Tawny stole another fry from Grace. "On a scale of one to ten for comedic value, I can only give it a two."

"Hello. I'm sitting right here."

Tawny reached for another fry. Grace batted her hand away.

"You seldom mouth off. When you do, we're like

what-what?"

Elaina smirked. Tawny was spot-on. Usually it was the other three tearing things up. But one couldn't be in their midst without some of the quirky spilling over. Plus, she was no longer weighed down by frustration for not having made it to their bed and breakfast. They'd get there, eventually. "It's because I'm more reserved."

"Yeah, that's not it. You're just caught up in making sure everything goes right. When you zing us with your wit it throws us for a loop."

"You were saying Grace made eyes at the cop."

"Did I mention that once I drank water, my foot stopped cramping?"

"Nice deflect." Tawny passed around her plate that was heaping with shrimp. Elaina took a couple. Steph shook her head no. Grace aimed her fork in pretend warning for Tawny to drop the subject or she'd be dropping the plate.

"Did the cop write you a ticket?"

Grace squirted more ketchup onto her plate.

"Well?"

"You already know he didn't."

"Grace has a way with men in uniform. First Officer T. Marley in Ohio. Now Officer J. Chapman. Maybe it's the handcuffs she likes." Elaina toed Grace's shin under the table. "Was Johnny Appleseed hot?"

"How would I know? He's from the 1700's."

* * *

Elaina held her breath when the navigation screen advised they'd soon be in Maine. "This is so happening."

Tawny grabbed Elaina's arm. "Is that a snow plow?"

"Yep." It shouldn't come as a surprise. There was a good inch of snow piled on the side of the road.

"Turn the car around. Head back to Ohio. Pronto."

Elaina tilted her head to reject the idea.

"Ha. Fake out. Had you going there for a minute."

"No you didn't. You and I both know you wouldn't leave Ferdinand in Maine. You love him almost as much as you love Stony." They'd shipped Ferdinand a.k.a. Tawny's Chevy Malibu and Steph's Ford Escape along with their household goods. It would've been silly for all four of them to drive separately. Although, it would've been a lot more peaceful if they had. Elaina chuckled to herself. It had been a crazy trip from the second they set out but she wouldn't have missed it for anything.

"Look at that sign. Instead of a deer crossing it shows a moose crashing into a car."

Elaina was too busy paying attention to traffic merging onto the interstate to gawk at signs. "Well then, we'd better be on the lookout for moose."

"Is the plural for moose, meese? Like goose, geese?" Tawny guffawed.

"You're wound up."

"It's because I'm so freaking happy. We should stop at a grocery or wine store and pick up a bottle. To celebrate."

"You should be more concerned about moose."

"Got it. Watch for meese and for a sign with a wine bottle."

The navigation screen was interrupted by an incoming call from Rachel.

Elaina didn't answer right away. "There was something weird going on in the background the last time she called. It's like she didn't want us to know she had an overnight guest. Steph thought so too."

Tawny made a face at a house lit up with Christmas lights. "It boggles the mind. How can people get Christmassy when Thanksgiving hasn't even arrived?"

"Don't knock folks who jump the gun and decorate early. It's their thing." To keep Rachel's call from going to voice mail, Elaina pushed the button to answer. "Hey, Rach', what's shakin'?"

"I got a dog."

Elaina smiled at Rachel's lead in. No hello. No how are you. Just a blurted surprise. In one of their many conversations at the winery they discussed pets. Rachel acknowledged a fear of anything with four legs, especially dogs. Now she had a pooch? "That's great! What kind did you get?"

"A Pomsky – part Pomeranian, part Husky."

Tawny's love for dogs gushed forth. "Sweet. A miniature Stony mixed with Pomeranian. I can't wait to see him."

"Her," Rachel clarified. "We're going to breed *her*." She swiftly corrected. "*I'm* going to have her bred."

Elaina and Tawny exchanged smirks. "No kidding."

"I know this comes as a shock to y'all since I'm not a dog person. Not by a long shot. At least I wasn't until we...until *I* paid a visit to..."

Tawny didn't beat around the bush. "You have a guy in your life."

Rachel didn't respond. She'd shocked them with the bit about the dog and Tawny must've shocked her right back.

"You can tell us. It's not like we're going to spread the word in Maine."

"I'd like to but I can't. Not yet."

Tawny leaned in close to the nav-screen and tried to pry the truth from her with a whisper. "Is he someone we know?"

"Possibly."

"You've dropped hints that you have a new man but you won't let on who he is. Mean girl. You might as well flash a chocolate bar and then hog it for yourself."

Rachel brushed over Elaina's feeble tactic. "I also called to see if y'all adopted the New England accent? They drop their R's, right?"

Tawny rolled her eyes.

"We've not assumed the accent because we haven't made it there."

"But you left a week ago."

"It feels like we've been gone for a week. It's actually only been a few days. Lots of," Elaina cleared her throat, "interesting obstacles."

"You call a hillside dangle interesting? You're one whacked chick, Samuels. It was NOT interesting. It was damned scary."

There was an unmistakable sharp intake of air too loud to have come from Rachel.

Elaina pictured Rachel's guy resting his chin on her

shoulder, listening in on the conversation.

"Tell me your vehicle didn't teeter on the edge of a mountain."

"No. There was no teetering."

"Then what's the bit about dangling?"

"The dangling bit is a discussion for another time."

Rachel's snicker was dramatic. "You're withholding information to get back at me, aren't you?"

"Would I do that?"

"Nah. Tawny would though. Are you coming back to Ohio soon? You could meet Neil and we could kill a bottle of Reisling. You could tell me all about being a hillside dangler." Rachel laughed. "That sounds downright creepy."

"It's doubtful we'll be back before summer." Or ever. "When we do visit, you can drink Reisling. I'll have Merlot or Sangria. Tawny goes for dry red."

"Deal."

"So your guy is Neil. I knew if we applied pressure you'd drop his name," Tawny said cockily.

Rachel made the sound of a buzzer going off. "Neil's not my guy. She's my dog."

"You call your female dog Neil? Bwahahaha. You're joking."

"I'm not. I don't follow convention. I named her after someone who won me over the first time we met."

"Did you meet him at the pet store?"

"Your detective skills are seriously lacking, Snoop Westerfield. Noooo, I didn't meet him at the pet store." Rachel's amused tone faded to serious. "I met him in the hospital." Her voice cracked a little. "He's probably not going to make it."

Tawny apologized straight away. "I'm sorry, Rachel. Had I known, I wouldn't have laughed."

"No worries. You have to be you."

Elaina chipped in with, "Or she'll implode."

"You've got that right."

"In less than five minutes we should cross over into Maine." Elaina was getting an odd vibe from Rachel and only a small portion of it had to do with her getting a dog. Something felt off.

A shuffling noise and the sound of a door closing could be heard.

"One more question, then I swear I'll leave it be. Is your anonymous guy from Cherry Ridge?"

"Maybe."

"Are you seeing Grady?"

Elaina flinched at the abrupt question. Tawny's ex was supposedly seeing someone he met online. Even with all the secrecy surrounding Rachel's new man, Elaina doubted it was Grady. Rachel was in her twenties. Grady was almost fifty. Even though it was no longer taboo for younger women to date older men, and vice versa, there was a huge gap in their ages.

"Who's Grady?"

"So that's a no?"

"You said one question. That's three so far." Rachel huffed out a sigh. "Stop digging."

Tawny tried to make light of her meddling. "Stowing my shovel."

Elaina didn't want things to get awkward with Rachel. "When you're ready to tell us you will."

"Thanks, Elaina. Wait a minute. When did I hint I had a new man in my life?"

"Talk about a light-bulb moment. Sheesh. We said it like five minutes ago. It just now sank in?"

Elaina gave Tawny a significant flick.

"Oww. Stop flicking me." Tawny popped the tab on a can of diet cola.

There were a few long seconds of dead air space, broken only by the sound of Tawny enjoying her first taste of soda.

"Rachel? Are you still there?"

"I'm here. Damn. I kept telling him to be quiet."

Elaina smiled at the 'Welcome to Maine' sign.

"He's a noisy one, huh?" Tawny prodded.

Rachel gave into a laugh. "You have no idea. Generally, I'm not a kiss and tell kind of girl. In this case, however, I can honestly say I've never met a more affectionate man. He can't keep his hands to himself no matter where we are. Yesterday at the grocery he got caught squeezing more than the produce." She lowered her voice to almost a whisper. "He's a lot to handle."

Tawny had no filter. "A real sex machine?"

"That's an understatement."

Rachel had let down her guard but she pulled it back up in a rush. "I've got to go."

"No. Stay. I didn't mean to apply too much pressure."

"That's not it, Tawny. He's coming out of the bathroom." Rachel said a hurried goodbye and must've thought she hit the end-button to disconnect the call.

They heard her giggle. "I can't believe you shaved... that." Rachel's pleasure rocketed through the phone. "It looks... Oh my gosh.... I like it!"

Elaina made a move to end the call. Tawny's hand shot out to keep it from happening.

"I want to hear," she said in a hushed voice.

Elaina said a quiet "no" and used the button on the steering wheel instead to disconnect the call.

"Killjoy."

"She got a Pomsky."

"That's the thing you keyed on?"

* * *

Elaina could barely keep her eyes from closing. She and Grace had made a pact to get to the new 4 Hussy Homestead by daylight. Sunrise wasn't far off. According to her nav screen they were almost there. She used her thumb and forefinger to hold open her eyelid. It wasn't the safest thing to do, but she could one-eye the road for a few more blocks.

Tawny was fast asleep with her face smashed against the door, and according to Elaina's conversation with Grace a few minutes ago, Steph had her cheek flattened against the window.

Beautiful Day by U2 came on the radio and in the middle of a yawn Elaina smiled. It was definitely going to be a beautiful day both weather-wise and personally. Instead of the temperature falling overnight, it climbed;

melting the snow – at least on the roads. There were still some slushy mounds on the berm.

Elaina sang along with Bono to let the music and lyrics penetrate her weariness. When Bono hit the high notes, she did too. Expecting Tawny to crack open an eye and tell her to shut her pie hole, she was surprised when the only reaction involved a loud, nasally snore.

"We have to be close." Elaina tapped the nav-screen. "It says we're here. But we aren't." A series of hard yawns took hold of her as she proceeded another block. Craning her neck to look for the street sign that seemed to be missing, her foot slipped off the brake and her vehicle lurched forward. At the same time, a souped-up truck with a lift kit that raised it high above other vehicles barreled through the intersection. The driver laid on the horn and Elaina's lethargic reflexes kicked in. She slammed on the brakes and scolded herself. "You drove all the way here without incident. Now you're within spitting distance of your destination and you almost got t-boned." She took several deep breaths to get oxygen flowing to her sleepy brain.

Tawny jerked awake. "Did you hit a moose?"

"Nope."

"Then what happened?"

Elaina's mouth dropped open. "There it is."

"There what is?" Tawny was still in a fog.

"Our three-story, ten-bedroom slice of heaven."

Chapter Seven

~ *Ohm!* ~

"Halle-freaking-luiah!" Tawny uncoiled with a languorous stretch then bounded out of the vehicle.

Elaina sat back against the seat and stared in awe at their new home. It was more than she could've hoped for or imagined. The pictures Steph had shared upon her return to Ohio a few weeks prior, hadn't done the place justice. Studying the inn that was white-farmhouse-meets-Cape-Cod, Elaina realized the hasty decision to leave everything familiar had been better than good. *This is it. This is where I'm supposed to be.* She tapped the steering wheel, admiring the wrap-around porch that transitioned to a deck on one side while the other side gave way to a sunroom. The intricate wrought iron fence that started at the sidewalk and enclosed the entire property, offered more charm than protection. Her pleasure darted all around but she kept going back to the porch where white rockers with crisp blue nautical pillows sat waiting for them. The quaint setting turned into a snapshot of the past. Her mom had loved everything nautical. Trinkets of anchors, boats, sails, and more, had been tastefully situated throughout the house when Elaina was growing up. A giant quilt with a ships' helm had covered her parents' bed. The sudden bittersweet memory of her mom once saying she wanted to someday live by the ocean stirred emotion deep inside. Elaina's eyes misted but a smile took the corners of her mouth. "You put Tawny, Grace, and Steph in my life. Now you've led me here."

Elaina rested her head against the window, deliriously happy but so tired she could barely function. She almost fell out of the Escalade when Grace opened the door. "Geez. Give some warning."

"I would've caught you before you smacked your head."

"Uh huh. I hear ya."

Grace clapped her hands. "I'm ready to check out every nook and cranny."

Steph, on the other hand, appeared drained of energy, like Elaina. "Why's my throat so scratchy?"

"It might have something to do with you snoring with your mouth open for the last hundred miles."

Steph frowned. "If you weren't such a control freak I could've taken my turn behind the wheel."

"Just because I prefer not to have my body parts mangled due to a crash, it doesn't make me a control freak. Right, Elaina?"

"Leave me out it. I'm tired, hungry, and thirsty. My mouth is so parched my taste buds are about to fall off."

"Can taste buds fall off?" The couple hours sleep Tawny had been able to catch was enough to revive her sense of humor.

Elaina shrugged. "Tawn', flip a coin. Heads, Grace is a control freak. Tails, she's a control freak." Wandering to the back of the SUV, she opened the hatch and snapped a leash on Stony.

Grace started to laugh, but stopped. "Ert. I'm not a freak; control or otherwise. Am I?"

Steph grabbed Lula before she bolted. "If the freaky snow shoe fits..."

Tawny put her hands on her hips. "No squabbling. We've arrived at our new digs in one piece."

Elaina watched their expressions soften.

Grace opened her arms toward the incredible residence. "This is our destiny."

Steph nodded but Elaina saw something peculiar flash through those green eyes. Without question, Steph had an issue or situation that needed to be addressed sooner or later. *Later*, Elaina thought. *Much later*. She was too weary to take on anything serious right now. The thing about being overtired though – at least for her – was her mind fastened onto stuff and wouldn't let go until she paid attention and did the whole over-thinking thing. Right now her fatigued brain conjured up the possibility Corbett would lure Steph back to Ohio. If that indeed was the case, it would be tough to keep her mouth shut and not persuade Steph to stay in Maine. Elaina wanted to shout to the sky that Steph wasn't a convenient yo-yo or boomerang for Corbett's pleasure.

She was a sweetheart of a woman who was trying to get her bearings just like everyone else and that Corbett-the-snake needed to leave her the heck alone. "Stone-man, it's time to find your new sprinkling area."

The second Stony's paws hit the pavement he was raring to go. Elaina held him in check when Grace handed her a bottle of water.

"Have a swig."

Elaina winked. "Mighty kind of you."

"Whatever. Just drink." Grace chuckled. "Is it too early for wine?"

"There are no rules when it comes to wine."

Tawny reminded her that the plan to stop at a wine store had been forgotten, hence no wine.

"It was your plan, not mine. Do you really think I'd leave home without provisions?" Elaina raised her eyebrows up and down. "Check my paisley bag. You'll find a bottle of Merlot."

* * *

"Holy sprawling estates!" Elaina had been struck spellbound by the house but the backyard, or rather, the abundant acreage, was a fascination all its own. Steph said the bed and breakfast took up a full city block. It was more like two city blocks; at least compared to what was considered a city block in Ohio. To Elaina's surprise, there was a separate small garage-loft type apartment nestled behind a row of pine trees that Steph failed to mention. It reminded Elaina of a romantic bungalow.

The cogs started to turn. In order to get folks to choose their bed and breakfast over the many others in the area would require something unique. The garage-loft was definitely unique and would be the clincher. They could tout it as the perfect honeymoon suite or lovers' escape. They could also advertise it as a quiet getaway for writers or harried business people in need of a serene place to get their heads back in the game. Excitement prevailed over Elaina's exhaustion. She went in search of the grape arbor and found it struggling to survive, just as Steph had said. It had been planted in a shady corner of the property. The potential to grow grapes was there but the canes and vines were in need of attention and the trees overhanging the arbor needed trimmed away to let in sunlight. The plants resided in a low spot and were being suffocated by a plethora of weeds and tall grass. When it rained, they were surely gasping for air. As soon as she could, Elaina would take care of all that ailed the arbor. She had much to learn when it came to producing grapes but she was willing to put in the time and effort. The same applied to the bed and breakfast. The book she'd downloaded only gave so much information. As with most things, real knowledge came from hands-on. At least they weren't going in blind. They had the basics.

Stony sniffed and peed; peed and sniffed.

Elaina spied the gazebo Steph had gone gaga over. It was as dreamy as she'd said. There were trellises of roses on two sides. The delicate flowers had turned brown from the cold, although they gave her a rough idea of what to expect in the spring. There was a wealth of wide open yard for sunshine and plenty of shaded space as well from maple, oak, and birch trees. Flowering dogwoods sectioned off a private patio. Hmm. Guests could reserve that area for a special occasion. There were lots of things that made the backyard exceptional. One thing stood out from the rest – the huge stone fire pit surrounded by benches constructed from the same stone. What an awesome gathering place for folks to come back to after a full day of sightseeing. The original owners clearly had a vision for the place. Elaina couldn't believe they'd unloaded it to the Kirbys – parents of the a guy Steph dated for a short time after Corbett – who then sold it to them.

Stony heard Tawny's gravelly voice and gave the leash a solid tug.

Elaina tightened the leash. "Take it easy, Stonewall Jackson Westerfield. There will be plenty of time to get some exercise. Look, a birdbath. Word to the wise." She shook her finger. "If you knock it over trying to get a taste of our tiny feathered friends you'll be in big trouble."

Stony blinked as though telling her it wasn't him she had to worry about.

"Don't throw Lula under the bus. You're supposed to be buddies." She bounced with a small laugh at the reality that sleep deprivation was making her squirrely.

They rejoined the others who hadn't moved an inch from when they left. Elaina took a deep, satisfied breath and smiled with the exhale. "I'm going to love it here."

"Me too." Tawny held up four plastic glasses and a corkscrew. "Aren't you the clever one for thinking to bring these?"

"What good is a bottle of wine if you can't get it open? And I prefer to have a glass to drink from rather than to pass the bottle around."

"We don't have cooties." Steph wandered around to the open hatch of the SUV and hoisted her suitcase to the sidewalk.

"I don't know that. You could have worse than cooties."

"I'd laugh if I had the oomph. I'm currently oomph-less. Done in. Defunct. " Steph leaned against the Escalade and closed her eyes.

Tawny shoved the sharp tip of the corkscrew into the cork.

Elaina tossed out a suggestion. "We could do this inside."

"My motto is: why wait?"

Grace wrapped her quilted jacket tighter around her to block out the cold air. "Pour if you're going to pour. It's freezing out here."

Elaina couldn't resist, "Technically we're supposed to let the wine breathe."

Tawny pasted on a fake scowl. "Are you insane?"

"As a future wine entrepreneur I've done some homework. Wine under eight years old should aerate for one to two hours; over eight years, thirty minutes."

"The dog ate my homework so I'm drinking wine that hasn't been aerated."

"Rebel."

"Bossy wine person."

"Whatever."

A heavy gust of wind blew into them from the Atlantic.

"I'm with Grace – it's freezing. I'm taking this party inside." Elaina jangled the keys, hurried up the front steps, and had the door unlocked before she remembered the security system was activated. A shrill blast, loud enough to rattle the rafters, just about sent her into cardiac arrest. "Damn." Her heart thumped hard while she scrambled to enter the code to quiet the ear-piercing sound. "Four, seven, eight, zero?" Nope. "Four, eight, seven, zero?" Bingo. "Ahhh! Sweet silence."

Grace stuck her head in the house. "What on God's green earth are you doing?"

"Trying to wake everyone in Portland." Elaina gestured to the keypad beside the door. "A neon-pink sticky note was attached to the front of the paperwork from my lawyer's office. It warned me the security alarm would go off upon entry. That slipped my mind. Since we haven't put the landline telephone in our name yet, I imagine it's disconnected. The security company won't be able to call to verify everything's fine, which means any second now we'll get a visit from Portland's finest." She made a goofy face. "Run a brush through your hair, pop in a breath mint, and work your mojo, Grace."

"Funny girl," Grace said with dry sarcasm.

Elaina couldn't stop a grin when she watched Grace fluff the back of her hair.

Tawny and Steph clamored inside with Stony and Lula.

"Way to let the neighbors know we've arrived." Tawny

maintained a firm grip on Stony while trying not to spill the opened bottle of wine.

"Our nearest neighbor is a block away."

Blue and red strobe lights flashed in front of the house. Elaina exhaled theatrically. "They're here."

Stony barked.

Tawny put the bottle of wine on the fireplace mantle. Steph stowed the glasses beside it.

Grace pulled her shoulders back and sucked in her belly. "Watch and learn."

Two policemen with their hands firmly planted on their holstered weapons met Grace at the bottom step of the porch. "Ma'am, we're responding to an entry alarm."

Grace appeared unaffected by the strong presence of authority. She put her hand out to the tall, slender, dark-haired cop. "Grace Vivian Cordray – part owner of the bed and breakfast."

The policeman kept his hand on his weapon and stared without batting any eyelash. "Do you have anything to back up that claim?"

"My birth certificate."

"I'm not referring to the validity of your name, ma'am. I'm talking about ownership of this property."

Grace swiveled around to look at the others. "Elaina, we need to show this kind officer proof that we're the proprietors of this property, or he'll slap on the cuffs and haul us to jail. I'm not a fan of orange jumpsuits so you'd better hurry."

Tawny was on her game. "But you ARE a fan of handcuffs."

Elaina swore she heard one of the men snicker, although their serious expressions remained intact. She was tempted to get Grace's goat by saying, "We don't have any proof." Since she didn't want to tick off the police she raised her palms. "I'll get it. It's in the Escalade." On the way to her vehicle, she was shadowed by the second cop. Without saying a word, the blond officer intimidated her with his height and muscled body. Yowza! With a built-to-the-hilt cop like him, the seedy underbelly of the city wouldn't stand a chance. "We arrived ten minutes ago, officer. I was so tired from driving through the night that I forgot about the security system."

The policeman didn't utter a word. Like the first officer, he had his scowling skills down pat.

An unexpected bout of annoyance took hold of Elaina. It had to be fatigue messing with her mood. "Look, we're not Bonnie and Clyde. We're Elaina, Tawny, Grace, and Steph from Ohio. We bought the place from the Kirbys."

"We'll soon know, won't we?"

Elaina had the utmost respect for law enforcement so she curbed the urge to sass further. "Do you trust me to rifle through my tote? Or would you prefer to do it?" Gah. She shouldn't have said rifle.

The slightest hint of a smile edged the corners of the cops' mouth. "I believe you are who you say you are. Please get your paperwork to back up my trust in you."

That was probably the best thing he could've said. The exasperation building in Elaina vanished in a heartbeat. "I understand where you're coming from." She fished a bundle of papers from the tote and handed them to him.

The officer flipped through the pages. "Which one are you?"

"Elaina Ashlynn Samuels."

Deep-green eyes glittered with something indefinable.

Steph sidled up next to them. "I'm Stephanie Irene Mathews. Our friend who's trying to restrain Stony J. Westerfield, is Tawny P. Westerfield. Don't believe her when she says the P stands for Pia."

Elaina tried to keep a straight face.

Grace giggled. "If anyone's suspicious, it's Tawny. Pia just doesn't fit with the rest of her name."

The hard-squinting officer that continued to bear down on Grace wasn't fazed by their humor. It didn't seem possible for him to tighten his eyelids even more, but he did.

"Everything's in order, Lorenzo." The blond cop handed the paperwork back to Elaina with a nod.

Grace repeated the name. "Lorenzo. Are you Italian?"

Lorenzo didn't confirm or deny the assumption.

"My son's in Italy. He married an Italian girl – Isabella. I now have a granddaughter Karina."

"Information overload," Tawny spouted.

Dark, bushy brows raised a fraction of an inch. "Since your paperwork is in order you're free to go back to whatever you were doing." Officer Lorenzo removed his hand from his gun and used it to tip his hat. "Thank you for your cooperation."

Elaina apologized for causing a ruckus.

"No worries, ma'am. We're here to serve."

Tawny hollered from the porch. "Grace likes men in

uniform; especially Italian men. And my middle name IS Pia."

The policemen walked to their vehicle and paused before getting in. They looked at one another...and smiled.

Steph was now wide awake and feisty. "Pia my arse."

* * *

Grace scooped cat food into Lula's dish. "Does anyone else get the feeling we're police magnets?"

"It's better than being a refrigerator magnet." Elaina snorted.

Tawny mocked with an eye roll. "You used to be quiet and demure, Samuels. What happened?"

"You guys happened. A person can't live with three zany cohorts without some of the zane rubbing off. You made me sing karaoke, for crying out loud. It's been downhill from there."

"Yeah. The karaoke thing. Damn, that was a fun night. We should do it again." Tawny ran a hand over the smooth glaze of the fireplace mantel.

Steph's reddish-brown eyebrows dipped into a V. "Is *zane* even a word?"

Elaina's chuckle was languid and hoarse. "It is now."

Grace wouldn't let go of the bit about the police. "Cops seem to find us. They materialize out of thin air."

"Or they're stalking us via satellite." Tawny peered over the edge of her wine glass.

"I don't think cops have satellites."

Tawny used Grace's own buzz word on her. "Ert. No, they don't. If they did, they'd have better things to do with them than track us. My intuition tells me fate is messing with your love life, Ms. Cordray. You're destined to either sleep with a cop or get hauled off to jail by one."

"Why me? Why not you? Or Steph and Elaina?"

"You're the only one who drools the second you see a badge. You had the hots for Cherry Ridge's own Officer Ted Marley. On the trip here you made eyes at Johnny Appleseed. I heard some accelerated breathing when you saw Officer Lorenzo."

"The evidence does support your claim. Officer Ted was a cutie. The sweet officer in Pennsylvania was an eyeful too. And Officer Lorenzo played hard to get but I think we had a moment." Grace fanned herself. "My temperature went up a few degrees when he entered my personal space."

"You didn't have a moment. You were the recipient of a scowl."

"Elaina, you have a lot to learn about men."

Men were mysterious creatures with penises. What Elaina knew about them – men, not penises – could fit into a teacup. Just when she thought she had a bead on what they were about, they proved her wrong. She had been married to Arden for over fifteen years and only knew what he allowed her to know. "You are spot on, Grace. I know practically zip. I was, however, keenly aware that Officer Lorenzo was ready to wrestle you to the ground and not in a fun way."

Grace's blue eyes glistened with amusement. "Some

guys go all bad-ass in front of a woman to get their attention."

"That's the most ridiculous thing I've ever heard."

Tawny allied with Elaina. "When they're in sixth grade, maybe. Forty-something men, on the other hand, don't resort to prepubescent behavior as a means to attract a woman."

"Wanna bet?" Steph ran a finger around the rim of her glass. "Corbett did it and I lost my head over him."

Grace didn't mince words. "Corbett's a douche."

The comment caught Elaina off guard. She broke into a hearty laugh and almost upended her wine glass. "How do you really feel, Grace?"

"It's true. Corbett's into douchebaggery. He broke Steph's heart and tried to bully her in the bar the day we met."

Steph clamped her mouth into a tight pucker. The fact she wasn't telling Grace she was a hundred-percent wrong, only deepened the likelihood she had a renewed interest in the snake.

Tawny exchanged curious glances with Elaina and Grace.

Grace was determined to get to the bottom of things. "Am I the only one who recalls Steph sliding under the table when Ditty Douchebag and his gum-snapping girlfriend came in?"

Tawny spit a spray of wine into the air.

Grace squinted at Steph. "You should be slapping your thigh with laughter instead of looking like you've been forced to drink ammonia. What gives?"

"Nothing gives. I'm tired. Let's take a tour of the house so we can go to bed already."

The Corbett-discussion was tucked away, for now.

Elaina encouraged Steph to be their guide.

Steph yawned. "Do you want the fifty cent tour? Or the five-dollar one?" She held out her hand.

"You're going to make us pay? Like you made Arden fork over the loot?" Tawny hip-checked Steph.

"I'm currently unemployed, so yeah, hand it over."

Maybe the vibe about Corbett was way off. Perhaps the only thing bugging Steph was finances. "Start me a tab," Elaina joked, hoping to lighten things up. The humor fell short. Steph's stiff expression didn't change one iota. Beyond the living room was an alcove. "Is that a library?"

"It can be."

"Lead on, little tour guide." A barely audible wince from Steph met Elaina's ears. This was not the time to delve into what it meant. Soon, she and Steph would reopen the conversation. Hopefully, her dear friend would be forthright with what was ailing her.

The alcove had a long, padded window bench with bare mammoth bookcases on both sides. "We have some book buying to do."

Tawny threw in that she had gossip magazines to contribute to their library.

Steph gestured to a winding staircase. "To your right, steps leading to the second and third floors; to your greater right, heaven."

Elaina placed a hand on Steph's back. "Not all women

view the kitchen as heaven. Some consider it a special kind of hell where things scorch or burst into flames."

"Your cooking has improved. You haven't burned toast or water in months."

"Suck up much, Mathews?" Tawny stepped back as though anticipating a swat.

Steph ignored the taunt. "Look at the skylight. It brightens the kitchen."

Despite being fatigued, Grace had enough vigor to heckle too. "You're a walking brochure."

"Don't knock it. We need to highlight all that's great about our new place. We have guests to entice. Steph, do you think you could jot down a few things you think are spectacular? Not now. After you get some sleep."

Steph bobbed her head. "I'd be happy to."

"Excellent." Elaina felt a twinge of guilt for using psychology on Steph. The more Steph realized how extraordinary their home was, the less inclined she'd be to leave.

Grace suggested they breeze through the 'brochure' so she could find a cozy corner to curl up in.

"Speaking of breeze, follow me." Steph took them to a breezeway off the kitchen. It was lined with windows. Below the windows were shelves filled with empty crocks and Mason jars. "Isn't this remarkable?" The question didn't require an answer and she kept talking. "What do you think about transforming it into a wine cellar?"

Tawny was quick to point out nothing above ground could be considered a cellar.

"You know what I mean. We could store wine here

until we build our tasting room."

Elaina picked up one of the medium size crocks that happened to be etched with grape leaves and held it out for the others to see. "A coincidence? I think not. It's a sign that Steph's on to something."

"Wait." Tawny backtracked to the kitchen. "There's something missing."

Elaina's belly rumbled. "Food?"

"Furniture. We don't have our table, chairs, sofa, or anything else. The moving company left a day ahead of us. Our stuff was supposed to be here already."

"I hate to admit I didn't notice. The cops descending on this place right away was a huge distraction. Factor in no sleep, no food, a little wine, and my brain turned to mush. It's a wonder I even know where I am." Elaina held up her phone and wandered into the empty living room to make the call. "This is Elaina Samuels calling from Portland, Maine. Your fellas picked up our furniture and belongings from Cherry Ridge, Ohio a few days ago. They've not made it here. Any idea where they might be?" She sighed when the customer service representative asked for the invoice number. "I'll get back with you once I locate the invoice." After ending the call, a few cuss words slipped out.

Tawny's light-brown eyes darkened with anger. "Don't tell me they lost our stuff."

"They didn't lose our stuff." At least Elaina hoped they didn't. "I'll get it sorted out."

"But we need our stuff," Tawny whimpered. "I need my bed."

"You could sleep in the Escalade."

"Meanie." Tawny went off on a tangent about inept movers and how they'd better have a good excuse for the delay.

"Wine needs to breathe for an hour and so do you, Tawn'. Relax." Grace sank to the floor and assumed a meditating position with her legs crossed, arms out at her side with her thumb and forefingers forming an O. "Ohm."

Steph got in on the act. She sat down and mimicked Grace. "Ohm."

"I could strangle them."

Elaina grinned. "Ohm."

Chapter Eight

- A chocolate meltdown! -

An odd noise roused Elaina from a deep sleep. One eyelid parted, then the other. It took a few seconds for her foggy brain to remember where she was and why a jacket covered her instead of a blanket. The peculiar disturbance happened again. Was that a knock? Half-dazed, she rose from the plush carpet of the first-floor bedroom and homed in on the sound to make sure it hadn't been imagined. The distinct rap of knuckles on wood made her scamper from the bedroom and to the front door. Smashing an eye against the peek hole, Elaina held hope it was the spiky-haired, brawny mover she'd worked with in Cherry Ridge. The wish was short-lived. A tall, slim, redhead with a county logo patch sewed on his jacket stood scratching his forehead. Without thinking, she opened the door and dang if the security alarm didn't go nuts again. "Shit!" In a flash, the code was entered and her fingers were crossed that the police wouldn't make a big deal out of it with another appearance.

Tawny stumbled into the living room with a murderous look. "What in Sam hell is going on?" She spied the guy standing in the doorway and something miraculous happened – her annoyed veneer changed to a full-face grin.

"Sorry. I'm still half-asleep." At the man's weird stare, Elaina further explained, "We drove all night to get here, so we had to take a nap." The sun beamed between barren branches on the trees situated on the west side of the property, which meant it had to be three o'clock or later.

Tawny scuttled up beside Elaina and pointed to the little dog stitched on the sleeve of his jacket. "Are you the dog warden?" The implication registered with her the same time it did with Elaina. They said, "Stony!"

"I'm not sure who Stony is, but I have a Husky in the back of my truck. A woman a block over found him in her garage. Needless to say, 9-1-1 got a call. The police notified me to take care of the problem. Officer Ferguson led me to you."

Elaina bit down on her bottom lip when she pictured the blond cop. Officer C. Ferguson had come through for them.

"You have Stony?" Frantic, Tawny pushed past Elaina and the county worker, and rambled as she ran. "He'd been cooped up for a few days so I tied him to the fence. He needed fresh air and to stretch his legs. There was plenty of leeway in the chain for him move around and get familiar with his new home. How did he get loose?"

The guy fell into a brisk run beside Tawny. "He's fine.

Although, he wasn't too keen on being locked up."

Tawny stopped mid-run. "You didn't subdue him with a... I can't even... You didn't shoot him with a tranquilizer."

"I didn't have to. He was stubborn, but in no way vicious. I spoke to him with a firm, non-threatening tone when I put him in the back of my van."

Elaina sidled next to them. "The same one you're using on Tawny?"

A delicate shade of red hit Tawny's cheeks.

Elaina's gaze moved to the dog warden. He had a deeper tint of color going on too. She had the distinct feeling she'd intruded on something. Hormones? There was a good chance those clever little suckers were ricocheting all around at that very moment. Not wanting to obstruct them, she took a step back. If it wasn't hormones, it could've been the smell of tobacco messing with Tawn'. The dog warden reeked of cigarettes. "I'll be in the house if you need me."

A series of warning beeps, the kind a truck makes when it backs up, made Elaina stretch her neck like a periscope. "Another van! The kind that carts furniture and boxes. Sweet mother of pearl, they made it. I should do a cartwheel."

"We've already had the cops here. And now the dog warden." Tawny winked at the guy who was just a breath away. "Why not an ambulance? When the No Sweat Pants Allowed – Wine Club decides to put down stakes, we make people notice. Not on purpose, but hey, it happens."

"I'll nix the cartwheel then." Elaina made haste to the driveway and around to the drivers' side of the long vehicle with her hands planted on her hips.

The driver exited the truck with a request for clemency. "Please forgive us, ma'am. We've had a rough trip. A flat tire came first. Then the transmission went out. Dispatch sent a replacement truck, which took forever to get there. We had to offload your belongings from the first truck onto the second one. None of that was our fault." He fired off the word "sorry" at least six times.

The second mover climbed out of the truck. "The only thing *we're* guilty of is running out of diesel." He grimaced. "Sitting along a busy highway while we waited for someone to bring us fuel, was the opposite of fun."

"Your company filled me in." Elaina had gotten a full accounting of why they were delayed and was promised a partial refund of their fee. She would've felt like a hypocrite not letting them off the hook with regards to the wait and the reimbursement, since she'd encountered a few difficulties getting to Maine too.

"Did they also tell you that all the nonsense would've only put us two days behind?" The skull tattoo on the drivers' Adam's apple bobbed when he spoke. "The mechanics that maintain the fleet failed to send a reliable replacement." He dropped the f-bomb. It must've dawned on him the language wasn't appropriate to be said in front of a customer; especially a female one. Again, he said, "Sorry." Making air quotes, he continued. "The *new* truck did some funky grinding when we crossed into Massachusetts." He kicked the moving van's tire. "That put us in this heap – truck number three."

"Life throws an occasional curveball." *It also hurls UTI's and slippery trips down grassy slopes.*

Impatience rolled off the second mover, who was all of eighteen if he was a day. He was agitated and unquestionably in no mood to hear about life and curveballs. "Are we going to stand here? Or are we going to do our job?"

"Asking if you'd like a cup of coffee is probably moot then."

The driver ignored his co-worker. "I could go for a cup of joe." He fidgeted. "More than anything, I need to use your bathroom – if that's okay."

"Of course it's okay."

"We have coffee?" Tawny asked from where she still stood with the dog warden. Stony was out of the truck and sniffing on the county employee who didn't seem eager to leave.

"Like I said earlier, I don't leave home without provisions. I brought a can of coffee and four mugs. We're good to go."

Elaina heard Tawny ask the dog warden if he'd like to stay for a cup.

"Maybe another time. It looks like you're going to have more than enough commotion going on for the next couple of hours. I don't want to be in the way. Besides, I'm on the clock until five." He crouched to come face to face with Stony. "You're a beautiful dog. Stay in your own yard, okay?" Gliding his fingers through Stony's fur, he did something uncharacteristic for someone who picked up strays for a living – he nuzzled Stony.

Tawny's mouth unhinged at the jaw. Elaina was sure hers had opened wider than normal as well.

"Thanks again. What did you say your name was?" Tawny had a dreamy glow going on.

The dog warden cleared his throat and shied away from the question by climbing into his van.

Tawny brazenly tapped the glass of the passenger side window and kept at it until he lowered it. "You probably didn't hear me ask your name."

Elaina left the moving crew to share a whispered thought. "He might be married, Tawn'."

Tawny had been bent over to peer into the van. She straightened in an instant. "I didn't give that a thought." Under her breath she mentioned he wasn't wearing a wedding band.

"Not all guys do."

As quietly as they tried to keep the conversation, he'd still heard. "I'm not married. Well, not anymore." Again, he cleared his throat. "I'm Bartholomew Simpson."

Elaina almost said "Bart Simpson" out loud.

Tawny didn't seem to put two and two together to come up with an animated TV character by the same name. "I'm Tawny Westerfield."

Elaina walked away when Tawny poured on the sugar with, "The offer is open-ended. When you get a hankering for coffee and conversation, stop by."

The moving crew had the back doors of the truck open and a fork truck ready to start the unloading process.

Elaina remembered the driver asked to use the

bathroom. "Follow me. Coffee and a bidet await you."

"A bidet?"

The co-worker explained that it was a fancy butt washer.

"I know what a bidet is. I didn't think people actually had them."

Elaina snorted a laugh. "We don't have one. I was just being mouthy."

The driver cocked an eyebrow. "I like mouthy chicks."

"Really?" Elaina said with a boatload of exaggeration. "Too bad I live in Jersey."

"Yeah, that is too bad." Elaina laughed herself inside the house. It had been a crazy day and she was sure there was a lot more crazy to come. Rather than fight the wacky, she'd embrace it.

* * *

Tawny nudged Steph with her foot. "Hey, sleepyhead, you might want to wake up long enough to tell these gentlemen where you'd like your dresser."

Steph pulled the jacket-sweater that was draped over her, higher.

"I tried to be nice." Tawny increased the volume of her voice to a shout. "Wake up!"

Steph flipped to her side with a moan.

Tawny crossed her arms. "Your butt crack is showing and these men are gawking."

The youngest guy grumbled about the weight of the dresser. He shifted his hold.

Steph gruffly encouraged Tawny to go away. "I'm trying to sleep." The remark about her bottom must've sunk in. Her green eyes zinged open. "What the French is going on?"

Elaina extended a hand to help Steph up. "Where would you like your dresser?"

"It made it to Maine?"

"Yes. Now hurry up and decide."

Steph stretched and yawned and motioned to an expanse of wall without windows on the north side of the room. She changed her mind as soon as they put the dresser in place.

Elaina put her foot down on behalf of the movers. "They're not interior decorators. They're the muscle we need to get the furniture in the house. That's it. They'll set it where you want it, once. The second time is on you."

The young, cranky mover showed his appreciation with a knuckle-bump. "Damn, boss lady, you rock!"

"I'm not the boss lady. We're equal partners."

"Pfft. Don't let her kid ya. She's the boss."

The guy roamed his eyes over Elaina. She reacted by giving him the evil eye.

Tawny said what Elaina was thinking. "She has a few years on you."

"I like a confident woman who's got looks and experience."

The older mover smirked. "Don't mind him. He thinks he's a Casanova who can win women by..."

"Smooth-talking them?" Elaina jested.

"Stretching the truth."

Elaina instinctively chuckled but she wasn't sure what to make of the comment. She wouldn't waste time trying to figure it out.

"Come on, Casanova." The driver guided the smooth-talker toward the stairs.

Grace stepped into Steph's bedroom with tufts of hair sticking every which way. "Who are those men?"

With a straight face, Tawny fibbed. "Gigolos. They're Elaina's gift to us for agreeing to come to Maine. They'll be right back. They forgot their credit card machine." She clicked her tongue. "The oldest profession has gone high-tech."

Grace turned to Elaina. "And the real explanation?" She looked and sounded like she could chop off a head or two without regret. Sleeping on the floor must've made her irritable.

"Those men are here to put you in a good mood; not in the way Tawny suggested. They've brought your bed."

"Oh, sweet Jesus, thank you!" Grace's eyes glazed with a teary mist.

If ever there was a moment of brutal clarity that was it. Elaina's chest constricted and for a moment she couldn't breathe. The cold, hard truth was that she'd encouraged three awesome women to quit their jobs to start over in a place only slightly familiar to one of them. She'd sold them on how great things would be. Then she put them through a hellish trip to get there. And for what? A possible slow boat to financial ruin? While she had money tucked away for essentials and emergencies, it wouldn't take long to use it up. She'd promised Tawny, Grace, and Steph medical and dental insurance, a 40lk plan, the ability to pay their car loans, and more. In a nutshell, she'd promised them the world. The undertaking so far had been physically strenuous and had taken a mental toll on them all. Steph suffered a UTI. Grace oozed exhaustion. Lord only knows what Tawny was dealing with. What it boiled down to was that she'd stressed her friends to the max...and herself. An abnormal amount of dread and self-doubt washed over her, along with a dozen other emotions. They pooled into one overwhelming mix and destroyed what was left of Elaina's calm. Her pulse thrummed loudly in her ears, the air in her lungs refused to move, and she broke out in a cold sweat. She buried her face in her hands for a few seconds, and then without any forethought, she raced from the room, down two flights of stairs, and out the front door. The tears she'd cried on that grassy slope in Pennsylvania were nothing compared to the water pouring from her eyes now.

The guys carrying the sofa almost dropped it when they saw her. "Lady, what's wrong?"

Elaina looked both ways, darted across the street, and down an alley. A brisk wind blowing in off the Atlantic made her shiver and trek faster.

Huffing and puffing at the waterfront, she put a hand on the wooden railing for support, and bent at the waist. After she caught her breath she walked the length of a dock and sat on the end with her legs hanging over the edge, almost touching the water. A great blue heron swooped down nearby. She also saw an Atlantic puffin propel itself underwater and come out with multiple fish.

Embarrassed for losing it, she sniffed and hung her head.

Elaina wasn't sure how long she sat there but she could now see the beacon light from a lighthouse and ferries were headed back into the harbor from trips to the islands.

"I wondered when you were going to crack."

Elaina closed her eyes and dropped her head to her chest again.

"You've been this remarkably strong woman."

Opening her eyes, Elaina swallowed hard.

Tawny sat beside her. "I read a headline the other day that applies here: Even monkeys know which rock will break the toughest nut." There wasn't a trace of mirth in the statement. "We're your monkeys, Elaina. You said so yourself. If we unintentionally found a rock to break you, we're sorry."

"You didn't break me."

"Are you sure?"

"I'm sure."

"You took off like someone set a firecracker under your butt."

Elaina twisted a loose string from her jacket around her pinkie, sniffed again, and shared the raw truth. "I had a panic attack." She ran her hands across her tired face. "It hit me hard back there when I realized how selfish I was. I talked you guys into giving up everything...for me."

Tawny swiped at the tears leaking from the corners of her eyes. "We didn't give up everything for you. The opposite happened. You gave up everything for us. We were in need of a fresh start. You provided it but you didn't muscle us. We're in Maine because we chose to be here. Are we freaking scared? Hell yes." She smoothed a hand over Elaina's shoulders.

Elaina pulled two tissues from the pocket of her jacket and handed one to Tawny. They both blew their noses. "Sorry for the meltdown."

"I'm glad you got it out of the way." Tawny flinched when a gull squawked overhead. "The others would've come along, but Grace thought she should hang back with Stony given his fondness for leaving the premises. Steph volunteered to work with the movers." She stood. "Come on, fearless leader. Let's go have a different kind of meltdown. One involving chocolate. I hear there's a restaurant on Terwilleger Boulevard that serves molten lava cake." A soft smile kinked the corners of her mouth. "We deserve it."

Elaina nodded. "We do."

* * *

"Good evening, ladies. I'm Nick. I'll be your waiter tonight." Nick handed out elegant menus laced together with burgundy satin ribbon. "Would you care to see a wine menu as well?"

Grace blinked up him. "Is the earth round?"

Nick met her snark with some of his own. "They say

it is. Don't believe everything you read."

Steph tapped his arm. "We don't need a wine menu. We already know what we want." She pointed to Elaina. "Blackberry wine for the boss lady." Gesturing to Tawny, "Give the hot brunette a bottle of your dry red. The woman who doesn't know a thing about planets loves white Merlot. And Sangria for yours truly."

Nick's gaze travelled around the table as if questioning whether she was pulling his leg.

"You heard right. We'd like four different bottles of wine." Elaina snagged a cheesy breadstick from the basket he'd placed on the table.

"Is this a celebration?"

Tawny fibbed ever-so-slightly. "No. We're just a bunch of middle-aged winos out on the town."

The numerous empty wine bottles they hauled to the recycle center every month could bolster Tawny's claim, but it didn't tell the whole story. Yes, they killed a bottle every now and then – not individually. One bottle equated to a full glass each. Along with the great taste, it helped four high-strung women relax. Elaina reflected on the last time they tied on one – the day they met. Over too much wine, they'd poured out their stories and got to know one another on a deeply personal level. A fast and easy friendship developed, and they formed the No Sweat Pants Allowed – Wine Club. In the wee hours of the morning they moved the wine club meeting to her house. At some point they'd fallen asleep only to wake up with phenomenal hangovers. It had been an amazing night and morning-after that changed their lives.

"A lively group. My kind of people." Nick's grin extended from one ear to the other. Maybe the smile was genuine; maybe not. Whatever the case, he knew the first rule of business – tune into your customers. They could take a lesson.

Elaina laid aside the garlic bread stick. "We're not winos. Not by a long shot. And this is definitely a celebration. We're now the proud owners of a bed and breakfast."

"Yeah? Which one?"

Elaina shared the details.

He snapped his fingers. "I know the place. It's awesome. My fiancé and I got engaged there in the summer."

"Congratulations, Nick!"

"Back at ya. Operating a bed and breakfast will eat up a lot of your time. Good thing there are four of you." The sound of a waitress dropping and breaking a plate curbed the conversation. "I should take your food orders and get those bottles of wine underway." The twenty-something blond started to walk away, but retraced his steps. "My dad owns the restaurant. He's also a member of the Chamber of Commerce. If you have questions about Portland or would like to join the Chamber, I could send him over when you're finished with your dinner."

Grace suggested they meet him before they got jiggy with all that wine.

"Good plan. I'll see what I can do."

Steph drummed her fingers on the table. "You might as well take our dessert orders while you're at it and deliver the goodies with our entrees." She slapped a hand to her chest. "Beef bourguignon, parslied red skin potatoes, sesame green beans, and my life would not be complete without your bread pudding."

"Excellent choice. The bread pudding comes with rum sauce."

Steph pulled at her bottom lip with her front teeth. "I know. More alcohol. Did we mention we're taking a taxi home?"

"I wasn't pointing it out because of the alcohol." A small chuckle moved his broad chest. "Who am I kidding? Yes, I was."

Elaina liked Nick. He was friendly, on the ball, and honest.

Grace made a face. "Bread and pudding doesn't ring my bell. No offense but who decided to combine those two things?"

"Don't be a food snob, Cordray. Sure it's made from stale bread but it's so much more." Steph's passion for food and cooking came out clear and strong, and she spoke with her hands as much as her mouth. "There's cinnamon, vanilla, brown sugar, butter. Oh my god! It's heavenly. I'm salivating just thinking about it."

"Sing it, sista," Grace playfully mocked. "Yeah, you can have stale bread with rum." She raised her cheeks high with a smile. "Key lime pie for me. Umm, for my entrée, the wild rice with mushrooms and salmon basted with honey, garlic, and butter will make my taste buds dance."

Nick punched the information into a tablet that

advised the cooks in the kitchen.

It was Tawny's turn. "Did we mention Steph's one heck of a chef who's writing a cookbook?" She didn't leave room for Nick to answer. "No? Well she is." Again, not giving him time to respond, she placed her order. "My palate is screaming for triple chocolate cheesecake and a cheeseburger with all the trimmings. Add sweet potato fries and we're good to go."

"We have dancing taste buds, a screaming palate, and someone who needs bread pudding to live." Elaina snickered and ran a finger over the fancy menu. "I'd like the   heavy-on-the-calories-but-comforting-to-the-soul molten chocolate cake. Oh, and since I'm supposed to be the health nut of the group, I should probably have the honey mustard grilled chicken and a tossed salad with no dressing – a lemon wedge to squeeze over it, instead."

"Thanks, ladies. You're a refreshing change from the clientele I'm used to." Nick took back the menus. "I'll return with the wine ASAP."

Tawny waited until he was well away before she said, "Down, hormones, down. Woo-wee, he's a cutie."

Elaina held her breath, not wanting anyone to say Tawny was old enough to be his mom. The mom-reference might send Tawny into a tailspin. There was only one meltdown allowed per day. She'd personally used up the allotment.

Steph spread her cloth napkin across her lap and took a sip from the fancy-smancy water goblet.

No one commented on Tawny's age. Elaina released the pent-up air. "This unofficial meeting of the No Sweat

Pants Allowed – Wine Club is now called to order."

Tawny clanged her fork against the glass vase of silk autumn flowers. As though she anticipated blowback, she defended her action. "We don't have a gavel."

Elaina bit off a small bite of breadstick and chewed fast. "First on the agenda, it might be wise to refrain from calling ourselves winos. If the wrong person heard it, they wouldn't hesitate to spread the gossip."

"Oops."

"It's okay, Tawn'. We clown around. It's what we do. But now we have to live by a different set of rules. Be ourselves at all times, with one tiny exception – when we're in public we have to portray serious women of business." Elaina backpedaled just a bit. "Business women have fun. It's just that we have to choose our words carefully until the community gets to know us for who we really are."

"Four delightful hussies?"

* * *

"I've been told you're writing a cookbook." A good looking guy with the same brown eyes as Nick, set his attention on Steph and put out his hand for her to shake. "I'm Nicholas Augustine the second."

"I'm Stephanie Mathews the first." Hot-pink embarrassment raced up her neck and into her face. "Yes, I'm a cookbook in progress." She corrected. "My cookbook is a work in progress."

A smile curved his mouth at the snafu but he didn't

linger on the mistake. He nodded in greeting to Elaina, Tawny, and Grace and then focused on Steph again. "That's incredible. I've wanted to write one as well." Nicholas sighed. "My wife tossed me aside for someone else a couple of years ago forcing me to shelve the idea and pour all my time into making a go of this place." He looked away for no longer than a moment. "I didn't mean to make things awkward by over-sharing. I'm not sure why that came out of my mouth. I don't make a habit of battering customers with personal information. Please forgive me."

Elaina tilted her head to the side and watched Steph turn to goo.

Steph placed a hand on his sleeved-forearm. "I've never been married but I've been tossed aside a few times myself. I know how it can crush a person's spirit." Warmth emanated from her words and her eyes. "If it wasn't for these ladies I never would've made it through the pain and I certainly wouldn't have started writing a cookbook."

All eyes jetted to Tawny when she slurped from her water goblet.

The Nicholas-trance was interrupted. Steph removed her hand from his arm. "These are my friends – Tawny, Grace, and Elaina."

"Nice to meet you, ladies. My son informed me you bought the bed and breakfast once owned by the Kirbys." The comment was meant for them all, although he still keyed on Steph.

Steph sat up a little straighter. "We did." In a voice

laced with sexy undertones, she invited him to stop by and check it out.

"I might just do that." He moved a little farther into her personal space. "Maybe we could spend an afternoon discussing cookbooks."

"I'd like that."

The soft lighting of the restaurant struck Nicholas's brown eyes just right. Damn he had great eyes.

"Excellent." Without asking he grabbed the bottle of wine setting in front of Steph and topped off her glass. "We can also talk about you joining the Chamber at that time. Would tomorrow be too soon?"

"Tomorrow works for me."

"Noon-ish?"

There was a small quiver in Steph's voice when she said noon would be fine.

The younger Nicholas arrived with an oval tray loaded with entrees. His dad took one of the dishes and sat it on Steph's place mat.

"How'd you know this one is mine?"

His eyes slid across Steph like a private embrace. "I just knew."

The flush in her face hadn't settled down from the first rosy tint caused by Nicholas, now it blazed to a deeper shade. "I've only had beef bourguignon one other time. I'm excited to taste you." She awkwardly tried to cover blunder by clearing her throat. "Your beef." She cleared her throat a second time. "Bourguignon."

Elaina had all she could do not to burst into raucous laughter. She dared not look at the others because she'd lose it for sure. Poor Steph was tripping over herself, big time.

Nicholas crouched beside her. "I'd appreciate your feedback."

Nick the third broke the trance this time. "Dad, Carson needs to speak with you."

"Duty calls." Nicholas straightened to a stand and looked around the table. "It's been a pleasure, ladies." He smiled at Steph. "I'll see you tomorrow."

"Okay," Steph said breathlessly.

Nicholas rushed off to address whatever Carson needed.

Nick watched his father hurry away. "Someone want to catch me up?"

Tawny took a sweet potato fry from the cheeseburger plate still in Nick's hand. "Your dad is paying us a visit tomorrow. Cool, huh?"

Nick's gaze darted back to his dad. "I guess it's cool." He shrugged. "Maybe the Chamber's welcoming committee makes house calls now." He commenced dispersing the rest of the food.

Grace took a bite of salmon. "Oh yeah, that's what I'm talking about. My taste buds are doing the cha-cha."

The hostess sat a young couple at an adjacent table. When she passed Grace on her way back to her podium at the front of the restaurant, she leaned in. "Mine do the same thing when I have the salmon."

They shared a laugh.

"Stephhhh." Elaina clutched Steph's hand. "That was...umm..."

"I know. I'm freaking. I may not look like I'm freaking, but my heart is pumping hard."

"Nicholas the second. His name sounds like he could be a czar or emperor." Grace dragged the tines of her fork through her key lime pie and then stuck them in her mouth for a taste. "He might not rule a country or kingdom but he rules pie." She licked her lips.

Tawny put her hand up and pointed behind it. "I think someone has had a bit too much wine."

"I think we've all had a little too much everything. It's time to eat dinner, head back home, and sleep off the side effects of leaving Ohio. Tomorrow morning we begin anew. I've made a list of things we need to do and I'm not afraid to delegate the tasks." Elaina grinned at Steph. "You already know what you have to do."

"Charm the Chamber member?"

"Laundry."

Chapter Nine

~ Hot flashes and handcuffs! ~

Grace hobbled into the living room holding her hip. "I feel like I tent-camped in the mountains and slept on a boulder."

Elaina sat at the table looking over the to-do list. One of the things on the list was to assemble their beds. She raised her head a fraction of an inch to level a look at Grace through her eyelashes. "You made a comfy nest of blankets on your mattress."

Grace poured a cup of coffee and joined Elaina at the table. "This birdie somehow fell out of that cozy nest. I woke up in the middle of the night because it was stinking hot in my room. I stumbled in the dark to use the bathroom and when I went back to bed I couldn't find half the blankets I'd shoved off."

"You could've turned on the light."

"Once my eyeballs detect light there's no going back to sleep." Grace yawned. "I woke up, covered only in a sheet. Was the excessive heat real? Or am I getting sick?

Feel my forehead. Do I have a fever?" She emitted a lengthy groan. "I don't have time to be sick. There's too much to do."

Elaina placed a hand at Grace's temple. "You're fine. No fever." She tapped the handle of her coffee cup. "Maybe you had an H-flash."

"What's an H-flash?" It took less than a nano-second for Grace to answer her own question. "Ohhhh, that's just plain mean. I didn't have a hot flash. Don't ever say those words in my presence again or I'll have to circle your neck with my hands and give it a squeeze."

Chuckling, Elaina sipped the piping hot Arabica brew and studied her friend over the rim of the cup. Shortly after they'd moved in together, Grace had gone into a hissy fit when Steph said the word menopause. Turns out, Mrs. Grace Cordray was petrified of that stage of life. With her forty-second birthday looming in the distance, there was a good chance she was experiencing some pre-birthday anxiety. "We've been all over God's green earth and somewhere along the way you might've picked up the flu bug. I have a bottle of Vitamin C stashed in my tote bag." She held up the bag that lay on the chair beside her and then produced a mega-size bottle of chewable orange C's. "Don't be shy about taking these today. Even if you aren't getting the flu we've put our bodies through a lot lately."

"What about our bodies?" Tawny padded into the kitchen in bare feet, dressed in the same clothes she wore yesterday, only now they were wrinkled indicating she'd slept in them.

"Grace thinks she might have the flu. She was hot in the middle of the night."

Guilt splashed across Tawny's face.

"You did something. 'Fess up," Grace ordered.

"I was cold so I edged the thermostat up a wee bit."

"How much is a wee bit?"

"Are you toasty warm now?"

"I could strip down to my underwear and still be hotter than toasty; both literally and figuratively." Grace made a sizzling sound.

"I jacked the heat up to eighty."

Elaina winced. "Tawn', if you were that cold you might be getting sick too."

"I'm not. I just thought since we were sleeping on the floor we'd need extra warmth. So I bumped it up." Tawny put her teeth together in a non-repentant grin.

"We didn't sleep on the floor. We slept on our mattresses."

Tawny half-rolled her eyes at Grace. "Which were on the floor." She looked at Elaina while she washed out the coffee mug she'd used the day before. "How was sleeping in the basement?"

"Not bad. There were some creaking noises to get used to."

"You don't have to sleep down there, you know. Stony and I would be happy to share our room with you." Tawny filled her coffee mug all the way to the top, leaving no room for creamer. Slurping the excess, she went bug-eyed. "Aye yi yi that's hot."

"Like we were last night," Grace interjected.

"You haven't ventured to the basement, have you? It's as nice down there as it is up here. There are four large carpeted rooms with wainscoting that matches the woodwork. The Kirbys left behind a sofa bed." She couldn't stop a smirk. "I slept like a baby."

Grace narrowed her eyes to a squint. "Must be nice."

Elaina shoved off her chair and opened a cupboard door. "Would these make things better?" She pulled out a box of assorted donuts and rolls. "There's a bake shop down the road. Stony and I enjoyed a morning walk through the snow so you could start your day with something sweet." She took one of the glazed donuts. "Grocery shopping has to take place today. We have to get back on track with better food choices. After the donuts are gone."

Tawny nodded. "I'm for that."

Grace agreed.

Steph lumbered down the stairs with some phenomenal clomps. "We need an elevator." She appeared in the kitchen wearing fuzzy plaid pajama pants and a t-shirt with a frayed collar. Her gorgeous head of red hair was matted like she'd taken a shower and went to bed without combing it.

"We have donuts."

Steph eyed the sugary pastries. "Nah. I'm going to be good."

"Be good tomorrow. This morning it's the only thing we have to eat." Tawny had already wolfed down a jelly donut and reached for another. "You might as well have one because Elaina is going to shove salad and broccoli down our throats from here on out."

"She loves succotash, so we'll have that too." Steph whapped Elaina on the back as she made her way to the coffee cups.

"I do loooove succotash."

"You hate succotash."

"Not the way you make it. I used to gag at the mere sight of it, now I look forward to a heaping dish of the gnarly combination of corn, lima beans, bacon, and carrots."

"Don't forget I add jalapeno." Steph dropped her bottom in an empty chair. The rough movement spilled her own cup of coffee and sloshed some of Grace's onto the table.

Elaina retrieved a roll of paper towels from the counter.

"Speaking of chefs," Tawny began the inevitable conversation, "would turning away donuts have anything to do with Nicholas the second?"

Steph squared her shoulders. "Yes and no. As you're well aware, I'm easily coerced by food and men." A grimace crimped the corners of her mouth. "I fall in love with both," she snapped her fingers, "just like that."

"That's not necessarily a bad thing."

"Since it was unbearably hot in my bedroom last night, which made it difficult to sleep, I stared at the ceiling for hours – even though I couldn't actually see it – and hashed over my past mistakes. I don't want Nicholas to become just another misstep."

Elaina bumped Tawny's arm with her elbow. "You're

grounded from the thermostat. Do not even go near it. Continue, Steph."

Steph tried to finger-comb her hair, unsuccessfully. "Nicholas got to me. I mean really got to me. If he would've said 'let's make love', I would've ripped off my clothes right there in the restaurant." She moaned. "What is wrong with me?" She swung a finger in the air. "I don't want to hear the word hormone come out of any of your mouths."

"Nothing's wrong with you. You're just ready for something intimate and real." Elaina tried to keep from sounding like a know-it-all and her inner-voice warned her to err on the side of caution, but it was hard to hold back. "I've sensed some internal strife going on with you, Steph." Why couldn't she shut her yapper while she was ahead? Because she was wired to mother people, that's why. She'd never be a mom but she had maternal instincts that were going to waste. "I worried you might still have feelings for Corbett."

Steph splayed her hand, palm-side down, on the table. "He wants me back."

I knew it.

Tawny dropped her half-eaten jelly roll on the table. "I'll bind you with duct tape and stuff a dirty sock in your mouth before I let you run back to... What did you call him, Grace?"

"Ditty Douchebag."

"There was pain in your eyes when you saw him, Steph, and I hear it in your voice when you talk about him. No way are you going back for another round of hurt. Ditty Douchebag doesn't deserve you."

"You can't dictate what I do with my life."

"I'm not kidding about the duct tape and dirty sock. I'll do it."

Steph's gaze went around the table, like she was canvassing opinion. "Corbett can jump off a lighthouse for all I care. Or I can push him off." She sighed. "We're not getting back together. I gave it some serious thought though. He broke up with the woman he left me for because he says he still loves me."

Grace didn't sugarcoat anything. "Chances are she broke up with him, not the other way around."

Steph had a distant look in her eyes. "That's probably the case. When she and I bumped into each other at the grocery that time, she told me the truth about everything and said she wouldn't stay with him."

"You were tired of digging pothole after pothole on your road to happiness, Steph. Maine is your chance to stop digging."

Steph tasted her coffee and made a face. She liked her coffee weaker than what Elaina made. "I know."

Elaina adjusted the direction of the conversation to give Steph time to think. "How's the heartburn, Tawn'?"

"Not bad today despite the fact my sons are still treating me as if I have a communicable disease. I am so over their selfishness. As far as I'm concerned they can kiss my pasty white arse."

Tawny wasn't over the rejection. Not by a long shot. Bo and Quentin Westerfield would soon get an earful from Elaina if they didn't stop being dipsticks. "On a lighter note, here's the list I promised. I've divided up the tasks." She shoved the lined piece of tablet paper to the center of the table.

"Aren't you the smart one? There are four squares. One for each of us. With assignments."

"Don't whine. I bought breakfast."

Steph inched a cinnamon roll topped with pecans from the box. She nibbled the edge. "This is good, but mine are so much better."

Tawny tapped the list. "That's why you get to buy the groceries. And do laundry."

Grace hawked the piece of paper. "You want me to hire a professional photographer? What's that about?"

"We should update the current bed and breakfast website with our picture and other pertinent information. There's a chance we might make a whole new site. For now, we'll want to introduce ourselves as the new owners. I thought a picture of us in front of the fireplace would be good. Stony and Lula have to be in it too. Our customers need to see us and they need to know our pooch and feline are part of the package. If they have pet allergies, this might not be the place for them. What do you think?"

"I think you're awesome." Tawny pulled up off the chair. "Looking at that list, you've thought of everything."

"I'm sure I've missed some stuff but we'll address whatever it is as it comes along."

Tawny started to refill her coffee cup but stopped. "You said you walked through the snow this morning. I heard you but I was more interested in donuts." She leaned across the sink to get a better look out the window. "Holy snowballs!"

* * *

Elaina's phone vibrated on the counter where it sat charging. She'd turned off the ringer so it wouldn't wake everyone if it rang, since they all needed a little extra shut-eye.

Tawny craned her neck to check the phone screen. "Ahhh, Rachel. I'll bet she has a dog story." She tossed the phone to Elaina. "I still can't believe she named her female dog Neil."

Elaina hunched her shoulders in a shrug. "She said she named her after someone special. Weird that she never mentioned anyone with that name before, but hey, we only know this much about Rachel." She pinched her fingers together to show an inch. "Maybe Neil is the guy who lurks in the background while she's on the phone."

"It couldn't be the lurker. Can you imagine if Rachel said, "Come here, Neil. Which one would obey? The dog or the guy?" Steph snorted.

Grace set them straight. "In case your gooey brains have forgotten, she named her after someone who's in the hospital; someone not expected to make it out of there. Sheesh, get with the program."

"Yeah, that tidbit didn't get stored in my medial temporal lobe." Elaina answered Rachel's call with Steph hee-hawing over her use of anatomically correct wordage. "Rachel, hello."

"Good morning, y'all. How goes the travels?"

A series of low yips could be heard in the background.

"We finally made it to the X on the map yesterday morning. I hate to admit we forgot to call you. In our defense we were so tired we didn't know up from down. Then the movers arrived." Elaina ran out of reasons.

"No worries. I've been preoccupied too. Neil is driving me insane. She's peed on the floor twice in the last five minutes."

"I would too if you named me Neil." Tawny said it low enough that Rachel couldn't hear. Elaina gave her the stink eye anyway.

"You wouldn't want a Pomsky, would you?"

"I hope you're kidding."

"I'm sort of kidding. I'm sort of not." Rachel hollered at Neil to stop chewing the table leg. "Just a minute."

Elaina took her phone temporarily off speaker. "This is your field of expertise, Tawn'. Maybe you can give her some pointers."

"Rule number one: don't name a female dog Neil."

"There's no need to tick her off. She seriously could use some tips. Be nice." Elaina returned the phone to speaker mode.

"I had to put Neil in her crate. Oh geez. Now she's crying like a baby."

"Rachel, this is Tawny. The first thing you should do is take a breath. Neil can sense your distress and it's confusing her. The reason she's crying like a baby is because she is a baby. As far as why she's gnawing things, it's because she's teething. I hate to be the bearer of bad tidings but she's going to teethe for at least six months, maybe longer. Whatever you don't want chewed, don't make it available."

"Am I supposed to clear the furniture out of the room?"

"Nah. They make doggie deterrent you can put on the furniture. It's supposed to be bitter. I'm not sure if that stuff works but it can't hurt. Your best bet is to teach her what she can and can't chew. She has no idea at this point. If she starts sharpening her teeth on the table, calmly say no and remove her from there. Sidetrack her with something she can chew." She also suggested Rachel not scream at the dog because it will make them both anxious.

"I can't do this."

Elaina pictured Rachel throwing her hands in the air and giving up. "Sure you can, Rach'. I wasn't a dog lover either, mostly because I wasn't comfortable around them. But Stony won me over on day one. Now I can't imagine life without him."

"Wasn't he a full grown dog when you met him?"

"Yes. But Stony sheds like crazy. That was the biggest adjustment for me. My ex just about had a conniption fit when he stopped by and saw a few dog hairs on the furniture."

"I hear ya."

Elaina exchanged glances with Tawny. "Is Neil shedding already?"

"Uh, no, I was...uh...speaking hypothetically."

Grace moved closer to the phone. "Does the man in

your life know anything about dogs?"

"The only thing he knows is how to get pissy when Neil does her business on the kitchen floor. He is so not a dog person yet he pressured me into getting her. If he wasn't so hot I'd tell him to take a hike and to take Neil with him when he left."

"Sounds like you're completely whipped over this mystery man." Elaina went on to say maybe the guy has a hidden love for dogs but also a bit of OCD and the two sets of feelings are battling it out.

"You hit the proverbial nail on the head. He's definitely obsessive-compulsive and for reasons I can't fathom, I dig it. He and I aren't stark opposites as much as I'd like to think we are. I hate clutter. He hates clutter. I have to disinfect the shower every day. He automatically grabs the bottle of disinfectant cleaner after he bathes. You won't see dishes in my sink. I either wash them by hand right away or load them in the dishwasher." She didn't take a breath. "Confession time – even if there are only a few things in the dishwasher I can't let them set until there are more. I run it half-empty. That's not the most economical or environmentally responsible way to go about it, but I can't help myself. I hit the start button. He does the same thing at his place. Recently, he hired a cleaning woman but there's nothing for her to clean. Regarding the dog, he gets as giddy to see the Neil as Neil is to see her. My mystery hunk gets down on the floor and plays with her. The second the dog piddles though, he loses his cool. Neil gets scared and squats right in front of him. I have to intervene so he doesn't toss the

dog out on her ear. Essentially, I'm training two babies."
Rachel groaned. "Like I said, if he wasn't so good looking
I'd kick his fine tush to the curb." Still not leaving room
for anyone else to say a word she continued. "I'm usually
not drawn to guys who can flip on a dime. One minute
he's amorous, the next, he's scrubbing something or he's
complaining about the dog."

"You absolutely have a situation."

"You know it and I know it, but I want him in my
life. It was a love-at-first sight kind of thing. I used to
scoff at the idea of instant attraction so strong it distorts
reason. Then it happened to me. Every time I see him my
brain short-circuits."

"Send us his picture to see if the same thing happens
to our brains."

"Nice try, Grace. We're still keeping our relationship
on the down low. When he gives me the green light,
I'll flood your phones with pictures. Until then, you'll
just have to wonder. Well, wine chicklets, I have to go.
Someone's knocking on the door. We're glad...I mean
I'm glad you made it to Maine safe and sound. Buh-bye."

"She hinted we knew him. I'd bet a hundred dollars
she's dating the mayor. He's recently single and rumored
to be," Tawny made a face of aversion, "handsy. Ick. The
thought of her with him gives me the willies."

"I've never heard he's handsy. I did hear he buys spray
disinfectant by the case." Steph glanced at the clock,
shifted in her chair, and shot the clock another quick
look.

Elaina wasn't convinced Rachel was dating the mayor.

"I can't see her panting over someone with nose hairs so long they should be put up in curlers."

Grace lifted one shoulder in a shrug. "Despite his lengthy nose hairs he's a fairly attractive man."

"Still." Elaina shuddered for effect.

"The mayor may not be someone you'd pick, but he fits the profile to a tee. He's single with OCD tendencies. He's all hands. And he's well-known."

Elaina wouldn't correct Tawny. When they tried to drag his name from Rachel during their last phone call, she'd said they may know him. She didn't say he was well-known.

"You guys can discuss the mayor and Rachel. I have to get ready for a very special visitor." Steph almost upended the table when she got up. Her clumsy departure from the kitchen turned into a brisk run up two flights of stairs.

"I wanted to discuss the name for our bed and breakfast this morning. Maybe over dinner we can decide." Elaina put a hand over her coffee cup when Tawny tried to top it off. "I'm going to unpack a few boxes and then head downtown. I have stops to make at the courthouse and the various utility companies to get things switched over to our name."

"Good plan." Tawny grabbed the reservation ledger the Kirbys left for them and flipped to November. "It appears the Kirbys cancelled reservations until the week of Thanksgiving. Thank goodness for that. We have some leeway to get this place in ship-shape. According to your list, it's my job to get the main living areas up to snuff.

I'm no decorator but I'll give it a try." She turned to leave, then twisted back around. "After Steph came home from her visit with the Kirbys, she'd described four-poster beds with quilts and floral settees, bookshelves filled with books, a grandfather clock, and more. The Kirbys weren't here long enough to go out and buy all that stuff so it must've come with the place when they bought it. When they decided to sell to us, we should've stipulated in the contract that the furnishings remain."

"Everything happened so fast. Furniture was the last thing on our minds."

Tawny rubbed her forehead above her brow. "How do we proceed since we don't come close to having enough furniture to fill the rooms?"

"There's money in our business account for whatever we need. Would you mind checking out the furniture stores today? I trust your judgment and your taste. If you find something you like, buy it and have it delivered."

Tawny smiled as big as the day she'd gotten Stony back from Grady. "Thank you for that."

"For what?"

"For trusting my judgment."

"I was married to Arden. I needed his permission for everything. After having been under his thumb for so long, I get downright giddy when I get to make decisions without him looking over my shoulder with a critique. So, I know what you're feeling."

Tawny traipsed back to Elaina and gave her a half-hug. "You're awesome."

The sound of a car door slamming made Elaina look

at the clock. "If that's Nicholas, he's too early." She started to get up.

Tawny motioned for her to sit back down. "I'll check it out."

"Good. I'm still cold from the trip to the bakery."

Tawny parted the curtains in the living room. "Uh oh. Now what did we do?"

Elaina was out of her chair in a flash. "Don't tell me Portland P.D. is going to read our pedigree again."

"Not in an official capacity. He didn't bring the squad car and he's out of uniform."

"Officer Lorenzo?"

"Nope."

* * *

Elaina took a series of quick glances out the oval shaped window above the security keypad. Her heart did a small flip at the sight of Officer C. Ferguson in tight blue jeans and a leather bomber jacket. "What do you suppose he wants?"

Tawny automatically said, "Grace. She's meant to join forces with the law. And by join I mean..."

"Yeah, yeah, I get your drift." It was a logical conclusion. Elaina secretly winced. It was just a matter of time before Officer C. Ferguson and Grace hooked up. It would probably happen in a few minutes; not the actual 'hook up', but the plan to 'hook up' would be put in place. Elaina remembered how she'd felt in Officer C. Ferguson's presence yesterday. He'd snagged her attention from the moment she laid eyes on him. She'd watched the way he moved, how his facial expressions changed, the way the corners of his mouth quirked at the corners when he smiled, and how his blue eyes sparkled when the misunderstanding about the security system was resolved. She didn't think he paid much attention to Grace, but men weren't always obvious. Maybe once he and Officer Lorenzo got back in the cruiser they discussed the dark-haired, blue-eyed cop magnet, and now Officer C. Ferguson was here to explore her magnetic pull.

Tawny opened the door at the exact moment he was set to knock. She exaggerated her greeting. "Officer Fergusonnn, how good to see you."

"Uh, hi. Is Elaina home?"

"Why yes she is." Tawny latched onto Elaina's wrist and tugged her into view.

Elaina straightened her blue cable-knit sweater and sucked in her belly. "Officer Ferguson."

Their eyes met and held for a few seconds.

An awkward, shy smile splashed across his face. "It's Chad Ferguson."

Tawny pushed at the small of Elaina's back to move her closer.

With a brief narrowed-eyed look she threatened to beat Tawny to a pulp if she didn't stop.

In Tawny's usual over-the-top style she feigned innocence by putting her palms up before walking away.

Elaina locked eyes with Chad again and a tremor of delight rocked her from head to toe. She detected a quiver in her voice too, when she spoke. "Did you come for coffee? Or are you here to ticket me for Stony running loose?"

"I'm not here to ticket you." A bigger, less-reserved smile curved his generous mouth. "But he's my excuse for stopping by."

"Stony made it home safely, thanks to you."

"You're welcome. When I heard the description of the dog I knew where he belonged." He shifted his weight from one foot to the other. "He's a beautiful dog. I'd hate to see harm come to him."

"I have a fresh pot of coffee with your name on it. Or do you have to get back to the precinct?" Elaina wouldn't assume he was off duty just because he wasn't in uniform. Cops were known to dress in street clothes when they took part in drug busts or other types of take-downs.

Chad rubbed the back of his neck and stumbled over his words. "It's...my day off."

Elaina tried hard not to convey surprise. "So coffee?"

"Sure."

Steph peered over the banister. "I heard commotion." She pointed at Chad. "Aren't you..."

Chad answered the unfinished question. "Yes."

Steph hollered loud enough to echo through the house. "Run, Tawn', they're on to you. They found out your middle name isn't Pia."

Tawny stuck her head around the archway of the kitchen to glare at Steph. "Pia IS my middle name, knucklehead." She looked at Elaina and Chad, wrinkled her nose, and took off up the stairs.

"Aaaand, it's game-on. Welcome to the loony bin."

Elaina inclined her head to the right. "This way."

"I grew up with four sisters and two brothers. I know all about game-on and loony bins."

Elaina noticed all four cups were dirty. "We haven't unpacked so give me a minute. Help yourself to a donut."

Chad's eyes laughed before he did. "You know the cop and donut thing is stereotyping, right?"

Elaina smirked and pushed the box toward him. "You don't like donuts?"

A larger laugh bounced in his broad chest. "I love donuts."

Filling the sink basin with just enough soapy water to wash their cups, she flicked a bubble in his direction. "I can tell by your physique that you only indulge in stereotypical behavior occasionally." Lame. When she tried to sound intelligent with a sense of humor, things sometimes came out cockeyed.

"I can't remember the last time I ate a donut. They're not something I keep on hand or think about. As far as physiques go, you're in good shape too. Are you a runner?"

The realization he was taking stock of her, made her even more nervous. "I like to run. I'm not hardcore though. I haven't run a marathon or half-marathon. I run on the treadmill sometimes. How about you?"

"Same here. In the summer I run every day; in the winter, not so much. If it isn't at least fifty degrees, I run on the treadmill. I also lift weights, and... Don't laugh. I'm into yoga."

"I'd never laugh at anyone who does yoga. The benefits are endless. Increased flexibility and muscle strength.

Improved respiration. More energy and vitality." His eyebrows rose ever-so-slightly, and Elaina realized she was rambling. "I used to own a gym, so I'm all about taking care of your body. Not your body. Bodies in general."

If he thought she was coming off as a moron, he didn't let on.

Chad never took his eyes off her. "Exercise is second-nature to me. Despite my parents having a slew of kids, my mom and dad made time to work out every morning before they went to work. We did the routine with them."

"That's pretty amazing. Most people I know couldn't imagine exercising first thing. For them, their morning routine involves slurping coffee, brushing their teeth while getting dressed, trying to get the kids out of bed and fed before sending them off to school, and then making a mad dash to their jobs. You know the drill."

"Actually, I don't. I've never had to deal with that kind of morning chaos."

What exactly did that mean? Elaina didn't have a chance to ponder the possibilities because Grace stuck her head in the kitchen. She was wearing an eye patch.

Chad laughed straight away.

Grace joined them with her hands in the air. "I swear I didn't do it."

An irresistible grin covered Chad's face. "Didn't do what?"

"Whatever is amiss that brought you here."

Elaina dried the mugs and filled them with coffee. She placed a cup in front of Chad and watched the good-humored interaction. The heady delirium she'd felt at seeing him for a second time, was replaced with a tiny bit of jealousy. She scolded herself for the reaction.

"Nothing's amiss. I came to check on your dog." He cleared his throat and glanced at Elaina. "To make sure he was back safe and sound."

Grace sat in the chair next to Chad. "Oh really? Is that a service offered by law Mainiacs?"

Chad's blondish-brown eyebrows twitched.

"By Mainiac she means someone who lives in Maine not maniac the lunatic." Elaina quirked her mouth into a lopsided smirk. "Forget it. By explaining, I'm becoming a maniac of the lunatic variety."

"You're fine. Like I said, I grew up in a version of a loony bin and my job sometimes becomes one. So we're good."

Grace laid a strong bead of curiosity on Chad. "You didn't answer the question. Don't make me interrogate you, officer."

Chad glanced at Grace but centered his attention on Elaina.

A squishy warm feeling infiltrated her whole being. "Don't you have a photographer to line up?" She asked Grace, without removing her eyes from Chad.

"It can wait."

"Noooo. You should do it now."

An emergence of understanding must've dawned. Grace toed Elaina under the table. "I'm on it." Ever the heckler, she put a hand on Chad's shoulder. "I hope you brought handcuffs."

Elaina tried to fend off the mortification heating her

cheeks by pointing to the back door. "Photographer."

"All right all ready." Grace clicked her tongue. "Those handcuffs would go great with your dominatrix personality."

That was no Freudian slip, and Elaina wanted to throttle her. "It's domineering, Grace, not dominatrix."

"My bad." Grace cackled her way out of the kitchen.

Elaina made a low hissing noise to sound irked, even though she wasn't. "Not my circus, not my monkeys."

Chad's laugh was masculine and downright sexy. "They might not be monkeys but they're certainly entertaining." He drank half his coffee in one swallow. "From what I've seen, you're four sassy chicks who feed off each other."

Elaina leaned across the corner of the table to put a hand on his bicep. "You just gave me the name for our bed and breakfast."

"I did?"

"You definitely did. I won't tell you what it is though. You'll have to do a drive-by after we get a new sign made. Would you like more coffee?"

He looked at his watch. "I'd love to stay for more but I have to be going. The lady who cuts my hair gets cranky if I'm a minute late. She has a *domineering* personality."

"You'd fit in perfectly with this bunch of loons."

"You think so?" Chad glanced at his watch again. "I have nine minutes to go four miles. I'm going to get a rotten haircut for being late. Good seeing you again, Elaina. Take care of that adorable pooch. By the way, where is he?"

"Upstairs. I wore him out when we went for donuts."

Chad held out a gentlemanly hand to help Elaina from her chair. "The nearest donut shop is over three miles away. You went on foot? In this weather?"

Delicious tingles from his touch generated a gasp.

Chapter Ten

~ *Suck it up, buttercup!* ~

Shortly before noon, another visitor arrived.

Steph raced down the stairs with Stony fast on her heels. "Is he here?"

"I think so."

Steph shook her hands nervously.

"Take a breath. He's not here to take you to prom. You're going to discuss cookbooks."

Stony dropped down in front of the door.

"Stone-man, what are you doing? I can't open the door unless you move."

He didn't budge.

Steph ran her fingers over the velvet of his ears. "What do you think his behavior means?"

"He got his second wind and is in full-protection mode."

"But he isn't barking."

Elaina twisted her mouth in contemplation. "True."

A louder knock prompted Elaina to drag Stony away by the collar.

Nicholas graced Steph with a smile. He also gave one to Elaina. "Hey, boy." Without a second's hesitation he put his hand out for Stony to sniff. Of course, Stone-man had to share some DNA by rubbing against Nicholas's trousers. "Steph, you look lovely today. I've watched the clock since I got up this morning. I didn't think noon would ever get here."

Nicholas the second was one sweet-talking man. And Steph was soaking up the sugar.

"I've paced for the last forty-five minutes." Steph's admission brought more gush from Nicholas.

"I circled the block four times because I was early."

For two people, one fifty-ish and the other forty-ish, Nicholas and Steph were acting like lusty teenagers. Elaina was more amazed at Stony's behavior though. He was not acting like the dog who usually stole the limelight. It dawned on her that Lula hadn't made a fuss all morning either. In fact, she'd been missing in action. Were they homesick? People longed for familiar. It only stood to reason pets did the same.

Steph apologized for the grey and white dog hairs coating the front of Nicholas's dark pants.

"It's no biggie. I love dogs. Hair comes with the territory."

Any latent tension in Steph seemed to ease. "Thanks for understanding."

Nicholas became aware of Elaina's presence. "Forgive me for not remembering your name."

"It's Elaina. I was just leaving. It's time to discover downtown Portland. You two have fun discussing food." She wanted to slide in "or whatever", but Steph might not appreciate the insinuation. Tawny and Grace wouldn't have a problem with her side comments. Steph was more sensitive. "Stone-man, would you like to come with?" His tail wagged so fast she could feel the air it stirred. "I'll take that as a yes."

Steph gave Elaina a thank-you smile.

Elaina sauntered to the breezeway where Stony's leash hung on a hook. She overheard Steph say to Nicholas that they could work in the kitchen since it was the only room in the whole place not in disarray.

Nicholas spoke so softly Elaina couldn't make out everything he said. One word, however, stood out from the rest. It sounded like bedroom. She must've misheard. Nicholas and Steph were newly met. Surely he wouldn't be bold enough to suggest going to the bedroom. Elaina was tempted to hang back to find out. Her inner-critic told her to let it go; that Steph was a grown woman. If she chose to do something radical, like sleep with Nicholas right off the bat, it was her decision. Elaina led Stony into the garage. "Please don't mess up, Steph."

* * *

At the courthouse, Elaina stood in line for half an hour. There were sufficient employees, just a mad rush of people who picked today to transact business. When it was her turn with a clerk, she was informed that since they were a ten-bedroom establishment, one of the four co-owners would have to take an eight-hour course and subsequent exam to become a Certified Food Protection Manager. Had it been five beds or less, they would be exempt. There was also an exemption if they served a continental breakfast like rolls, juice, coffee, etc. No way would Steph agree to simple breakfasts. She had plans to put her cooking skills to good use with omelets, quiches, biscuits and gravy, eggs Benedict, tater tot casseroles, pancakes, dairy-free and gluten-free selections. There'd even be vegetarian and vegan choices. The night before, the guests would fill out a breakfast form and when they arrived at the table in the morning, voila! Dining elegance! Elaina almost complicated the whole shebang by saying they'd be serving mimosas for guests celebrating special occasions. At the last second, she withheld the information. That particular tidbit was still up in the air. The way she was feeling right now, they'd probably shuck the idea. After the bed and breakfast was registered in their names, Elaina agreed to be the one to take the online course and produce the certification before they opened for business.

A weird look passed over the clerk's face. "I need to check something."

"Is there a problem?" *Please say no.*

"I recall an issue either with your address or one close to your address. For the life of me, I don't remember what it was. Maybe it had to do with zoning." The woman frowned at her computer screen. "The commissioners might've turned it down for commercial zone." She tapped her screen with her fingernail. "The zoning box is blank. That's odd. Give me a minute." She disappeared into what appeared to be a storage room.

Elaina clutched the edge of the counter. What if the Kirbys had found out after-the-fact that the business wasn't zoned commercial and had gone to City Council to get it rezoned, only to be turned down? Perhaps the same thing happened with the original owner. That would explain the sell-off. The house was fairly new, yet Elaina and the girls were the third owners. What was wrong with that picture? She tried not to stress. The more she thought about it, the more it made sense and the more her blood pressure rose.

The clerk returned with a hard-to-read expression. "You're in luck. Your address is zoned properly. I must be thinking of another place."

Elaina breathed a sigh of relief. "Halleluiah."

"No doubt."

With things squared away, Elaina inquired about a place to get lunch.

The clerk gave directions to a grill and raw bar not too far from the courthouse. "You have to try the fish tacos. They make them with blackened pollock, jalapeno slaw, avocado cream, and pico de gallo. If you love your fish with some spice, that's the place to go."

Elaina's mouth watered. "I'll check it out. Thanks."

The clerk smiled. "Welcome to Portland."

Life was good. The bed and breakfast was registered and would soon be available for occupancy. There was an extra spring in Elaina's step. Spotting the marquee for the restaurant, she crossed the street and made her way past a jewelry store. A platinum bracelet with a tiny anchor charm and matching necklace caught her eye. She backed up and stared through the window. Her mom would've loved those. On impulse she went inside the store.

An older gentleman with white hair and reading glasses welcomed her with a warm smile. "Can I help you?"

"Would you mind showing me the bracelet and necklace with the anchor charm that you have in the window?"

"I'd be more than happy to, young lady." He moved slow and steady to a glass display case on the opposite side of the room.

Young lady? If only. She'd turn forty-four on January twelfth.

The gentle way he removed the jewelry from the satin lined box said he loved his job. "These are almost as beautiful as you."

Elaina smiled. "What a sweet thing to say."

"More honest than sweet, my dear." He studied her. "Fisherman's daughter?"

She shook her head. "No."

"Sea captain's granddaughter?"

"No. My mother loved everything associated with the sea even though she lived inland."

Aged bluish-grey eyes beamed with intelligence. "It would be interesting to know why the sea was so special to her."

Elaina took the comment for what it was – a challenge to discover the reason. "I agree. Should I ever find out why, I'd be happy to share the information."

"That would be most excellent." He handed her the necklace for her to inspect. "Would you care to try it on?"

"I'd love to." Elaina hooked the necklace around her neck and snapped on the bracelet. A feeling of calm came over her when she touched the anchor that sat at the hollow of her throat.

Kindness emanated from the wise man. "I have a feeling this purchase is more about your mother than it is about the jewelry."

Elaina looked in the mirror that sat on the counter. "She's my stabilizing force. My anchor."

"What a lovely sentiment."

After the purchase and a few minutes of small talk, Elaina was on her way again. Wearing the necklace and bracelet, she felt stronger than she had all day. Her world was upright and she was ready to dive into those famous fish tacos.

Elaina walked past the last plate glass window before reaching the restaurant door and did a double-take when she saw who was sitting next to the window. Chad Ferguson was smiling at a long-haired blonde seated across from him. "Special," she muttered with monumental sarcasm. "Good one, Elaina. You talked yourself into thinking there was a spark." The cynicism rolled out of her in waves. "You assumed he came to see you when he said he was there to check on Stony."

Elaina took a deep breath, shoved Chad Ferguson to the back of her mind, and proceeded to the license bureau to register her vehicle.

The DMV employee looked as if she'd had the day from hell. Her demeanor and posture were rigid. "Did you say you wanted to register your boat?"

"My SUV." Elaina forced a smile despite her own foul mood. She produced the necessary documents. While the registrar took care of the formalities – stamping this, stamping that, Elaina looked around. A huge wooden anchor hung on the wall. She nodded to herself. Her stabilizing force was telling her everything would be okay.

* * *

The electric, gas, cable, and telephone companies were a piece of cake. Elaina headed to the security company who maintained the alarm system to explain about the two accidental alarms and to sign up for their service. She sent Steph two text messages asking what they were having for dinner. It was now six-thirty and she hadn't received a reply.

Elaina drove into the four-car garage to find all but one stall filled. Grace's Chevy Equinox was gone, which meant she was running an errand, probably for Steph who'd forgotten something at the grocery.

On her way into the house she rubbed her hands together, anticipating delicious smells coming from the oven, crock pot, or stove.

Flicking on the kitchen light, the only aroma that met her nose was the lingering smell of pine-scented cleaner she'd used in the morning to clean the counter and appliances. No cooking had taken place and the rest of the rooms were dark. "Tawn'. Steph."

Slinging her purse on the counter, Elaina checked out the living room and a small smile slid into place. Tawny had arranged their existing furniture into a pleasing floor plan with plenty of room for their guests to be comfortable without invading another guest's space. The sofa Elaina brought from home was the focal point of the room. She was thankful Arden had insisted on that particular piece of furniture. He couldn't stress enough that it was timeless and elegant with its deep-button tufting on the padded rolled arms, back, and seat. It was polyester beige with plush cushions. She snickered at the memory of Arden's OCD kicking in and him placing a fitted cover over all that awesomeness. Once he moved out, she didn't bother to remove the cover. Today, the sofa had been unwrapped and looked perfect in its new home. It too, was getting a new beginning.

Out of the corner of her eye, she caught sight of something bold...and gaudy.

A deep-purple gothic, Victorian loveseat sat angled in a corner. It might've been the 'in' thing way back when, but it was currently the 'out' thing when it came to the stylish, modern bed and breakfast. "What on earth?" The loveseat wasn't tragic; although, it did serve as a powerful yank on the flimsy thread of Elaina's mood. She walked away from the hideous piece of furniture but returned to stare at it. What had Tawny been thinking? The more she looked at the darn thing, the madder she became.

Emitting a low, feral growl, she marched to the

refrigerator. "It had better be full." The anchor charm on the bracelet slapped against her skin. It was as good as a flick to the forehead. "Okay. I get it," she grumbled. "You're trying to put out the lit end of the dynamite." Easing open the refrigerator door, she gritted her teeth when the only *thing in there was an* opened box of baking soda to absorb odors. Elaina drew in a deep breath, exhaled it, and headed to the stairs. After a few steps, she paused. Losing her temper about the lack of progress and Tawny's objectionable purchase, wouldn't fix anything. Her mind – or her mother – sent her a subliminal message, Suck it up, buttercup. She wasn't a freaking buttercup and no way did she want to suck it up. Not this time.

Elaina's gaze flew to the back door. Where was Grace?

Releasing the tight grip she had on the banister, she went to the kitchen to try to calm down.

Elaina leaned against the counter and considered why she was so upset. Was it seeing Chad with someone else? She huffed air at that possibility. They didn't know each other well enough for her to be upset. She began pacing back and forth in front of the sink, and didn't stop until she fully understood where the jagged feelings were coming from.

She proceeded to Tawny's bedroom and rapped her knuckles on the door. "Tawn', you in there?"

No answer.

She knocked a little louder in case Tawny was in the shower.

Not a peep.

Privacy only went so far. Elaina opened the door. "Tawn'?" She flicked on the light. The bed had been put together and a bedspread was in place. Unopened packing boxes were stacked so high they blocked the set of double windows.

Returning to the staircase, she stomped her way up to the second floor.

Steph's door was ajar and she was lying across the bed, texting.

Oh sure. Steph could text whomever, but not her.

There were stacks of unopened boxes in her room, too. They'd been shoved in a corner. Even though the door was open, Elaina knocked to make her presence known.

Steph startled and turned with a creased forehead. "Make some noise, will ya?"

Once again, Elaina's temper bubbled to the surface. She shoved it down and bit back a sour reply. "I made noise when I came up the stairs."

"I make racket when I climb the stairs. You don't. You have a light foot."

Elaina deliberately scanned the room to let Steph know she was aware little progress had been made. "How'd it go with Nicholas?"

Steph pulled her lips in for a second then she broke into a full-face smile. "I think I'm in lo*ve!*"

Elaina stiffened. "No kidding?" It was then she noticed Steph's messy hair and that her clothes were haphazard like she'd dressed in a hurry.

Steph fluttered her eyelashes. "He's awesome!"

"Did you work on the cookbook?"

"Actually..."

"You didn't discuss cooking," Elaina surmised. Nor did you make a trip to the grocery. Stay calm. Breathe. Stay calm. Breathe. She repeated the mantra until she no longer wanted to put Steph in a sleeper-hold.

"We sat at the kitchen table to go over recipes...for like two minutes. When we looked at each other I swear the earth moved. We literally threw ourselves at one another."

Elaina covered her mouth to stop herself from giving Steph a sermon about shovels and potholes. She didn't want to kink Steph's happiness or Nicholas's. They'd both had been wronged by past loves. Maybe they found something today that fixed all those wrongs – each other. It was hard to scale back her displeasure to be exuberant for her friend, but she managed. "Wonderful, Steph."

Steph's grin was priceless. It was part mischief, part love-struck. "He didn't hide his attraction last night...or today. Boy can he kiss!"

Elaina forced her cheeks up, so the corners of her mouth would turn up as well.

"I know what you're thinking." Steph tucked the bottom of her camisole into her jeans and buttoned her blue-plaid over-shirt. "We didn't sleep together. Le sigh. But we did get familiar with each other. If you know what I mean."

Elaina put a hand up to st*op the flow of private information. "I* kno*w what yo*u mean."

Steph fanned herself like the mere thought of their

actions made her warm all over. "If Nicholas the third hadn't called twice, we would've christened the place." She either felt guilty or expected a reprimand for her loose behavior. "Don't judge."

"It's your life." You can mess it up any way you see fit.

"I know, right?"

"Any idea where Tawny might be?"

"Honestly, I haven't paid much attention to anything but Nichol*as.*"

No kidding. "She's not in her room and Ferdinand is parked in the garage."

"Did Stony come running when you came home?"

"No."

"Then she probably took him for a walk or out back to do his business."

"Grace isn't here either."

"Haven't seen her."

Steph had been bitten by the lust bug and her mind was on Nicholas, nothing else.

Elaina's stomach rumbled loudly. "I'm going to order pizza."

"I promise to get groceries first thing tomorrow."

Whatever. "Thanks." Elaina proceeded to the third floor in case Tawny was hard at work placing more gaudy furniture in the guest rooms. She poked her head in each room, including Grace's bedroom. Tawn' was nowhere to be found and there was no evidence Grace had returned from her quest to find a photographer. Back on the second floor, she did a full sweep of the rooms, except for Steph's. On the first floor, she started at the breezeway and worked her way through the house. No Tawny. No Stony. She checked the hook for his leash and found it there. The only places left to search were the basement and the romantic loft out back. She nodded with the knowledge that the basement wasn't just her personal quarters. It was also storage central. Tawny was probably down there, organizing things they seldom used. That theory dissolved when Elaina opened the basement door and it was pitch black. She sighed. Groaned. And sighed again. There was no need to worry. Tawny could take care of herself, just like Grace could.

Steph bent over the banister. "Do you mind if Nicholas joins us for pizza?"

Elaina left the questioned unanswered. She went to Tawny's room for another look. A noise that sounded like it came from the bathroom reached Elaina's ears. "It had better not be a case of déjà vu." They'd had a falling out in Ohio when Tawny went against the rule of no smoking in the house. Surely Tawn' wouldn't risk another argument by puffing away in the bathroom with the window open to get rid of the smoke.

Steph stuck her head inside Tawny's room. "Is that a yes or no?"

"What?"

"Can Nicholas join us?"

Still leaving the request hanging, Elaina trekked to the bathroom and discovered what she already knew – the door was locked. Anger exploded inside her. "Open up!"

"Go away."

"Same ole. Same ole. Different day." She threw her hands in the air. "Not my freaking monkeys. Definitely not my freaking circus. I give up. I was under the illusion this would work for us. It's another epic fail on my part. I should have my freaking head examined."

"You're throwing a lot of 'freakings' out there."

Elaina glared at Steph. "Yeah? Well there are a lot more where those came from." That sounded ridiculous but it was better than battering them with the other f-word.

Stony barked; not just a single bark, a tirade of barks.

Anger, heavier and hotter, zapped every one of Elaina's nerve endings. "You can roost in there until you," she almost said 'rot', but she didn't hate Tawny she was just thoroughly ticked at her, "are ready to face me. Let Stony out."

The lock clicked and the door swung open just enough to let Stony bolt from the bathroom and through the bedroom. Steph stepped aside so he wouldn't knock her over. Elaina set chase.

She found him at the back door, turning in a circle. "I'm hurrying."

Steph shouted from the doorway of Tawny's room. "You might want to come here before you take him out."

"His bladder is about to burst."

Once outside, Stony didn't wait for his designated sprinkling area. He hiked his leg on the first tree – a Pagoda dogwood. On a normal trip outside he'd choose a tree alongside the fence and give it a little spray, run to the next tree and do the same, then repeat the process until he'd visited ten to twelve trees. Not tonight. It was just him and the dogwood.

A snowflake hit Elaina on the nose, followed by a few more. She looked at the dusk-to-dawn light that illuminated a good portion of the yard. Snow sifted through the beams of light. "Grace, where are you?" No sooner had she uttered the question when the sound of the garage door going up permeated the stillness of the night.

Stony tugged on the leash and Elaina let him have his way. He'd been cooped up for God knows how long. He deserved some exercise.

In the darkness, with snow falling all around, Elaina let Stony drag her to the farthest tree on the property. Of course he'd take her there. Why wouldn't he? Emotion came at her hard. Tears spilled by the bucketful. Freezing from not taking the time to put on a hat, scarf, and gloves, she fell apart. Between hiccupped sobs, she pleaded for Arden to come to Maine to rescue her from...herself. The heartless bastard had been right about so many things. He'd once said people needed to deal with their own grunge without her offering a shoulder. At the time, she assumed the comment stemmed from him wanting her undivided attention. Reflecting on his words now, she understood them to be wise advice. Had she not stuck her nose in Grace's weepy business that day at the jewelry store everything would be fine. She wouldn't be in Maine, in the dark, cold as an ice cube, crying for a multitude of reasons.

Stony didn't understand her tears but he must've understood her angst and leaned into her. Elaina knelt beside him. "As the saying goes, I've bitten off more than I can chew, Stone-man." She brushed the tears from her cheeks and searched her pockets for a tissue.

"Elainaaaaaa." Grace's voice bellowed in the darkness. "Elainaaaaaa."

Elaina was tempted to ignore the summons. Since she wasn't a petulant child, she let Grace know she'd be there in a minute. Then she told Stony to lead the way.

Stony only knew one speed – fast.

Elaina tripped in a divot in the grass and landed belly first on the frozen ground. "Awesome."

Stony circled back and put a paw on her.

Elaina blew out a breath and pulled to a stand. She pressed the button on the retractable leash. "I'm giving you no more than five feet of latitude."

When she got to the house, Grace was standing on the deck without a coat.

"You didn't need to come find me so I could order pizza. You're capable."

"What the French are you talking about? I came to get you because Tawny's a mess."

Chapter Eleven

~ Hideous purple beasts and nude women! ~

Not bothering to wipe down Stony's paws or unhook the leash from his collar, Elaina let go of him and ran to Tawny's bedroom. She found her sitting on the corner of the bed with red puffy eyes and a clump of used tissues in her hand.

Elaina shoved aside her own torment and sat down to comfort her friend. "I didn't mean to make you cry."

Steph and Grace stood in the doorway, abnormally quiet. Elaina raised questioning eyes to them. Steph shrugged.

"I belly flopped a few minutes ago."

Tawny blew her nose and stared at Elaina with watery eyes. "What?"

"Stony thought it would be fun to see me wipe out." Her attempt to alleviate or lessen the distress by saying weird stuff was another classic fail.

Tawny's voice cracked. "H-he didn't mean to make you fall." Tears gushed from her eyes.

Elaina moved off the bed and broke into a rant. "Stop! Just stop! All of you!"

Her bark shocked Tawny's tears into damming up.

"Now that I have your full attention I'm going to have my say. I've had it up to here." Elaina put a hand under her chin. "I love you guys, but dammit, we only have a few days to get things sorted out and you're behaving like we have all the time in the world. I need your help." Shoving her hands on her hips to strengthen her point, she went to the window and looked out. "I gave you tasks to do and it doesn't appear anything other than those I assigned to me got done." She turned around and locked eyes with Steph. "You fell in love when you were supposed to be shopping and doing laundry." She moved on to Grace. "You were supposed to line up a photographer."

Grace didn't blink.

"Yeah, that's what I thought." Elaina walked to Tawny. "That loveseat is hideous. Cry if you want, but it's going back to wherever the heck you bought it. We're not doing purple."

Tawny fell over on her side and buried her face in the bedspread.

"Way to *freaking* go." Steph pushed past Elaina to spread protective arms over Tawny. "She's bawling her heart out and you're brow beating her about the loveseat. What's your problem?"

Elaina stood her ground. "My problem is the three of you. We pledged to start over. The only things I've seen are desperate attempts to cling to the past."

It was Grace's turn to jam her hands on her hips. "I hired a photographer. He's coming tomorrow morning at nine. The reason I took all day to line him up, is that he and I clicked." She arched an eyebrow as if to dare Elaina to voice her opinion. "I'm warning you ahead of time not to give me that judgy look."

Elaina tightened. She withheld a response. Both must've ticked off Grace because she went into a rant that made Elaina's pale in comparison.

"When you disapprove, you don't have to say a word, we get 'the look'." The featherlike lines at the corners of her eyes deepened. "We aren't your children or your employees. We're your friends and equals. You said so yourself. Yet you've assumed the role of commandant. It's okay to guide but you can't rule; not without stirring a shit ton of resentment."

The accuracy of Grace's claim was a knife-like pain that circumvented the ribs and went straight to her heart. Elaina had overstepped, not just today, many times and they'd let her go until now. "Oh god. I've turned into Arden. I'm so sorry."

Grace smoothed a hand across Elaina's back. "You haven't turned into the barracuda. You just caught up in trying to make everything go right. We're partly to blame for you acting like a dictating buzzkill. It was easier to put the bulk of responsibility on you because you do the homework and because you have more energy than the three of us put together. There's also the matter of the money it took to buy this place. We contributed to the pot, but let's get real. What we put in was a drop in the bucket compared to what you ponyed up. Subconsciously, we handed you the reins because this place is yours, despite what the deed says." She sifted air through her teeth. "Damn. I just highlighted the real problem. It's not you. It's us."

Elaina closed her eyes to deal with an overload of emotion. Despite Grace's denial, she had become a female adaptation of her ex.

"Elaina," Grace softly said, "you don't have anything to apologize for, we do. From now on, we'll assume a greater role. We'll make you proud."

Elaina opened her eyes and sniffed back the salty brine filling her eyes and nose. "I'm only going to say this one more time and you'd better get it through your stubborn heads. It doesn't matter how much each person put in. We have an equal share in this adventure. Although, there's an unwritten clause in our pact that I forgot to address. Should any of you decide to opt out, I won't hold it against you. I want you with me, but dreams change. If this enterprise isn't what you want for you, I'll understand. Whew." She blew out a breath. "I'm getting preachy. I have a few more things to say then I'll shut up. We're going into this thing mostly blind. We'll mess up. Once in a while we'll get on each other's nerves." She swung her gaze back to Tawny who was taking in every word. "And we'll buy purple loveseats."

Tawny cracked a smile.

"When things get tough we'll say our peace. Hopefully our friendship will be stronger than our blunders." Elaina received nods of agreement. "If there ever does come a time when you want out – of the bed and breakfast, not the friendship – we'll be okay. There won't be any hard feelings. They say life begins at forty. We're all in our forties. We have a lot of life ahead of us. I won't delude myself into thinking it'll be the four of us for all time. Grace, you might end up moving to Italy to be with your new little family. Tawny, your boys live on the west coast. It would be selfish to bind you here when realistically you'll want to be near them and eventually your daughters-in-laws, and if you're lucky, grandchildren. Steph, you might stay in Maine and become Nicholas the second's happily-ever-after. Or not. And me? I haven't a clue. I'm going to take it one day at a time. One moment at a time. I'm an only child. My folks are gone. The sea has beckoned. I'm where I'm supposed to be."

Grace rolled her eyes. "You do give a good talk. Here's how it's going to go down. We're here because we want to be. We're a hundred percent with you, Elaina. This bed and breakfast means as much to us as it does to you. I can't foresee moving to Italy. I'll probably visit there a lot, so there are times I'll leave you short-handed. Steph may or may not give her heart to Nicholas but she loves it in Maine. Even if she gets married and becomes rich and famous from the many cookbooks she's going to write, she'll also be part proprietor of this amazing B & B and wants to pour her heart and soul into it too. Right, Steph?"

Steph bobbed her head up and down in concurrence.

"Then there's the matter of Tawny. I saved her for last because she's in the middle of a crisis."

Elaina shook her head. "I didn't mean to make a big deal about your smoking."

"Oh puh-lease. She's wimpy sometimes but she wouldn't cry over cigs."

Tawny stretched her neck from side to side and then explained, "Bo called and blasted me for moving to Maine. He said he and Quentin aren't happy with me for putting more distance between us." Her voice trembled. "They laid a major guilt trip on me."

"Sweet mother of assumption." Elaina chastised herself for jumping to an unfair conclusion. "Tawn', I'm sorry."

"It's okay. Really. You have to stay on me about the smoking thing. I can't conquer the animal on my own." Tawny released a weighty breath. "My sons are a whole other story. They're on my case for no reason. They're such pains in my rump."

"No they're not. They're your children."

"I don't get why they're upset. They live in California and Oregon. What's the difference if they fly to Maine or to Ohio?"

Steph spouted that they'd add another stop on their flight plans because she didn't think there were nonstop flights from California to Maine.

Grace raised her eyebrows and held them in the up position. "Not helpful."

"I was trying to be."

Grace backed off. "I know you were."

Elaina kissed the top of Tawny's head. "There's more to this story, I'm sure of it."

"Like what?"

"I don't know. My gut says there's more. You can't let this rest. You have to fly out to see them and find out the real reason why they're being pissy. Tomorrow morning we're taking you to the Portland Jetport and you're going to Cali first, then on to Oregon."

Tawny rejected the plan. "They hurt me for no reason. I'm staying here."

"I'm slipping into the commandant role one more time. You ARE going and that's that. Once they see you, they'll soften and so will you. Besides, they came home to Ohio a while back. It's your turn to go to them."

"You just got done saying we all need to pitch in to get our business up and running. Now you're trying to shove me out the door."

"Tawn', it's family first; now and always. Take as long as you need. We'll be here when you get back and so will the bed and breakfast. Make sure Bo and Quentin know they're welcome here anytime. Even if we're filled to capacity when they come, we'll make room. They can have the basement and I'll bunk with you. Got it? Now about that purple monstrosity in the living room..."

* * *

"Never in a million years would I think to put cheese, scallops, scallions, and bacon on a pizza. But hey, it's wicked good." Grace took another slice, nibbled the corner, and let her eyes roll back in her head.

Steph had gone gaga over the descriptions of the

unusual pizzas in the pizzeria's ad in the phone book and cited the need for culinary inspiration. So they ordered a variety – the one Grace was currently hogging with scallops and scallions, one with ricotta cheese and mushrooms, an olive and feta pizza, and a safe bet with pepperoni, sausage, and banana peppers.

Grace shifted in her seat. "Now that we have something in our bellies, I have to tell you about Philip."

"Philip?" Steph asked with an airy tone of inquiry.

"He's a hunky dunky, handsome photographer and artist extraordinaire. I talked to a handful of photographers prior to meeting him. They were okay but didn't offer anything exciting. Then I met Philip. He won me over right away. Did I mention he has long greyish-black hair that he pulls back in a ponytail? Oh, and he has a diamond stud earring in his left ear. He wears leather bracelets and listens to music from the sixties. Do guys call them bracelets?" Grace took a short breath. "His studio is filled with framed photographs, oil paintings, hand sketches, and sculptures. The man's a modern day Picasso with a dash of hippie for good measure. He has a replica of one of Picasso's famous paintings hanging in the foyer of his studio. I think he called it *Les Demoiselles d'* something or other."

"Les Demoiselles d'Avignon?"

"That's it. How did you know?"

"Arden." The one-word explanation generated sneers. Despite Arden being a kink in everyone's neck, he had exquisite taste. Elaina hadn't really thought about that particular quality until lately. He did have a keen eye.

The eye had wandered, but it was keen.

Tawny popped an olive in her mouth. "I'm familiar with that painting. Isn't it nude prostitutes in a brothel?"

Grace's forehead creased. "I don't think so. Doesn't the title mean 'The ladies of Avignon'?"

Elaina stifled a laugh. "It does. Those ladies just happen to be for hire."

A giggle shook Grace's slight frame. "That is so Philip."

Elaina had to ask, "He doesn't want to paint us, does he?"

"Would that be a bad thing?"

"Graaaace."

"He mentioned it. I told him we were looking for a photo for our website, not a painting. Philip balked at the early appointment because he stays up late and sleeps in. I told him we had to get this puppy done." Grace's eyes flicked open wide. "Wait. You're heading to California tomorrow."

"It's all good. Elaina booked me on a red-eye flight." Tawny took a slice of the scallop and scallions pizza. "You were gone a long time. Did Philip paint or sketch you?"

Grace grinned.

Steph said what Elaina and Tawny were thinking. "Tell us you didn't pose nude."

"I wasn't completely nude."

Elaina put a hand across her face and spread her fingers to peek through them.

Steph wanted a straight answer. "Sorta nude?"

"Ha. Gotcha. I kept my clothes on. He snapped a few pictures."

Elaina chortled. "You built the story slowly so we would think you and Philip got to know-know each other." She nudged Grace with her shoulder. "He listens to music from the sixties? How old is this guy?"

Grace engaged in a series of blinks for no other reason than she was rotten to the core. "Given the grey in his hair and his love for music from decades ago, you'd think he was much older than me. As it turns out, he just turned forty."

"Guys lie about their age just like women do."

"Speaking of grey hair..." Grace yanked a strand from Tawny's head.

* * *

Philip was nothing like Elaina envisioned. Due to Grace's description, she'd conjured up an image of an unconventional, carefree guy who spent his days and nights creating great art, and prompting his talent by smoking weed. She could try to duck responsibility for the supposition by pointing a finger at Tawny who was forever talking about marijuana, but this was on her. Elaina felt the need to apologize to Philip. What an awkward conversation that would be.

Philip made Grace laugh and she was holding her belly. That was awesome to see. The part about his long hair was precise. Today he was neatly groomed with his hair in a man-bun. Elaina generally wasn't a fan of man-buns. On Philip it wasn't bad. It gave him a sexy bad-boy edge. He caught her staring.

"Grace tells me we're going to include the dog and cat?"

Elaina joined them in front of the fireplace. "Good plan? Or bad plan?"

Dimples dotted the corners of Philip's mouth when he smiled. "Getting pets to sit still is like trying to catch a fish with a rock. It could happen; chances are slim."

Stony sniffed Philip.

Lula wouldn't come out from under the sofa.

"Should we alter the plan?"

"No way. We're going to give the formal setting with everyone, including your pets, a go. You might be surprised at the results." He fanned out his hands. "Imagine someone checking out your website and seeing the dog trying to get the cat, and the cat trying to get away. Action photos garner more attention than a still photo of well-behaved people and pets."

Tawny sidled next to Elaina. "I agree with Philip. We don't want to come off as a group of stiffs."

Philip was so close Elaina's nose picked up a variety of scents. One scent in particular verified her assumption. The need for her to apologize fell apart.

"Your content will list all the perks of your business but a slightly crazy photo will draw your customers. Trust me."

Steph looked in the huge wall mirror at the far end of the living room and messed with her hair. "We're crazy entrepreneurs. People need to know what they're getting themselves into when they stay with us."

Elaina wasn't sold on the idea. "We'll see how the

pictures turn out." She dropped to her knees with a treat to lure Lula from beneath the sofa. "Come here, you beloved feline."

Lula took the bait.

Stony saw an opportunity and pounced. He put a paw on Lula to hold her in place.

Lula hissed.

Stony didn't heed the warning.

"Stone-man, you're asking for it."

If dogs could say 'duh' Stony would've said it. He grazed her with a quick look but the center of his attention was Lula.

Philip snapped pictures as the chaos began to unfold.

The landline phone rang. The camera followed Grace when she made a mad dash for to answer it.

"Cody?" Grace squealed with delight.

Elaina advised Philip it might be a while.

"Not a problem. I have all day."

"Care for a cup of coffee?"

"Do you have tea?"

"No tea. We have coffee, water, and leftover pizza."

"What kind of pizza?"

"Ricotta and mushroom."

His eyebrows lifted with interest. "You don't say."

Tawny boldly put an arm around Philip's waist and led him into the kitchen. "So you're a fan of Picasso?"

Chapter Twelve

~ *Chaos times a thousand!* ~

The photo shoot was exactly as Philip predicted – a bunch of bungled pictures and retakes. Just when they'd get Lula to behave, Stony would act up. Then the two animal buddies switched up the bedlam with Lula misbehaving and Stony masquerading as an obedient pooch. Probably the most exasperating yet funny thing about the whole ordeal was that Grace blinked in just about every picture. Tawny threatened to tape Grace's eyelashes to her eyelids. Through it all, Philip laughed and clicked his camera. He seemed to enjoy the dysfunction. With everything being digital they were able to view the photos right away and delete the ones they didn't want to keep. One picture begged to be chosen. It was freaking comical – and completely them. Philip had captured Lula trying to escape from Elaina while Stony had his nose buried in Tawny's skirt. Everyone except for Grace was looking straight ahead. For reasons known only to Grace, she had her mouth open and appeared to be holding a conversation with the side of Steph's head.

"I vote yes on this one." Grace boogied in place even though there wasn't any music. "Philip, you're a genius. We wanted wacky. This one's wacky." She modified the quote from the movie *Field of Dreams*. "If we use it, they will come."

Steph and Tawny approved.

Grace polled Elaina. "What say you?"

Elaina was highly amused at Grace's idiomatic English. Regarding the use of the picture, she tried to decide if it was wacky or tacky. One look at her friends' faces and she decided not to be a dictating buzzkill. "I second the motion."

"You're actually fourth-ing the motion." Tawny put her teeth together in a toothy grin.

Steph nodded. "Yeah, what she said."

"I have a suggestion."

All eyes swung to Philip.

"With the website banner out of the way, you'll need to strike a balance with a few regular pictures. I propose you use them throughout your site. The banner will grab your prospects attention. To keep it, you'll also want to come across as serious in business. I'm going to follow you around with my camera. Do what you'd normally do and forget I'm here."

"I'd *normally* put Steph in a sleeper-hold."

Philip put his forehead on Grace's. "I know you would. Maybe a little less normal and a little more staged."

The phone rang again. This time it was potential customers wanting information. Before the conversation was finished, Elaina booked them in the garage-loft for the last week in April.

A knock on the door gave way to a group of people collecting money for Christmas gifts for disadvantaged families.

Stony had to go outside.

Steph unloaded the dishwasher.

They were doing regular stuff, hence regular pictures. An hour later, Philip announced he had what he needed. He promised to return to capture the comfortable essence of the bed and breakfast once they bought more furniture.

After he left, Grace declared it was time to exchange their finery for sweat pants.

Tawny stepped out of her sling-back heels. "Now you're speaking my language. Whoever invented sweat pants should win a Nobel Peace Prize."

Steph walked side-by-side with Tawny up the stairs. "Because?"

"They make me peaceful."

Steph grinned over her shoulder at Elaina. "Tawny's not all there."

Tawny shot back. "None of us are."

All in all, Elaina was beside herself with joy. They had pictures for their website. Tawny was no longer inundated with sadness and tears. Steph didn't make a big issue out of turning down Nicholas's request to join them for pizza last night. And Grace had accomplished more yesterday than she let on. Not only did she arrange for Philip to photograph them, she also paid a visit to the local newspaper and signed them up for a subscription.

She took it upon herself to speak with their advertising department about putting an ad together for the B & B.

"I didn't want to mention this earlier because of Tawny's fragile state with her boys, but Cody again confirmed that he, Isabella, and Karina would be here for Christmas."

Elaina wrapped an arm around Grace. "I'm tickled that they're coming."

"Me too. I'm probably the happiest person on the planet right now. The only way I could be happier..." Grace choked up and couldn't finish the thought.

Elaina planted a kiss on Grace's temple.

"I miss Brince so much and I feel guilty for even considering Philip."

"You already know this, but I'll say it anyway. Brince wouldn't want you to spend the rest of your days without male companionship."

"I know." Grace smiled but there was a tender ache in her voice. "Did I tell you that whenever I was in a slump, Brince would make me laugh and then he'd quote Mark Twain – 'Sing like no one's listening, love like you've never been hurt, dance like nobody's watching, and live like it's Heaven on earth'."

"Wise words from a great writer and from your husband, but honestly, I've heard you sing and I've watched you dance. It ain't pretty."

* * *

"Dinner is served my B and B'lings." Steph motioned for

them to have a seat at the table.

"When someone asks what I do for a living, I'm going to say I'm a B and B'ling." Tawny took a seat.

Grace filled a glass with water and chugged half of it. "We speak in secret code."

"You speak in code. I speak in food. Prepare your taste buds to be deliriously cheerful. Tonight's menu is gluten-free. Your dining experience will consist of grilled halibut fillets that have been basted with a palate-pleasing mixture of olive oil, dried basil, and lemon. I mashed cooked cauliflower and added tiny bits of jalapeno and tomatoes for color and flavor. Last but not least, we'll tantalize our tongues with spicy green beans coated with olive oil, minced garlic, and red pepper flakes. They've been grilled for just a few minutes to seal in the flavors."

Elaina rubbed her hands together and dropped a napkin across her lap. "I can't wait."

Grace spooned a big helping of mashed cauliflower onto her plate. "Don't you love how she gets into character with the dining-experience, palate-pleasing, tongue-tantalizing talk?" She winked at Steph. "You wasted a lot of years being an executive's assistant. At this stage in your life, you should have an executive assistant of your own because you're going places."

"Why thank you." Steph speared a green bean with her fork. "Are you volunteering for the position?"

"I don't know. Maybe. Just to check – when you said palate-pleasing you meant my appreciation for taste not the wooden platforms for moving things around with a forklift, right?"

"I meant forklift pallets."

"Not my circus, not my monkeys." Elaina smirked and took a halibut fillet from the serving platter.

"You keep saying that, but you know we are." Tawny licked her lips after tasting the cauliflower.

"Speaking of monkeys, I chose a name for our business. I couldn't wait. The courthouse needed one to process the paperwork."

"The Four Monkeys Inn?"

"Close, but no."

Tawny added green beans to her plate. "Don't keep the monkeys in suspense."

"I credit Chad for the inspiration. He called us sassy chicks yesterday. So we're officially *Four Sassy Chicks Bed and Breakfast*. They gave me a forty-eight hour window to change the name. We're down to twenty-four."

Elaina received a rousing round of approval.

"There's something I've been meaning to say." Tawny finished chewing a green bean. "We said we were going to be pet-friendly, and we still can be. As much as I love Stony, I'm concerned about his coat. The first time a guest finds a dog hair in the eggs, we'll be in trouble. He or she will post a negative review. Bad reviews can kill a business."

Elaina had thought about it a few times too. Not wanting to upset the delicate balance of things again, she kept her concern on the down-low. "What do you suggest?"

"You know that quaint little bungalow out back? Stone-man, Lula, and I will take up residence there."

"We can't ask you to do that."

"You don't have to ask. I'm doing it."

Steph laid her fork down with a clatter. Grace did the same thing. Elaina followed suit.

"Last one to the bungalow is a rotten egg."

Tawny reached the bungalow before anyone else and went inside.

Elaina, Grace, and Steph congregated at the door.

"I don't want Tawny to feel like she has to live separately because of Stony. She has a valid point about the hair. We have to come up with Plan B."

With a nasally whine, Steph made it abundantly clear that Stony and Lula were part of the family. She went on to say, "They shed hair. We shed between 30,000 to 40,000 skin cells every hour. There's a whole lot of shedding going on."

Grace made a face. "Gross."

"My point exactly. We leave DNA lying around, just like they do. We can complain about dog hair, but while we're doing it we're dropping skin cells right and left."

"That's the most bizarre viewpoint ever. Yet it's hard to dispute, Steph." Elaina turned the doorknob to the bungalow. "I propose certain areas of the house are off limits to Stony and Lula. It's a big house with many entrances and exits. Stony and Lula will have to get used to going outside via the sunroom door. That way they stay away from the kitchen. I think guests can ignore a minimum amount of dog hair, but we owe it to stay ahead of the hair. More importantly, we have to keep it out of the kitchen. The health inspector would agree.

We'll be obsessive about cleanliness and we'll need to make sure our guests see us being clean-freaks. l. We can do one thing that will go a long way to putting their minds at ease. After we pet Stony and Lula, wash our hands – not in the kitchen. That goes without saying, but hey, it's worth pointing out. When we walk back into the main living area – once we've washed our hands – we could comment how we love the scent of our new lemony anti-bacterial soap or something along that line, and then smell our hands. Here's another obvious tip: use latex disposable gloves when we prepare food or drink, even if it's to make a pot of coffee."

"That's not Plan B, that's Plan A. You've thought this out." Grace suggested they go convince Tawny.

They didn't have to say a word. When they entered the bungalow that could've easily been a ski lodge with its slab-stone brick fireplace and hardwood floors, Tawny admitted she couldn't live there. "There's a four-person tub with jets in the bathroom. Up in the loft, French doors open to the outside balcony. This is our money-maker."

"I thought the same thing the day we arrived. I can't believe we're just now getting around to checking it out."

Tawny rubbed her forehead above her eyebrow. "We've been preoccupied by men and odd pizza combinations."

Grace informed Tawny that Elaina had a plan.

"She always does," Tawny said matter-of-factly. "I'm not being a smartass when I say that. I mean it in the best possible way."

Grace struck again with a random comment. "Did

you know Maine used to be part of Massachusetts?"

Tawny cracked up laughing. "We could change the name from Four Sassy Chicks to Four Random Chicks. Stuff just flies out of our mouths. We went from tantalizing our tongues to freaking out about dog hair to random facts about Maine. I love you guys."

Elaina, Grace, and Steph echoed the same response. "We love you too, Tawny."

Steph reminded them their food was getting cold.

"I can't wait to dive back into those spicy green beans. I pity the unlucky passenger who gets to sit beside me on the airplane tonight. I'm going to reek of garlic."

"Speaking of reeking, I believe my new crush smokes funny cigarettes."

Elaina laughed behind her hand.

Steph suggested Philip might toke for medicinal reasons.

"Or he's a pothead." Grace giggled all the way back to the kitchen.

* * *

"What if I get to San Diego and Bo's not there? I should've called to let him know I'm coming. What if he gets pissed because I showed up unannounced? I'll be in a big city with an angry son."

"What if you stop panicking and enjoy the sneak attack? You're this funny, mischievous, no-holds-barred person with us. When it comes to Bo and Quentin you turn into someone else." Grace adjusted the collar on

Tawny's jacket because part of it had rolled under. "Stop letting those boys mess with your head. Knock their heads together instead; gently of course. While you're at it, show them your fun side. Drag their butts to karaoke. Sing. Dance."

Like no one's watching. "Yeah, what she said." Elaina was tickled that Grace was offering wisdom to Tawny. They both had sons who lived far away. Both had sons that tested their patience.

Grace continued the pep talk. "Cook their favorite food. Talk about things they did when they were younger. Shower them with love. They'll weaken."

"They're in their twenties. I shouldn't have to coax them to love me."

"It doesn't matter if they're thirty-five. Two words describe your boys: unmarried males." Grace snickered with a faraway look in her eyes. There was a good chance she was remembering going through with Cody what Tawny was going through with her sons. "Men need their mommies until they commit their hearts to someone else. Once they become parents, they go through another metamorphosis. All that knowledge you gave them over the years will hit home. They'll see you in a different light. Their respect for you will deepen."

"Not all unmarried males are buttheads."

Grace sighed and raised her eyebrows at Elaina. "And she thinks her boys are stubborn."

Elaina looped an arm through Tawny's as they walked to the security checkpoint. "What Grace is trying to say, is that kids – no matter the age – occasionally suffer from brain tilt. It's up to you and Grady to tip their craniums back where they're supposed to be. Since you haven't gotten a call from your ex, it appears as if your boys view you as the tilt-expert. In a weird way they're giving you a compliment."

"That's a steaming pile of horse dung."

"You can set their worlds right, Tawn'."

"You're stinking up the place with that logic. The bottom line: they're being selfish."

"They're not heinous jackanapes. They're your sons. They might have some latent anger about you and Grady breaking up."

"Jackanapes? Who are you? Shakespeare?"

"Duh." Elaina hugged Tawny. "It's going to be okay. Give them some mom-time."

"You're probably right about the anger. The boys were already in California and Oregon when Grady and I called it quits. We spoke on the phone to Bo and Quentin, but it's not like having a heart-to-heart talk in person where they could gauge our level of hurt and we could gauge theirs. When they didn't go ballistic I thought they accepted that divorce happens. When they showed up at your house, shortly after we moved in together, they didn't let on that their noses were out of joint. They said they came to check on me and to help me celebrate my birthday. Had I not freaked out about turning forty-seven, I might've picked up on the fact they didn't ask important questions about me and their dad."

"Maybe they shelved their feelings because they

couldn't deal with the loss of the family unit they once knew. And now they've taken those feelings out of storage and want answers."

Pain glistened in Tawny's eyes. "Baring my soul to them will be like reliving the nightmare of the divorce."

Grace put things into perspective. "You'll only have to slay that beast once. Well, twice – once with Bo and once with Quentin." She tucked a wisp of Tawny's hair behind her ear. "It'll be liberating."

Apparently Steph was the official timekeeper. She tapped the crystal on her watch. "Tawny, it's time to take a deep breath, board that plane, and do what you have to do to get your boys in line." She reared her hand back as though she was going to give Tawny a crack on the butt like some coaches do when they put a new player in the game. Instead of following through, she dropped it to her side. "Go to it, mama."

Before entering the line for screening, Tawny gathered them in a group hug. "I don't know what I'd do without you guys. You keep me sane."

Steph offered her slant on the topic. "Sanity is subjective."

"No it's not." Tawny also hugged them individually. "Thanks for everything. You're my boulders."

"Don't you mean rocks?"

"Nope."

They were blocking the entrance to the screening maze. A young couple with a small child wandered up and waited for the boulders to move.

"I've got to go."

Another quick round of hugs and Tawny joined the line.

Elaina gave Tawny a wave. "Fare thee well in thy travels, and may by fate we meet again."

The guy behind Tawny lifted his child into his arms and said, "Shakespeare." His wife asked if they'd just come from a Renaissance faire.

Grace fielded the question. "You'd think so, but no."

Chapter Thirteen

~ It's all about timing...and sticky buns! ~

Their dream was within their grasp. Tomorrow the doors would be thrown open and guests would descend.

Elaina was confident they were ready. She wanted to give the place one more walk-through. She'd just come from the garage where a shiny new van sat with a metallic sign on the side that read, 'Four Sassy Chicks Bed and Breakfast'.

In the spacious living room, she looked around, filled with pride at the end product. Together with Grace and Steph, they'd gone hog wild with furnishings. A Cleopatra chair that was as close a match to the sofa as they could get sat waiting for the first guest. If Grace hadn't insisted they go to one more furniture store during the shopping spree they would've missed the four over-sized recliners that were a definite match to the sofa. Elaina wanted to shy away from getting a flat screen TV for the living room because she wanted it to be a gathering place for reading or conversation. Grace muscled her with the argument that on many occasions guests would come during football season, or the Olympics, or even highly advertised local events and folks would want to root for their favorites in an atmosphere of camaraderie. Elaina countered that it was a bed and breakfast not a sports bar. She gave in though and was glad she did.

Yesterday, Steph invited Nicholas over to view the changes. She'd asked for his opinion but he clammed up. Elaina guessed the reason for his reluctance had to do with her. The night Tawny unraveled, she denied his wish to eat pizza with them. Tawny had needed her three best friends; not her three best friends and a guy she met once.

Elaina smiled at the recollection of Nicholas shooting her wary glances as they proceeded through the house. Only after she put an arm around his waist, guided him into the living room with the announcement they were wearing their big girl panties and would appreciate his input, did he loosen up. The self-assured restaurant owner came forth. Nicholas had worn a tie. That baby was pulled off and stuffed in his pocket. He walked around the room, rubbing his chin. 'You need floor lamps and paintings.' He directed their attention to the sofa. 'I don't see any decorative pillows. A colorful throw or afghan would make your guests feel like they could curl up with a good book. Where's the magazine rack? There are no vases or figurines on the mantel.' His eyebrows had bumped together. 'Where are your plants? I'm not talking silk arrangements. I'm talking the real thing. Plants are a healthy addition to any home.

They take in carbon dioxide and convert it to oxygen. With a lot of people in and out of this place, you're going to have a boat load of carbon dioxide.' He did another walk-around. 'Don't bite my head off when I give it to you straight. Ladies, I've seen hotel lobbies cozier than this. You're being stingy with the personal effects. Bring out your pictures, doilies, area rugs, and anything else you have boxed up. This is your business. You also live here. Make it comfortable. I have no data to back this up, but I'd say most people who stay at a bed and breakfast are seeking a warm and fuzzy experience. Give it to them.' He'd made a face at the purple loveseat. Surprisingly, he didn't say a word about it. Elaina had been prepared to negate any proposal to ditch it. Tawny had bought the darn thing. Therefore, the dreadful piece of furniture was staying and would most likely become a conversation piece. Later, Steph rewarded Nicholas for his critique with a private dinner in the sunroom. She'd served him pork chops drizzled with raspberry sauce, buttery-herbed potatoes, broccoli crowns jazzed up with sea salt, and grilled pineapple for dessert. They stayed in the sunroom for hours. Elaina hoped the only thing that happened in that time span was dinner and conversation. With the chemistry that sizzled between those two lust-birds, who knows. When they reemerged, Nicholas teased Elaina that he was replacing his head chef with Steph. At her protest, he chuckled. 'Made you sweat for a second. Lucky for you, Steph is dedicated to the bed and breakfast.'

Nicholas the second was quite the guy. Elaina could

see why Steph liked him. He fit into the misfit bunch like he'd been one of them all along.

They followed his advice and the place now looked like a home instead of a hotel lobby. There were framed pictures on the walls; including one Philip had taken of them. Pillows graced the sofa and plants had been placed in every room.

On the trip up to the second and third floors, Elaina inspected every bedroom. Each contained a four-poster bed, chest of drawers, a desk and chair, small flat screen TV, two recliners, a lamp table and lamp, a full length mirror attached to the back of the door, and a mini refrigerator. The adjoining bathrooms had thirsty monogrammed towels and scented soaps. Guests could tuck away in their rooms for privacy or take advantage of the entire house, except for the rooms with plaques on the doors that read 'personal residence'.

Returning to the first floor, she walked through the alcove that now contained a slew of books. They'd combed the used bookstores for contemporary romances, historical romances, the horror genre, books about vampires and dragons, children's books, how-to books, you name it they had it. There was also a selection of DVD's the guests could borrow.

Stony was fast on her heels when she headed for the kitchen. Elaina wagged her finger back and forth. "Ut. Ut. You have to stay here." The hairy Husky sat down but watched her every move. Someday he'd figure out he could back up, get a running start, and sail across the wooden barricades that kept him from the two places he wanted in. The morning after they dropped Tawny off at the airport, Elaina called around for a carpenter to build half-doors to cordon off Stony and Lula from the kitchen and dining area. Grace argued it would cheapen the look of the downstairs. Once the carpenter had them built and in place, she changed her opinion. Stony whined and pushed against the doors for a few days. He finally got the message that there were boundaries. Lula seemed to care less about the doors. Knowing the sly cat, she waited until they were in bed and then leaped across them with little effort.

Elaina straightened the pots and pans hanging under one of the cupboards, and ran fingers over the twenty-eight bottle wine rack that had been installed under another. She was pleased to find the stainless steel refrigerator crammed with food. Everything was neat as a pin, at least for now. When they opened for business, Steph would make the kitchen look like something exploded in there. It's what she did and they'd grown to accept that's the way it was. The guests would have to allow it too, since the kitchen and dining area flowed into one. They'd get a bird's eye view of the hardworking chef and get a memorable, mouthwatering meal to boot.

Steph had spent the past few days making different kinds of quiches, French toast recipes, one-dish breakfast casseroles, and sticky buns, for practice. She squeezed oranges and grapefruit for the juice but decided it was a lot of work for the amount of juice they needed and it wasn't cost effective.

Filled with awe at having pulled things together in a

short amount of time, Elaina had one last area to visit. It was the place nearest and dearest to her heart in the whole house – the room they converted to an exercise center. Elaina stepped into the room as if seeing it for the first time. She smiled at the walls covered with mirrors that gave the illusion the space was bigger than it actually was. The stationary bike, elliptical machine, treadmill, rack with weights, and rowing machine from her home gym in Ohio were ready to be used. There was a table stacked with freshly laundered towels and a small fridge with bottles of water.

They were a well-rounded B & B – roomy enough to accommodate large groups and fully conscious about dietary needs and restrictions. The guests would have a place to work off those sticky buns. As an added bonus, the bed and breakfast offered rides to and from the airport. The day-to-day operation was yet to be learned. Hopefully their mistakes would be minimal and the things that went right would be too numerous to count.

Stony saw his reflection in one of the mirrors and stuck his nose on it, leaving a mark. He went to every mirror and did the same thing.

"If you weren't so darn cute you'd be in the dog house."

Blue eyes stared in confusion.

Elaina was glad Stony no longer acted homesick. He loped from room to room like he owned the place. She had a sneaking suspicion though that he missed Tawny. Every night he went into her bedroom and laid his head on the edge of the bed. "I'm right there with ya, boy. I miss her too."

"Elainaaaaaa."

It was useless to holler a reply given the size of the house. If she shouted back, Steph would commence an entire conversation by yelling. She made a mental note to tell the girls to keep their cell phones on them at all times when guests were in residence. A text message, even if it was from the third floor to the kitchen, was better than hollering.

"Elainaaaaaa," Steph called again. The urgency in her tone prompted Elaina to break into a sprint.

"What's up?"

Steph tossed her the landline phone. "Tawny needs to talk to you." She whispered, "Things might not be going well."

Elaina muted a growl at the thought of Bo and Quentin making Tawny walk a gauntlet, or worse. "Hey, Tawny-scrawny, Stony was just telling me how much he missed you."

"You're a weirdo."

"That goes without saying." Elaina forced a laugh. "Where the heck are you?"

"Portland." Tawny sounded tired.

"Well, it's about time. Let me grab my keys. I'll come pick you up."

"That'll be quite a drive. I'm in Portland, Oregon."

Elaina's heart sank. "Really? Do you want me to come, Tawn', because I will?"

"That would be sweet. Doubtful it could actually happen."

"I'll make it happen." Tawny only called once while

she was gone. At the time, the mother and son reunion was a work in progress. She and Bo had talked about the divorce, went out to dinner a few times, took a trip to the San Diego Zoo, and visited the famous Hotel del Coronado where L. Frank Baum wrote *The Wonderful Wizard of Oz* series. She'd sent a text message when she left California and arrived in Oregon. That's the last they'd heard from her until now. Elaina assumed things had gone smoother with Quentin, but maybe he was a tougher nut to crack.

"Do you have the inside track with the weather gods?"

"This isn't about Quentin?"

"Nooo. It's about the weather. Haven't you watched the news?"

"We've been getting things ready for the first round of guests so the TV has stayed off for a week. Are you stuck in a blizzard?"

"Portland doesn't get blizzards. That hasn't stopped the wicked weather wench from going on a rampage. We've had freezing rain off and on for the past two days. My flights have been cancelled four stinking times. What a mess. The way things are going I won't make it home in time for the grand opening or for Thanksgiving."

They couldn't delay the grand opening. Guests were scheduled to arrive promptly at check-in time – three in the afternoon. Realistically, Tawny would miss it. Thanksgiving wasn't for three more days. Surely she wouldn't be stranded that long. "Maybe the Good Lord has a reason for keeping you with Quentin a while longer."

"Are you kidding me? I got to see him a handful of times, in fifteen minute increments. That's a stretch, but you get the idea. He took me out for sushi the day I got here. Over an order of spicy tuna I realized he didn't have a problem with me at all. His head is in the clouds over a girl named Melinda. Poor guy is whipped. He gave me hope I'd have a daughter-in-law in the foreseeable future. He and I are good, Elaina. Bo's the one who was holding a grudge because I walked away from his dad. Now we're good too. Thank you for shoving me out of Maine so I could fix things. When I get back, the four of us are going to celebrate."

"You're on."

Tawny cleared her throat. "Stony hasn't gotten loose lately, has he?"

Elaina read between the lines. "No, Bartholomew Simpson hasn't stopped by." *And neither has Chad*. Oh well. It wasn't meant to be for them.

Tawny cracked up laughing. "I detest you."

"I know, right? Now get your butt home so I can hug your neck."

* * *

"I'm so excited!" Steph paced back in forth in front of the large picture window.

"Stop pacing. You're going to wear a spot in the carpet." Grace placed a crystal dish filled with wrapped candies on the coffee table.

Elaina was beyond excited but she tried to appear

calm. "There's no need to pace. The guests won't show up unexpectedly. I'm going to the airport to get them. When you see the van pull up out front, you can pace. For like two minutes. Then you'd better open the door, greet them with a big smile, and help with their bags."

"It was nice of Nicholas to donate gift cards to his restaurant for our grand opening." Steph fanned the envelopes that lay on the corner of the mantle. "He's an amazing man." She walked to the ficus he'd sent as a congratulations-gift and straightened the silk ribbon at the base.

"He's also a major suck-up," Grace kidded.

Nicholas was also hot for Steph and knew how to stay on her good side. Smart man. "Be nice, Grace." Elaina shrugged into her jacket.

"I am being nice. I could've called him a horn-dog."

Steph disregarded Grace's comment. "I can't believe this is actually happening. We're about to open for business." In an abrupt move she clutched her stomach. "Oh no! Not again!" With lightning speed she was up the stairs.

Grace lifted an eyebrow. "That can't be good."

"She's got herself too worked up." Elaina wrinkled her nose. "She might need something."

"I'm on it." Grace stopped mid-stride. "Pepto Bismol or Imodium?"

Butterflies had taken flight in Elaina's stomach as well. Luckily they were just fluttering not causing bathroom mayhem.

* * *

Elaina had done a trial run to the airport earlier in the morning. It had been a breeze. Easy in. Easy out. At the moment, there was nothing easy or breezy about it. Traffic on I-95 was crazy. She didn't know if it was due to the time of day or the fact it was a holiday week. Whatever the case, she should've left a half-hour to an hour earlier. Glancing at the clock on the dash did nothing to calm her nerves. In fifteen minutes she was supposed to meet four guests at baggage claim. She breathed a sigh of relief when the road sign indicated Jetport Road ahead.

Some things in life are all about timing: that precise moment when you decide it's best to do a particular thing. At that exact second, Elaina made the choice to accelerate beyond the posted speed limit. *Terrible* timing. A police car materialized out of thin air. Red and blue flashing lights hit her rearview mirror. "Noooo." Was it the temporary license tag that drew their attention? Or had the van been shot with the handy dandy police radar gun? Who was the lucky cop who would get to write her a ticket? She envisioned Officer Chad Ferguson and Officer Lorenzo cautiously approaching with their hands touching their weapons. It happened once. It could happen again. She'd die a thousand deaths. Chad would possibly say something to the effect that she'd only been in Maine a few short weeks and already had two encounters with the law. He wouldn't be able to let her off the hook, not with his no-nonsense partner in tow. "Please. Not today." Thinking a traffic stop was unavoidable she looked for a place to pull over. Just before the exit there was a space big enough for two cars. Before she got there, the cop car buzzed past like she was sitting still. Elaina let out a squeal of joy. "Thank you," she murmured to the heavens. "Thank you. Thank you. Thank you." Accepting she wouldn't make it to baggage claim on time, she hoped their flight was a few minutes late or that they'd stop to get coffee at one of the airport shops. Yeah, she'd caught one break, it was doubtful she'd catch two. Elaina checked and double-checked her speed.

An impatient driver in a black Mercedes honked behind her.

"I can empathize, buddy. I'm in a hurry just like you, but I'm not going to put the pedal to the metal to make you happy. Go around if you want."

He honked again.

"Geez." She glared in her side mirror. "Unless you're trying to tell me I have a flat tire or my gas tank lid is open, you'd better knock it off."

The expensive car moved so close it was practically on her bumper.

Elaina wanted to hit the brakes to give the guy heart palpitations. That was a form of road rage. God-fearing women didn't engage in that kind of behavior. She wouldn't get in too much trouble with the man upstairs for wishing for a flock of birds to target their droppings to the pinheads' windshield.

The driver of the Mercedes must've tapped into her

thoughts. He sped around the van and cut her off. Elaina jerked the steering wheel to the right to avoid a collision. Rattled, with her heart thumping hard against her ribs, she was thankful her guardian angel had *great* timing. "Okay. Whatever. You win. No more hoping for bird droppings."

Elaina pulled into the parking garage, craning her neck to find a space. Level one - nothing. Level two – all parking spaces filled. Level three – one spot left and one pinhead in a black Mercedes taking it.

The driver spotted her at the same time she spotted him. A wicked smile dimpled his mouth.

The urge to give him the finger was overpowering but she vowed to be good. "Forget him. You're here to pick up guests."

He gave *her* the finger.

Elaina's eyes widened. "Oh no you didn't!" It was fortunate for the arrogant buffoon that she didn't have time to leave tire tread marks on his forehead.

* * *

Breathing hard, pulse pounding, Elaina arrived at baggage claim with the Styrofoam-cardboard sign she'd made.

Two twenty-something guys who looked as though they'd just returned from Florida or the Caribbean given their tropical shirts with palm trees and cargo shorts, walked past Elaina.

The tall brunette backed up and gave her a salacious

grin. "I only see one."

Elaina was taken by surprise. "Excuse me?"

"Your sign says *Four Sassy Chicks*. I only see one." He hooted with laughter as though he'd made a huge funny.

"I can sass like four."

"I loooove sassy chicks; especially ones with amazing eyes."

The guys' friend grabbed his buddy by the back of the shirt. "Don't mind him. He had one too many drinks on the plane."

"That may be true but I know a fine looking woman when I see one."

Elaina fought a smile. "I'm old enough to be your mother."

"You're like what? Thirty-one-ish?"

"Almost forty-four-ish." Elaina stepped to the right so her sign would be visible.

"Bax, no way she's almost forty-four. No friggin' way."

The friend known as Bax – possibly short for Baxter – offered an apology. "He's usually not this obnoxious." He mimicked bringing a bottle to his lips. "Whiskey loosens his lips. But he's not wrong. You do have spectacular eyes. Take care." He increased his hold on his friends' shirt. "Let's go, Frank. It's time to get a taxi."

Could the day get any stranger? First, the guy in the Mercedes; now Frank and Bax.

The unspoken question answered itself.

An old gal with powder-white hair and glasses came up to Elaina. "Four Sassy Chicks. That describes us to a tee. Isn't that right, Flora, Hazel, and Josie?"

Accompanying the short, tiny-framed woman were three carbon copies. The four women were dressed in the same fake fur coats and floral bandanas.

The carbon copies nodded.

"We're in our eighties but we can be a bit cheeky." The leader of the pack smiled so big her eyes went closed. "I'm Adelaide. We've come from Tennessee to stay at your bed and breakfast. Sorry it took so long for us to get to baggage claim. We're not as spry as we used to be. The airline offered to cart us with one of those fancy four-wheelers."

One of the carbon copies spoke up. "They're not four-wheelers, Addie. I believe they call them shuttles."

Another of the four women winced. "A lot you know. They're called courtesy transports."

"That's our know-it-all sister, Hazel. What she doesn't know isn't worth knowing." Adelaide broke into a cackle that turned into a loose cough.

"I never claimed to know everything; although I do have more upstairs than the other three put together."

"You wish. I'm Flora, dear."

Elaina nodded. "Nice to meet you, Flora."

"I'm, Josephine, the prettiest of the Turlington sisters." She put her dentures together in a silly grin. "Boom."

Did she really say boom? Elaina kept her expression even. Inside she was jiggling with a laugh. She had a feeling it would be a fun few days. "I'm Elaina. Welcome to Maine."

Adelaide leaned into Elaina. "Several years ago we decided to vacation in every state before we kick the bucket. We're proud to say this is the fiftieth. Right, girls?"

Their heads wobbled when they nodded.

"How exciting! I'm sure you've seen a lot of great things in your travels."

Flora shook her head. "Not really. We don't get around so good, so we usually don't venture out."

"You don't leave the hotel or bed and breakfast?"

Hazel didn't hedge on the truth. "Nope. We play cards and drink wine." She made a weird noise that could've been a laugh. It was hard to tell. "When we get home we brag to our card club that we visited another state."

"That's remarkable."

"Oh it is." Flora winked. "I want you to know ahead of time that we collect those little bars of soap and bottles of shampoo. Some people collect trinkets. We collect toiletries."

"Collect?" Josephine scoffed. "We steal them."

Hazel set the record straight. "They think they're getting away with something."

Adelaide rebuffed her sister. "It's thievery all right. If you don't use it, you're not supposed to take it."

Elaina looked from woman to woman. "Are you ready to discover the Four Sassy Chicks Bed and Breakfast?"

"Can we make a stop?" Flora inquired.

"I'll bet she forgot to bring her Depends," Hazel said under her breath.

Flora leveled a scowl at her sister. She couldn't maintain it. An evil grin splashed across her weathered face. "You're just jealous that you have to use the bathroom when you have to pee. I never have to leave the card game."

Adelaide rushed to deny Flora's boasting. "She's teasing. Flora, tell this sweet lady you're teasing."

"Nope. I pee wherever and whenever I want. I'm peeing right now."

Hazel lifted her eyes in embarrassment. "Sorry about that, miss. I could blame it on her age, but age doesn't excuse everything."

"Booyah." Flora blew on her fingernails like she'd one-upped her sisters.

Elaina smiled at each Turlington sibling. "You remind me of my friends. Wait until you meet them. You'll see what I mean." Her cell phone chimed with an incoming text message. She ignored it to remain professional.

Her cell phone rang shortly after the text. Again, she ignored it.

Elaina addressed Flora. "Where would you like me to make a stop?"

"Wherever they sell wine."

Her cell phone rang yet again.

Josie was using hand sanitizer for a second time since their arrival to baggage claim. "Don't you hear your phone? I can hear it and I don't have my hearing aid in."

"I didn't want to be rude."

"Aww, hon, it's okay. Someone is trying to get a hold of you. Go ahead and answer. It could be important." Josie motioned for her to do it now.

"Thank you." Elaina fished her phone from her coat pocket. "Hello."

"I made it home. Woohoo!" Tawny shrieked with

happiness. "I was on three different airplanes but I made it. Can you pick me up?"

"Halleluiah, Tawn'! You're going to make it for the grand opening after all. Did your plane just land?"

"It landed fifteen minutes ago. I would've gotten a hold of you sooner, but I couldn't get Quentin off the phone. The second the plane touched down, he called. He was worried, Elaina. After I hung up with him, Bo called for the same reason. They love their mom again."

"They've always loved you. They just needed for you to remind them."

Josephine coughed.

"You'll find me and four awe-inspiring guests by carousel one."

"No kidding? I'm at carousel two."

"Excellent. You get to help with luggage. Perfect timing, eh?"

Chapter Fourteen

~ *Eight feisty chicks! Boom!* ~

Stony went nuts when he saw Tawny. He flew across the living room and jumped so high his paws landed on her chest. After a few licks to her face, she held him close and kissed his head several times. The unconditional love left few with dry eyes.

"Would you look at that, Adelaide? Winchester never jumps on you after you've been gone."

"Flora, he's a Yorkie who's all of eight inches tall. I doubt he could leap onto my chest."

Flora elbowed Josephine. "Her chest has fallen to her waist. Winchester would have no problem."

"Boom." Josephine knuckled-bumped Flora and then checked her watch. "Time to take your insulin."

Flora made a face. "You might want to stop bossing me, bosser."

Those ladies were over eight decades old, they behaved much younger. They knuckle-bumped and said things like 'boom' and 'booyah'. Their language occasionally got a little spicy. On the ride from the liquor store to the bed and breakfast, Hazel called Josephine a bitch. It had been said in fun, but still. Elaina had slanted a glance at Tawny who was in the front passenger seat. Tawn' mouthed the word 'Grace'.

Steph came from the kitchen carrying a tray with wine glasses and the bottle of blackberry wine Adelaide had bought. "Here's your bottle of wine. You'll have to wait to drink it though. Elaina says wine under eight years old should aerate for one to two hours."

Hazel cackled. "Screw that. I'm eighty-six. I could be dead in that time. Pour me a glass."

Adelaide shook her head with disapproval. "Such a potty mouth."

"Don't act so pious. When I'm whooping your butt in cards, you've been known to call me a..." Hazel caught herself. "It wouldn't be right to say it in front of you whippersnappers. But it rhymes with... I'd better not say it. Addie's give me the stink eye."

"Whippersnappers? Geez, Hazel, they're not kids. They've been around the block."

Grace chimed in. "I haven't been around the block."

Adelaide studied Grace. "A beauty like you? You've been around a few blocks. Not that it's a bad thing. If I were a few years younger..."

"You'd be eighty-one. Stop the chitchat and get the cards. I'm itching to whip on you." Josephine pulled a small bottle of hand sanitizer from her pocket.

Elaina noticed Josephine used the sanitizer almost as frequently as some people use lip balm – like every half hour.

Addie fired back at Josie. "You can barely keep score let alone whip me."

Flora whimpered that the wine could aerate for days as far as she was concerned, since wine and insulin weren't a good mix. She followed with a hodgepodge of indecipherable words. It could've been bad language cleverly disguised.

Josie advised Flora to stop bellyaching.

Elaina perceived some compassion in Josie's tone.

"I can beat you in cards with or without wine, Josephine."

"Oooo. She's calling you by your formal name, Josie." Hazel patted Elaina's arm. "I should warn you. We get a little vocal when we play."

"Not a problem. You're our only guests. You can wail on each other or trash-talk all you want."

Hazel smirked. "I'm allowed to wail on you, Addie."

Tawny mumbled under her breath. "You are so Grace."

* * * *

"They're party animals. Not." Steph cleared the table of the glasses and loaded them into the dishwasher. "It's seven o'clock and they're in bed."

"It might have something to do with the fact they ate very little and had wine. Factor in their age and it's a wonder they didn't tuck in at six." Tawny went to the fridge for a mozzarella cheese stick. She peeled back the protective wrapper and took a small bite.

"They're peculiar...and amazing. I swear they had four conversations going on all the time. I tried not to eavesdrop but they seem to have one volume – extremely loud." She put a hand across her heart. "I feel a strange connection with Josie. I think she was a nurse."

"Just because she mentioned blood draws doesn't mean she was a nurse. She might have a medical condition that occasionally needs to be checked."

Tawny cocked her head to the side. "I didn't get the whole conversation because I took a load of white clothes to the utility room and folded some towels. When I brought a stack of clean dish cloths to the kitchen I heard her say venipuncture. I doubt anyone other than a nurse or phlebotomist would use that term."

"You got me there."

Elaina cupped her ear to listen. "It's very quiet. I think it's safe for us to celebrate." She held up an opened bottle of Merlot. "And yes, it's aerated for an hour."

"You know, we don't have to sneak around. Like Nicholas said, we live here. We're responsible for providing a great place for our guests to bunk, interacting with them a little, and serving a tasty breakfast. Other than that, they're supposed to be on their own." Steph held out her glass for Elaina to pour wine into. "At the same time, getting to know those quirky ladies was fun. Want to know why?"

Grace hunched her elbows on the counter and steepled her fingers. "Do tell."

Steph looked from Grace to Elaina to Tawny. "Because they're us."

Tawny exaggerated a laugh. "You're bonkers. I'd never wear fake fur, or real fur for that matter. Nor will you catch me with a bandana on my head. It's doubtful I'll go to bed at seven unless I'm sick. Pinochle and bridge don't interest me." She stuck out her tongue.

"You're keying on the physical aspects, not their personalities." Elaina shoved a glass of wine across the counter to Tawny. "They're mouthy and fun. They have an unbreakable bond. Hazel called Josephine a bitch. I'd bet money if someone outside their circle called Josie that, she'd sock them in the nose. That's how we are. Tawn', I think you're afraid to picture an older version of you."

"I'm not afraid of getting older...bitch."

Elaina cracked up laughing. "You lie so much... Josephine."

They laughed until they cried.

Grace composed herself. "Josephine is..." She broke into laughter again. "Josephine is so you, Tawn'. Steph, dah-ling, you're Flora. Elaina, you're the leader of the brat pack. You're Adelaide. That leaves me. I'm Hazel. I totally am."

"You're crackers. All of you." Over the rim of her glass, Tawny's brown eyes glittered with irrepressible mischief. "Eight feisty chicks under one roof. Boom!"

* * * *

"Hey, handsome." Flora batted her eyes at Chad Ferguson. "Where'd you come from?"

Chad smiled at the tiny woman but Elaina could swear he also blushed. "I just got off work and thought

I'd stop by to congratulate the girls on making their dream a reality."

He was here again. Elaina's mind raced. Should she mention seeing him with the blonde?

"Uh huh." There was good-humored skepticism in Flora's reply. "Hot guys like you don't stop by to offer best wishes. You've come to scope out the babes. Which one of us has caught your eye?" She tapped her chin. "Is it me?"

Chad played along. "You are pretty cute."

"Josie, he thinks I'm cute."

"He thinks you're one step away from a straight-jacket."

Flora wrapped her hands around his forearm. "She's just jealous."

Adelaide came from the kitchen with the bowl of red grapes Steph set out earlier for them to snack on. "Unhand him." She sat the bowl on the coffee table and marched to Flora to pry her fingers loose. "He's not here for you, loony bird. He's here for Elaina."

Flora crinkled her nose. "How do you know?"

"It doesn't take a genius to figure it out. All you have to do is see the sparkle in Elaina's eyes."

"There's no sparkle." For a millisecond, the space between Chad's eyes creased, prompting Elaina to add, "Then again, I can't see my eyes."

Chad's follow-up smile blasted Elaina with warmth. Thank goodness Hazel stepped in.

"Elaina and crew have pampered us so much, we hate to leave. They're going to let us have Thanksgiving dinner with them tomorrow evening. You should come."

Chad's gaze darted from Hazel to Elaina.

"We'd love to have you."

Chad shifted from foot to foot. "Really?"

Josephine threw in her two-cents. "Who else is going to carve the turkey? We need you, hot stuff."

Chad met and held Elaina's eyes again. "I'd love to."

Elaina determined in that moment he wasn't in another relationship. She touched the anchor on her necklace and said silent thanks to her mom. "Excellent. Appetizers and wine start at four-thirty. Dinner will be served at five."

Still with their gazes locked, Chad took Elaina's hand.

His touch sent another blast of warmth spiraling through her body.

Bringing her hand to his mouth, he placed a soft kiss across her knuckles. "I'll see you tomorrow."

"Aww," Josie chirped from the overstuffed recliner that seemed to swallow her fragile frame. "Isn't love grand?"

"We're not in love," spontaneously came from Elaina.

Josie corrected the comment. "Isn't lust grand?"

Grace happened to walk in when the lust word fell. "What about lust?"

Josie jerked her thumb toward Elaina and Chad. "They just undressed each other with their eyes."

Chad whispered, "Time for me to go."

Elaina gave him a small nod.

To Grace and the spunky geezers, Chad said, "Have a good evening." He didn't wait for them to acknowledge the farewell. In a blink he was gone.

"I have to make a trip to town." Hazel shuffled across the room to the huge coat closet. "Can you call me a taxi?"

Grace jumped at the chance to get away. "I'd be happy to drive you."

"Hon, you don't have to do that. You've done so much already."

"It's okay, really. I don't mind."

"Whatcha getting? Preparation H?" Flora inquired with a giggle.

"None of your beeswax. Can't a gal go to town without getting the third degree? Come on, Grace, let's go."

Adelaide sprang from the sofa like a nimble little minx. "I'd like to go, too."

Flora was at the coat closet in a flash. "You're not going without me."

"Well hell, I just got cozy." Josephine struggled to get out of the recliner. "You're not leaving me behind." Her gaze slid to Elaina. "You're great company but someone has to supervise. Grace can't do it because she'll be driving."

Steph passed through the living room on her way to the kitchen. "Where are you going, Grace?"

"I have no idea."

Hazel cleared things up. "Out."

"Okay then." Steph gave Elaina a questioning look.

Elaina lifted her shoulders just enough to qualify as a shrug.

Tawny's bedroom door creaked open and she peered around the door jamb. "What's shakin', ladies?"

"We're on a secret mission." Josie put a finger across her lips. "Shh. Mum's the word."

Tawny chuckled without opening her mouth.

Steph spouted that Tawny sound like a ventriloquist dummy.

"Bite me."

"Before we leave, I need to get something." Grace flew up the stairs. In a heartbeat, she was back with five eye patches dangling from her finger. "Secret missions call for special attire."

Adelaide said what Elaina was thinking. "We barely have a decent set of eyes between us. I'm not sure eye patches are a good idea."

"I hate when you're right." Hazel took one of the patches. "Nothing says we can't wear them in the van. When we pull up to a traffic light, we'll lower our windows to scare the crap out of the people in the car beside us."

Tawny snickered. "Oh yeah, they're definitely us."

* * *

Steph added more butter to the mashed potatoes. "I can't believe it's Thanksgiving. Where'd the time go?"

"The older we get the faster it goes." Grace flicked on the oven light to check the candied sweet potatoes. "I can't wait to dive into these."

Elaina pretended to retch. "Sweet potatoes are evil."

Tawny inclined her head toward the living room. "Josie asked for them. So did Bart." She hip-checked

Elaina. "Thanks for letting him join us so he didn't have to spend the holiday alone."

"I hope his wife didn't mind."

"Ha, ha, funny woman. For your information he doesn't have a wife anymore. He's divorced and they never had kids. His folks and relatives live in New Jersey."

"How did he end up here?"

"He met someone online. He quit his job and moved here. They shared an apartment for a few months. Things didn't work out. He decided he loved Maine and stayed."

Philip walked into the kitchen. "What's with all the whispering?"

Grace put a hand on his chest and gave him a small shove. "You must have dog ears because we clattered enough utensils to cover the whispers."

An impish grin spread across his face. "You told on yourself. I didn't really hear you. I came in to see if you needed any help." He used the back of his hand to tap Tawny on the arm. "Stony is making puppy dog eyes at Adelaide. I thought you should know."

"She has a way with dogs. So does Bart."

Grace took a spoon from the drawer and scooped a small bit of mashed potatoes. She handed it to Philip. "You'd make puppy dog eyes at her too if she kept sneaking you treats."

The trip to town actually *was* for Preparation H. Hazel had left home without it. While they were at the store Adelaide bought a bag of treats for Stony and a bag of fish specialties for Lula. Stony hadn't left her side after she gave him the first treat. The self-governing cat, however, only came out from under the sofa when Addie lured her with a treat. She'd snatch it and wouldn't be seen again until Addie offered another bribe.

"You just did the same thing with Philip." At Grace's narrowed eyes, Tawny backed up and clarified what she meant. "Didn't you just give him a treat? The potatoes?"

Philip snorted. "What one of you doesn't think of, the other does. No wonder this works." He used his finger and made a circle to include Elaina, Tawny, Steph, and Grace. "By the way, thanks for inviting me. I took my parents to lunch. They wanted lobster rolls instead of turkey. Now they're headed to New Hampshire to spend a few days with my aunt." He sighed. "Thanksgiving is so different now."

By *now*, Philip meant since he'd become a widower three years ago. Yesterday after the shopping extravaganza with the eccentric octogenarians, Grace dropped in on Philip. Grace said they sat in front of his wood burning fireplace, sipped Mai Tai's, and talked until around midnight. In one of their many conversations, Grace asked him about smoking weed. Philip didn't hide the fact he used it to dull the mental pain of having lost the one woman who understood him. He also confessed that after meeting Grace he'd only smoked it once – the day he came to take their pictures. She asked why that day in particular. He'd said he was nervous about seeing her again. Grace didn't hold back with him either and shared how she'd mourned the loss of Brince for over two years – and would always mourn for him – and how she'd worn nothing but black garb until she met Elaina,

Steph, and Tawny. Elaina had a hunch some healing had taken place last night for both Philip and Grace.

Grace blinked up at Philip. "Have a seat at the table. Food will be out shortly."

The door bell chimed and Steph dashed from the kitchen.

"We have a doorbell?" Tawny looked dumbfounded. "Since when?"

"I had it installed while you were gone. I can't believe this place didn't have one. It has everything else." Elaina poured gravy into a fancy gravy boat.

Tawny leaned to look into the dining area. "Don't you find it surprising that we've been here less than a month and there are four men sitting at our dinner table? Actually it's more astonishing than surprising."

Grace was quick to clarify that surprising and astonishing meant the same thing.

Tawny forged a mean face. "Sure glad you're here to keep my English in check."

"I do what I can."

"Tawny," Steph hollered, "someone's here to see you."

"My boys? I just saw them a few days ago. Did they follow me home?" The questions and a boatload of hope rushed out of her mouth like she was hopped up on energy drinks. "Oh God, let it be them. Please. Let it be them. I need for it to be them."

Steph yelled again. "Hurry up, Tawn'."

Elaina hadn't had the talk with the girls about not using their vocal chords excessively while guests were there. She shouldn't have to coach them. Some things should be obvious. *Note to self: speak with Steph. Aww, hell... Note to self: stop making notes to self.* Steph would figure it out or get one heck of a sore throat.

Unlike Steph burning up the carpet getting to the door, Tawny dawdled.

Tawny wanted it to be her boys, yet she was doing a snail-like shuffle. Elaina assumed it was from fear of being disappointed.

Steph returned to the kitchen. "The food's ready. Let's serve it before we have to reheat it."

"Who's at the front door?"

"Delivery guy." Steph commenced scurrying about the kitchen. She took the sweet potatoes from the oven and handed them to Elaina.

Elaina waved them away. "I want no part of those sinister potatoes. I wouldn't be able to stop my throat from lurching. Nothing encourages our guests to enjoy their meal quite like a convulsive gag reflex."

"Give me those." Grace set aside the dish of green bean almandine and whisked the casserole dish filled with sweet potatoes from Elaina. "You get today's top prize for a theatrical performance. Is it because you're nervous?"

"Why would I be nervous?"

"Self explanatory – Officer Chaddy-boy is seated at the end of the table. How'd that come about? You never did say."

"You better watch it, Grace. He'll taze you." Elaina grinned from ear to ear. "All I had to do was ask. Actually, Hazel invited him."

"He had no prior plans?"

"That's a good question." Elaina hadn't considered that Chad might've had plans and cancelled them for her. He'd said yes without hesitation. Steph had gotten the same results with Nicholas. She'd asked, he said yes right away.

"Are you going to ask Chad? If I were you I'd want to know."

"I'm not as impulsive as you are. I'll have to think about it."

Steph was the queen of the kitchen and she had no problem reminding them who wore the crown. "Get a move on. I'm aging here and the food's getting cold."

Tawny placed a box on the counter. "They're from my boys."

Elaina glanced at the box labeled gourmet dipped strawberries. "How sweet, Tawn'."

"Yeah it is." Tawny sniffed back tears, grabbed the gravy boat and plate of garlic cheese biscuits, and shuffled out of the kitchen.

"Did someone just flip from happy to cranky?"

Elaina nodded. "She's going to need a lot of space today. With a crowded table and four guests that will be staying on after the meal, it will be difficult. We'll have to be careful."

* * *

"Succulent." Nicholas's comment made Steph's cheeks go red. It didn't stop him from expanding on the thought. "The turkey is juicy. I'm not a big fan of turkey because it's normally dry and tasteless. This, however, is extraordinary." He ran a tongue over his lips. "I can taste oregano. What else did you use? Inquiring minds want to know."

The blush in Steph's face lessened to a softer shade of pink. "I bought a fresh turkey instead of frozen." She went on to say she'd basted it with flavored olive oil.

Nicholas swiveled in his chair to face Steph. "You bought flavored olive oil? Or infused it yourself?"

Grace made them laugh when she advised Nicholas not to diss the queen. "She made it herself."

The Turlington sisters had been remarkably quiet for the last five minutes. Maybe the chemical in turkey that was responsible for making people drowsy had lulled them into a nap-like state. But they were wide awake now and the room became a boisterous mass of confusion.

Hazel, Josie, and Flora tried to hit on Bart more than once. It was comical to watch them sweep their lashes over their eyes and wet their lips in an attempt to appear enchanting. Addie crushed their efforts with the mention of Winchester, her Yorkie. She was speaking Bart's language. Needless to say, Addie received three slit-eyed glares.

Fierce competition for a man's attention didn't fade with age. Apparently.

Philip grazed Elaina with a glance, smiled devilishly, and turned to the feisty ladies. "What's it like living in Tennessee?"

While Addie soaked up attention from Bart, Josie,

Flora, and Hazel talked over one another to give Philip details.

Elaina would thank Philip later for averting a geriatric brawl by dragging three of the four away from Bart. If he hadn't, there might've been dentures knocked loose, hearing aids flying through the air, and the sound of support hose getting ripped.

The dinner plates, water glasses, and serving dishes had been removed to make way for dessert – pumpkin pie with homemade ice cream, cherry delight with walnuts and pecans, and raspberry jello.

Adelaide was delighted to get jello. "Thank you for making this. It's my favorite."

Hazel narrowed her eyes. "Why does she get her favorite? Mine is lime."

Addie didn't hesitate to sing her own praises. "Because I'm special."

"You're special all right. About as special as toe fungus."

Steph tried to smooth ruffled feathers. "Tomorrow I'll make you lime jello, Grace." The gaffe had been on purpose, Elaina was sure of it. "I mean, Hazel."

The ringing of the landline phone cut into the merriment.

Grace and Tawny almost upended the table trying to get to the kitchen first to answer it.

Elaina appeased her guests' curiosity. "It's either Grace's son, Cody, or Tawny's boys, Bo and Quentin."

"Or Norma from Pennsylvania." Steph handed Flora the whipped cream to go on top of her pumpkin pie.

Elaina had offered to listen anytime Norma needed an ear. It hadn't been lip service. She doubted Normal would call, especially on Thanksgiving.

"How nice." Josephine picked the pecans out of her cherry delight and piled them on the side of her plate. "We let our kids do their own thing for Thanksgiving but we get together for Christmas. It's the most wonderful time of the year, yet downright nerve-wracking. Our kids. Grandkids. Great grandkids. Great-great grandkids. Their boyfriends. Their girlfriends. Fiancées. People they dragged along. Whew! The list is endless. Love them to pieces. The day turns into a circus. An hour into the shindig and I'm ready for it to be over."

"Sometimes it's just a circus of four. Right, Elaina?"

"Right, Steph."

"Josie's a Scrooge." Flora wrinkled her face into a cheesy smirk.

"Am not."

"Chad, would you like more coffee?"

"That would be great." He was out of his seat and halfway to the kitchen before Elaina even moved.

Hazel tugged on Elaina's shirt as she passed by. "Bring the pot, honey."

"Can do."

No sooner had she and Chad stepped into the kitchen, than the phone was thrust into her hand.

"You have to take this call. And you might want to do it someplace else." Grace's blue eyes darkened a wee bit.

Interesting.

"Why?"

"Rachel asked for you specifically and said she wanted to speak with you in private." Tawny looped an arm through Chad's. "Come on, lover boy, back to the table we go."

"Elaina might need me."

Elaina's heart swelled with affection at his concern. "I've got this, Chad. Thanks."

In an unexpected move, Chad pecked the side of her head with a kiss. Elaina didn't mean to react by making big eyes but she couldn't stop her surprise.

Chad smiled warmly.

Grace brought them back to the matter at hand, "Don't leave Rachel hanging."

"Right," Elaina said breathlessly, in a mild state of bliss. The kiss hadn't been on the lips. In an odd sort of way it felt more intimate.

Chad smoothed his hand over her shoulder, grabbed the coffee pot, and let Grace lead him back to the dining room.

Elaina hurried to the utility room. "Happy Thanksgiving, Rachel."

"Happy Thanksgiving to you, too." Rachel paused. "I didn't mean to interrupt your meal. We...I..."

Rachel was back to doing the 'we' and 'I' dance. Elaina could hear coaching going on in the background. "Seriously?" She restlessly walked the length of the utility room and back. Lula sat on the dryer staring at her with those indifferent green eyes. The cat was probably wondering why her human seemed twitchy. "I'm wondering the same thing."

Rachel returned to the conversation. "What?"

"That was meant for my cat. Soooo," Elaina drew out, "how's it going with Neil? Is he being a good dog?"

Bypassing the question about the Pomsky puppy, Rachel squealed into the phone. "I'm engaged, Elaina!"

Elaina was stunned yet again. "That's wonderful, Rach'! I'm so happy for you! If you were here right now we'd be jumping around and hugging you, and telling you how great it is to be in love." It dawned on her that Rachel had singled her out to share the news. Odd. Then again, a woman's brain was known to go sideways when the love of her life popped the question. "Congratulations, sweetie."

"We're so happy. Never in a million years did I think I could fall so hard and so fast for a guy. It goes to show when a person least expects it, bam!"

"Are you finally going to tell us his name?"

Rachel circumvented the question. "Can I send y'all a picture of the ring?"

Still no name. Elaina decided to give him one. "Sure. I'd love to see what Rufus picked out."

"Hold on. Okay, it's on the way. Who's Rufus?"

"Your mystery guy is Rufus until you tell me otherwise." Elaina was able to check out the picture of the ring and stay connected to the call. The photo that came through was mind boggling. That wasn't an engagement ring. It was a sparkly paperweight. "Holy mackerel, woman, that's some ring!"

"I know. Isn't it gorgeous?"

Despite its size, it wasn't gaudy. Although, it wasn't

something Elaina would be comfortable wearing. "Who are you marrying? A billionaire?" She meant it in jest but the silence that followed made her feel like a heel for suggesting such a thing. "Rachel?"

"I'm still here."

"I didn't mean to offend you."

"You didn't."

Another awkward lapse of silence, except for some hushed exchange between Rachel and her guy.

"Elaina, there's something I need to tell you."

"You want me to be a bridesmaid?"

Rachel's laugh sounded forced. "We're not going the traditional route. A lavish affair would be too taxing on my future father-in-law given his state of health. We decided to have a quiet ceremony with our parents in the hospital chapel and we'll take a honeymoon at a later date."

"What an amazing and unselfish thing to do."

"Thank you."

"Back to the joy, Rachel. You and Rufus are getting married! Can I tell the others?"

"Soon. There's one more thing I...we...need to say first."

"I'm all ears."

"Elaina, umm..." Rachel cleared her throat.

Impatience was building in Elaina to get back to her guests, especially to Chad. "You can tell me anything. You know that."

"You're such a good friend. That's why this is difficult."

"I'll be signing up for Social Security by the time you

get out whatever it is you have to say."

"There's no easy way to say this."

"Just say it."

"I'm engaged to Arden."

Elaina wasn't sure she heard right. "What?"

Rachel repeated the announcement in a hushed voice.

Elaina went slack. The phone slipped from her fingers and hit the tiled floor. Good thing she had it stored in a shatterproof case. She put a hand on the clothes dryer to steady herself and with her other hand she picked up the phone. "I don't... I can't... Arden Samuels?"

"Yes."

Lula jumped off the dryer like she anticipated carnage.

A clog the size of grapefruit in Elaina's windpipe made it hard to speak. "T-that explains the secrecy."

"We wanted to shout it to the world but we wanted to be sure of our feelings before we told anyone. Arden struggled with the thought of upsetting your apple cart."

"My apple cart is fine." Blatant lie. The wheel had fallen off the damned applecart and most of the apples had rolled away. "I'm genuinely happy for you. For both of you."

"That means so much to us."

It took all her strength to keep her cool. "I have to ask how this came about."

"You can blame Tawny. Actually, it was a joint effort between Tawny, Grace, and Steph."

"They fixed you up with Rufus?" The heat of betrayal flooded Elaina's veins.

Rachel hem-hawed. "Not directly. Remember when

they had me steal his newspapers?"

"I heard about it after the fact. I wasn't pleased, but yes, I'm aware of their mischief."

"I think Steph called it sweat revenge, instead of sweet revenge. Grace told me about his security cameras so I skulked about in the dark wearing a black hoodie and ran from bush to bush."

That poked the memory of Elaina and the girls dressing in a similar fashion to mess with Tawny's ex, Grady, who had an aversion to textures. They'd smeared axle grease on a few of his things to get even for him dumping Stony's things in Elaina's front yard. The caper had gone off without a hitch. Evidently Rachel hadn't honed her get-even skills yet.

"I snatched his newspapers for a few days without being detected. Then Arden got wise and installed a motion detector along with the cameras. The blasted light went on and I got caught red-handed. He was lying in wait for me. I almost had a heart attack when he jumped out from behind a tree. Instead of calling the cops, like he had every right to do, he invited me in for coffee and to grill me. He's one smooth and handsome interrogator. When those blue eyes bore down on me, I caved. I didn't mean to. Then he kissed me and here we are."

Smooth wasn't the word Elaina would use to describe Arden. "That's the most ludicrous story I've ever heard."

"I'm not making it up."

"He cross-examined you and then kissed you?"

"Weird, right?"

"Uh yeah, it is. *Rufus* is a germ-a-phobe. Did he swipe

your lips with rubbing alcohol first? He prompted you to get a dog? Pardon my skepticism, but I can't wrap my head around any of it. He's making you say this nonsense in exchange for not having you thrown in the slammer for petty theft."

"He did kiss me. We do have a dog. We are getting married."

"You named your dog Neil...after his dad. Why didn't I put that together?" Elaina was dumbfounded by so many things that her brain couldn't process all of it. "Neil Samuels. Duh."

"You didn't put it together because the last person you expected me to get with was your ex." Rachel sounded certain and passionate. "We were meant to be, Elaina. If Arden and I hadn't connected in the midst of the newspaper escapade we would have when I asked him for the hot tub you said he didn't want. I hate to tell you, we've spent many a night in that thing. Please, don't be mad."

Arden had complained about that hot tub. He'd said he hated it. He'd called it a swirling tub of bacteria. Elaina kept her snort of derision quiet. Soooo, Arden wasn't afraid to flip-flop when it suited him. Anger tried to surface; Elaina shoved it back down. There was no reason to be upset. She pulled in a deep breath and let the air ease back out. "Love doesn't always make sense. It blind-sided you, Rachel. I get it. I hope you believe me when I say I'm not mad. I'm really am happy for you." She meant it too. "Could I talk to Rufus? Sorry. Arden?"

"Don't yell at him."

"I won't." She crossed her fingers.

There was additional murmured conversation in the background.

"Elaina."

"I understand congratulations are in order." While she was happy for him, a part of her still wanted to rip into him.

"Yes. Thank you. I've said this before but it bears repeating – I'm sorry for being a jerk all those years," he said softly, like she was a good friend and confidante. "Elaina, I've found love – with a thief no less. Rachel has rearranged my way of thinking. I can barely concentrate on work."

A tiny bit of jealousy for what wasn't, tried to steal Elaina's calm. She squelched it by remembering Arden's knack for micromanaging and how he'd held her back in just about everything. For sanity's sake, it was wise to let go of the past. At the same time it was good to have a lucid memory. "I'm sorry to hear about your dad."

Arden surprised the hell out of her when he broke down and sobbed hard into the phone. He explained that his father had been diagnosed with a rare type of blood disorder and wasn't expected to survive. He also apologized for not being there for her emotionally when she lost her parents. "I understand where I failed not only as a husband but also as a human being."

Elaina couldn't keep her tears in check either. "Please tell your dad I'm thinking about him and will lift him up in prayer."

"I will. It means a lot to me that you care."

"Of course I care." She swiped at the last of her tears. "Your parents were a part of my life for over fifteen years. And Arden...I forgive you."

"I don't deserve your forgiveness."

"You're not the guy you were then. You've grown. And now you're the guy who's going to work hard to make Rachel happy. If you don't take that responsibility seriously, I'll have no choice but to bring Stony to your house and let him scatter dog hair everywhere."

"I have to be nice to Rachel. She'll be picking out my nursing home in a few years."

Arden had made a funny – at his own expense? It was a sign the end of the world was near.

* * *

The inquiry began the second she returned to the table.

"Everything okay?"

Elaina reached for the pumpkin pie. "Better than okay." Putting a wedge of pie on her plate, she felt the pressure to say more.

"That tells us nothing, dear." Flora's tongue darted to the corner of her mouth to get the small splotch of whipped cream she'd missed with her napkin.

Elaina surveyed the curious faces. They wanted details. She wanted to eat pie and forget the phone call had taken place.

Grace lifted her spoon. "Will we have to spoon it out of you?"

Elaina sighed and turned the valve of information.

After a full accounting of the conversation, every mouth was ajar.

"Arden's the guy Rachel has been going bonkers over? The guy who squeezed more than the produce at the grocery store? The one with whom she shares a Pomsky? That can't be right. He's twice her age. He's an obsessive-compulsive lunatic. Rachel's yanking your chain."

Elaina's legs were restless under the table.

Chad put a hand on her knee to settle her legs.

She took a sip of water. "They're getting married."

Steph dropped her fork onto her plate with a clatter. "And this is better than okay?" She left her chair and went to Elaina to feel her forehead. "Just as I thought."

Adelaide leaned into the table. "Is she delirious with fever?"

"Nope, but there's a bonfire going on inside. She's burning up those memories like they're kindling."

Josie put her palms up. "You young people speak in metaphors. Just lay it out in terms we old geezers can understand."

"I can do that." Steph did a rewind and put her hand back on Elaina's forehead. "I'm sensing some real joy here. She's finally put her past where it belongs and now she's free to find out what Chad's all about."

"Now that I get. Of course she's torching her past and going after Chad. He's hot."

Elaina's gaze zipped to Chad. Instead of trying to clarify Josie's take on things, which she'd make a huge mess of by over-explaining, she simply agreed. "I'm not going to lie. You ARE hot."

"Atta girl." Josie knuckle-bumped Hazel. They said "boom" at the same time.

Chad smiled with his eyes. "You definitely get an Atta-girl."

Chapter Fifteen

- S or M? Both? -

"Of all the fifty states we've visited, this one has been the best. Thank you again for going out of your way to make our stay extraordinary." Adelaide hugged Elaina and proceeded to do the same to Tawny, Grace, and Steph.

"We'll be back some day – if the Good Lord's willing and the creek doesn't rise." Flora took her carry-on bag from Tawny. "Elaina let her man know how she feels. You should do the same with that cutie-pie Bart. Grace, Philip needs a haircut. He's one cool dude though. I think you make a sweet couple. And Steph, Nicholas adores you. You gals might not have known your men long but don't dilly-dally with your feelings. Go for it. Addie, Hazel, Josie, and I chased after our men. Once we caught them, we loved them with all our might. You should do the same thing and when you get to be our age you won't have regrets."

Josie struggled to get her driver's license from her wallet so she could give it to the ticket agent at the counter.

"Let me help."

"It's wedged." She handed the wallet to Elaina.

It wasn't wedged. It was Josie's arthritis preventing her from sliding the license from its protective cover. Elaina pretended to struggle too. "It was snug, that's for sure." Her eyes inadvertently skimmed the name on the license when she handed it back to Josie. "You have got to be kidding me."

Josie drew back with a baffled look.

"Your middle name is not Pia."

Tawny heard the comment and pushed her way over to Josie. "Your middle name is Pia?"

"After my godmother, Pia Lorraine."

Tawny smiled tenderly at the elderly woman. "MY middle is name is Pia, too. I've been dying to ask, were you a nurse in your work life?"

Elaina couldn't believe Tawny held off the question this long. It might have to do with the whole privacy thing since she'd overhead the blood draw conversation versus actually being in the conversation.

"Why, hon, yes I was. How did you know?"

Tawny took Josie's hands in hers. "It was more of a guess than anything. You reminded Flora to take her insulin and you were on Hazel all the time to eat more roughage. I saw you taking your radial pulse a few times. Once, you took your carotid pulse. Then there was the hand sanitizer thing."

Josie's face pulled into a wrinkly grin. "Germs are not welcome on my person."

Tawny pecked Josie on the cheek with a kiss. "Thank

you for taking The Nightingale Pledge all those years ago."

"Oh, sweet girl, you've made my day." Josie oozed joy. "Thank you, from the bottom of my heart."

Hazel scoffed. "Enough with the mush. Get a move on, Florence Nightingale, or our plane will leave before we get through security."

Josie stuck out her tongue. "It doesn't leave for two hours."

"Exactly. With your speed, we'll be lucky to make our gate by January."

Josie rolled her eyes. "See what I have to put up with?"

"I feel your pain." Tawny inclined her head toward Elaina, Steph, and Grace. "I have these three to contend with."

Josie squeezed Tawny's hand. "Aren't we lucky?"

"Yes we are."

Elaina offered a parting remark. "You ladies are wild and wonderful. We're so glad you came to Maine."

"Speaking of wild, did Josie tell you the time she pole-danced for her hubby?"

Josie swatted Hazel. "The plane. We need to get to the plane." She laughed as she made her way through the roped off maze of the TSA checkpoint.

Addie, Hazel, and Flora followed.

Addie was almost to the TSA agent. She turned and blew them a kiss.

Elaina did the same back.

Grace pointed to the exit. "Ladies, it's time to learn how to pole dance. Oh, and Tawn', I don't believe for a second that your middle name is Pia." She raced ahead of the others as if expecting repercussions.

* * *

The next few weeks were a blur of activity. Customers came from far and wide to partake in snow skiing, snowboarding, or to relax prior to Christmas. Elaina was surprised to discover even a few local folks had booked rooms because they wanted the bed and breakfast experience. Business was good.

Elaina combed over the reservation book. "Permission Daniels?" She stared at the entry and then confirmed it on the computer screen. Handwritten entries were old-school, but a necessary backup in case their computer went on the fritz. "Tawn', this looks like your writing. Are you sure the name is PerMission and not PerSimmon?"

Tawny twisted her mouth to the side as though contemplating a possible slip-up. She sifted air through her teeth. "I'm sure she said Permission."

"Just asking. I went to school with a Persimmon Daniels." What were the chances? Nah. The Persimmon she'd known wouldn't stay at a quaint bed and breakfast. "She was a bit rough around the edges." Colossal understatement. In school, Persimmon had gone for the shock factor in everything she said and did, which gained her plenty of timeouts in grade school and detention almost every day in high school. She was one of those people who were fluent in four-letter words. Elaina remembered the Health teacher discussing marriage and

Persimmon disrupting class with a vow to stay single for all eternity. She said marriage equaled putting leg irons on a person. It was strange that Elaina had committed that to memory. Maybe it was because the teacher lost control of the class that day. The guys squealed their approval to the no-marriage idea and left their desks to give Persimmon high-fives.

"Isn't persimmon a fruit?"

Steph walked into the office with her hair pulled into a high ponytail, reading glasses lowered to the tip of her nose, a pencil tucked behind her ear, and a spiral notebook in hand. "Yes. Why?"

"Elaina went to school with a girl named Persimmon."

"And?"

"It's an unusual name."

"You shouldn't make fun of someone's name. Whatever the reason her folks chose to call her Persimmon is nunya."

Tawny scrunched her face at Steph. "Huh?"

"Nunya business."

"I wasn't making fun of her name. I said it's unusual."

"Kind of like yours? Tawny Pia? Get real."

Elaina pressed her lips together to stifle a laugh. Those two would argue the color of the sky. If Tawny called it milky blue, Steph would correct her and call it azure.

Tawny motioned to Steph's notebook. "Did you come in the office to ask our opinion on something or to pick at me?"

"The latter goes without saying." Steph tapped her chin. "Now that you've mentioned persimmon I might concoct a salsa recipe using it as the base. I'll add cilantro, red onion, tidbits of carrot and celery for crunch, small slices of jalapeno to thrill your taste buds, a little olive oil, and a squeeze of lime juice."

"No thank you. I'll stick with something less thrilling."

"Is heartburn still having its way with you?"

"Every. Stinking. Day. It was getting better, and then wham! It came back like it never left." Tawny balled her hand into a fist and pressed it into her solar plexus.

Steph removed the pencil from behind her ear and tapped the notebook. "While doing research for my cookbook, I ran across a blog post about natural remedies for heartburn. The author suggested a teaspoon of bicarbonate of soda in eight ounces of water. Try it for a week and see what happens."

"Baking soda?"

"Why not?"

"That doesn't sound appealing. Stop drumming the pencil on your notebook or I'll break it in half."

"You can't break a notebook in half." Steph snickered. "If baking soda doesn't intrigue you, how about aloe juice? Down a half-cup straight. Aloe is supposed to reduce inflammation."

"I'm not drinking aloe." Tawny stuck her finger in her mouth and pretended to gag. "Instead of helping my heartburn, you're trying to make me throw up."

"Fine. Let your stomach acid eat away your esophagus."

"And then she paints a gruesome picture."

"Seriously, I'd give the aloe a try; which by the way

can also act as a laxative. Your heartburn would go away but you might have to stay close to the bathroom." Steph moved out of striking range.

"There are times I want to clean your clock, Mathews."

"Ditto." Steph beamed genuine smile. "I do want your opinion on something though. I've been jotting down ideas for the cover of my cookbook. Should I go with an assortment of mouthwatering food or something simple like a piece of cheesecake topped with strawberry sauce? The cover is what draws the buyers' attention first. I need something eye-catching."

Elaina said the first thing that popped into her head. "A picture of you wearing a chef's hat and apron, with your arms crossed, and a cocky look on your face. You could call it Food with Attitude."

"The title is cool. Ixnay the part about my picture on the front. I'm not photogenic."

Elaina tilted her head down but raised her eyebrows. "You always sell yourself short. You're stunning, Steph, whether you think so or not." Steph started to balk at the assessment. "Ut, ut. Hear me out. I'm not fluffing your feathers. I mean it. There are women who would kill for your shade of red hair. You have expressive green eyes. And the dusting of freckles across your nose gives you an innocent look, which is in contrast to the title. People flock to things that conflict. How can someone like her make food with attitude?"

Steph's chest rose and fell with a hearty laugh. "You're lying through your pearly whites, but hey, I needed some stress relief. I've spent the afternoon fretting over the cover when I should be compiling content."

Tawny wasn't done harassing. "Innocent? Not by a long shot. She is the direct opposite of innocent."

Steph issued Tawny a steely-eyed glare.

"Elaina, you're right. She has expressive eyes. Those expressive lasers are trying to burn my retina."

Grace walked into the office. "What did I miss?"

"We have a guest coming named Permission. Stomach acid is eating my esophagus. And Steph has amazing hair."

"So, nothing important." Grace parked her bottom on the edge of the desk.

"Just another day at the Four Sassy Chicks Bed and Breakfast."

Tawny sniffed. "Does anyone else smell burnt retina?"

* * *

Are you kidding me? Elaina exclaimed without making a sound or moving her lips, or changing her businesslike expression. "Persimmon?"

"In the flesh. These days I go by PerMission." Persimmon exhaled a nasally laugh. "I love the look on people's faces when I tell them my name."

Elaina's mouth started to drop open but she caught it. Tawny's chicken scratching in the reservation book had been correct. "It's good to see you again."

"I searched for bed and breakfasts in Maine and came across your website. There you were – the one person who didn't treat me like a disease when we were in school. I never told you how much I appreciated you being nice to me. Funny picture on your website, by the way. Stroke of genius."

"Thank you. Permission, you were nice to me in school, too."

"I was a real treat in school. In some ways I still am. I'm wired differently, I guess."

"Wouldn't life be boring if we were all wired the same?" Elaina noted Persimmon's blue-green streaked hair, multiple piercings, and fingernails that were painted an assortment of colors. Her classmate was still walking to the beat of her own drum. Where there was hardness to her in the early days, there was now softness. "I'm going to put you on the second floor, in a room with a view of the harbor."

Persimmon's small smile grew larger by the second. "That would be incredible. There's something about the water that soothes my soul. I sure could use the tranquility and comfort right now."

"Is everything all right?" Clearly it wasn't.

Persimmon's shoulders drooped. "I suck at relationships."

Elaina's mind went into fix-it mode. Her inner-critic told her to back down and assess the situation first. "I wish there was a how-to manual about relationships. I'd buy that thing in a heartbeat."

Hazel-colored eyes perked with curiosity. "You've crashed and burned, too?"

"Sadly, yes."

"How many times?"

Elaina snickered. "Are we talking marriages or dating relationships?"

"Marriages."

"Just one."

"Lucky you." Persimmon held up four fingers.

Elaina's eyes instinctively widened.

A sheepish grin slid into Persimmon's face. "I know. I know. I made a big to-do about never getting married. The thing about talking smack out loud, the gods hear and make you eat your words. I moved to Delaware and married the first guy who appeared to appreciate my uniqueness. Stupid move. I repeated the stupidity three more times. Essentially, I've made one stupid chess move after another. My head and heart goes nuts over guys with blue eyes and a proclivity for not wanting to settle down."

Elaina went around the desk and gathered Persimmon into an embrace. "There are roughly four billion men in the world. How are we supposed to find our one true love in a wolf-pack that size?"

"You were a gem then and you still are." Persimmon jiggled with a laugh. "I'm done with wolves for a while. Maybe forever."

"I may have stumbled onto my one true *wolf*. Time will tell." Elaina realized the error of over-sharing – once it was out of her mouth. She didn't want to be quizzed about Chad so she hastily changed the subject. "My friends and I are forging a new beginning with this enterprise." She gestured around the tidy office.

"Did your wolf come howling?"

She'd captured Persimmon's interest with the wolf reference. It would've been better to mention a less risky animal like a dog or cat, since danger seemed to appeal to her former classmate. "Would you care for a cup of coffee or glass of wine?"

Tawny poked her head in the office. "Did someone say wine?"

* * *

Grace placed a platter of blueberry pancakes on the table.

"Were those made with organic blueberries?"

Grace shot Elaina a look as if asking how to proceed. Elaina simply grinned. In the two days since Persimmon had been there, she'd complained about the hardness of the mattress and asked to switch rooms. Elaina happily moved her to the third floor, where the mattresses were firm but with pillow-tops. Persimmon griped about being too far away from everyone. Elaina agreed to let her switch again to a first-floor bedroom. Then the room was too cold. At the suggestion she turn on the fireplace in her room, Persimmon voiced her opinion for all to hear – 'If it was an actual fireplace with real fire and real wood, she wouldn't have a problem using it. Since it was electric, she'd rather not bother.' Elaina decided not to waste her breath explaining that real fire and wood in a guest house would be a headache, not to mention a huge liability. The eccentric guest had snubbed her nose at their coffee. Apparently, it had too much chicory. On and on with grievances.

Elaina now understood why Persimmon had difficulty with relationships and she was a hair away from letting her former classmate in on the conclusion. "They're not organic."

Persimmon shoved the platter farther down the table. "I don't want pesticides in my body."

"We washed them." The stiffness in Grace's voice indicated she was close to going off on the picky person who'd changed her name to PerMission.

A haughty nose with a diamond stud piercing, tipped up.

Grace's frustration came out as a long, loud sigh. "It's eight-thirty in the morning. Is it too early for wine? I think not."

Persimmon's eyes did a lazy travel to Elaina. "You've centered your world around sweat pants and too much wine. Neither is attractive. All of you have guys in your life. What message does it send to them and to your customers, when you don't dress for success and are willing to drink wine with your pancakes?"

For a second, Arden rang loudly in Elaina's ears. She gave her head a firm shake to clear the mad ramblings of the female who could easily be his clone. "Wine played a part in bringing us together, and yes, we named ourselves a wine club. We plan to someday own a winery. Fermented grapes happen to be our thing. On occasion, we seek the comfort of sweat pants. If our guests or the men in our lives don't approve, that's on them." Instead of letting Persimmon needle her into a bigger argument, Elaina took the high road. "We're an unusual blend of personalities. We're strong, confident, and the best of friends. Together, we've learned how to be happy again when we thought it wasn't possible. We laugh. Cry. Throw an occasional hissy fit. At the end of the day, we're four feisty misfits who fit perfectly together."

Air gushed from Persimmon and she revealed what Elaina had a feeling about all along. "I've been trying my whole life to find one good, true friend who understands me. You've found three."

Elaina sat up from a slight slouch. "I got lucky. When my world turned upside down, I didn't draw inward. I wanted to. Then I saw Grace struggling. Along came Steph and Tawny. Persimmon, you have a lot to offer folks, but you keep them at bay. It appears to me, that you look for reasons not to like people before they have a chance not to like you."

"That's absurd."

"Is it? You're abrasive when you don't need to be."

Persimmon squinted hard and her lips thinned into a straight line.

Elaina wouldn't back down. "We've gone out of our way to please you; not just because you're our guest, but also because you had a rough go of it in school and you confessed to four failed marriages."

Tears pooled in the corners of Persimmon's eyes. The emotion, however, didn't dampen her surly attitude. "I don't need your sympathy."

"We didn't offer sympathy. We offered kindness."

"I didn't ask you to."

Tawny walked into the dining room from the kitchen.

"I've been listening to your discussion." She cocked an eyebrow at Persimmon. "Elaina's summation of our behavior AND yours is accurate. We've been nice. You've been a pain in our derrieres." She raised her voice and wagged an accusing finger in front of Persimmon. "You have a horrible approach to life and love."

Persimmon still didn't soften. "You're right. I'm a mess; a hopeless, beyond repair mess."

"You're also a whiny baby. Geez. Give me a break with that woe-is-me mindset. You've made things awkward for our other guests. That's probably why a few crept into the kitchen earlier and looked around before taking a spot at the breakfast table. Had you been seated there, they might've tiptoed back to their rooms."

Steph pranced into the dining room with a plate of scrambled eggs and plopped down beside Persimmon. She forked a bite of eggs into her mouth and studied the faces of her friends. "Who's a whiny baby?"

"Late to the game as usual, Mathews."

"I was busy cooking."

"I'm the whiny baby. Apparently."

"And she's a mess; a hopeless, beyond repair mess." Grace volleyed Persimmon's sarcasm back at her. "Apparently."

Steph laid her fork down. "Tawn', no one is hopeless or beyond repair. I was a mess. A huge mess." She shifted in her chair to face Persimmon. "Thanks to these ladies, I'm mostly fixed. Because of them, I'm able to make my dream come true. Did I mention I'm writing a cookbook? And for once in my life, I'm in a relationship with a guy who isn't out to break my heart."

"They fixed you?"

Steph sprinkled salt into her hand to get the right amount and then dusted it over her eggs. "The repair work is an ongoing thing for all of us. Little by little our broken pieces are getting glued back where they belong."

Grace slid the platter of blueberry pancakes back to Persimmon.

Persimmon stared at them for an inordinate amount of time. She finally took one and poured a thin drizzle of syrup over it. Without looking at the others, she cut into the pancake and took a small bite. "These are delicious."

In a surprise move, Tawny left the kitchen and came back with an opened bottle of wine. "Care to wash it down with Merlot?"

Persimmon's baby blues jetted from woman to woman. "Wine and pancakes with the repair crew?"

"Yep. You in?"

A slow smile replaced the sour look. "I'm in."

"You're welcome to stay for as long as the repairs take. It could be months. Or years." Tawny went a little overboard, but hey, they'd never turn anyone away who needed a friend and a bottle of glue.

"You're letting me join the wine club?"

Tawny informed Persimmon she'd have to invest in a pair of sweat pants.

Elaina reached for the bottle of wine. Things were about to get real.

Chapter Sixteen

~ *Sassy chicks, psychics, or lovable psychos?* ~

Tawny hung another gold ornament on the live Christmas tree they would plant in the backyard after the holidays. "Could we talk? Privately?"

Elaina stopped messing with the red velvet ribbon that refused to become a decent looking bow. "I knew you'd eventually seek me out."

"You're psychic."

Grace leaned in with her two cents. "Or she picked up on your restlessness like the rest of us did."

"I'm not..."

Steph hip-bumped Tawny. "Yes you are." She used the back of her hand to wave Tawny from the tree. "You're in my way. Now would be a good time for you and Elaina to go to your room or to the basement."

"Can we take a cup of coffee along?"

"Do you even have to ask?" In the kitchen, Elaina filled insulated travel mugs with coffee that had been setting for a few hours. It looked strong enough to take off nail polish.

Tawny sliced into brownies that were still too hot to cut. She plunked two on a paper plate.

"Those are supposed to be for later when the guys come over."

"Steph won't mind."

"Wanna bet?"

"What can I say? I need coffee and chocolate right now."

"Won't it cause indigestion?"

Tawny shoved part of a brownie in her mouth. "Probably."

Elaina agreed that caffeine and chocolate were a must when it came to having serious conversations. She smiled, although her thoughts were now anything but cheerful. Tawny was going to throw a wrench into their well-oiled machine. Hopefully, it would be a single wrench, not two. One specific wrench could drastically change the machine altogether.

Tawny flicked the switch to turn on the electric fireplace in the basement and took a spot at the end of the folded-up sofa-bed. After a slurp of coffee, she gingerly sat the cup aside and began. "This venture is working out better than we thought."

"That's because we know how to do it. We've been in training forever."

"How so?"

"It amounts to keeping house, just on a grander scale. Instead of cooking, cleaning, mopping, and doing laundry for four, it's for fourteen or twenty four."

"It's not overwhelming, is it?"

There it was – the lead-in.

"Nah. It's all good. We're doing great."

Tawny tucked her legs up under her. "Can you believe how much snow we got overnight? I thought we got a lot in Ohio. Pfft. Maine gets a crap ton more."

"You don't have to make small talk or try to gently ease into whatever you want to say, Tawn'. Just put it out there."

Tawny put her legs down and adjusted herself on the sofa. "You're right. I am restless. I think I had the onset of restlessness the moment I said I'd be part of this amazing undertaking."

Elaina swallowed hard. "Are you leaving us?"

Tawny's brown eyes clouded with tears right away, like they'd been lying in wait to make an appearance. "Sort of."

"You're sort of leaving?"

"I want to remain a co-owner. I just don't want to be full-time in the day-to-day operation."

Elaina dreaded the words but she said them anyway. "You're relocating to California or Oregon."

"What? No." Tawny left her perch and cozied next to Elaina. "You thought I was leaving-leaving?" She scoffed. "I hate to tell ya, I'm here to stay. Quit trying to weasel out of hanging with me."

Elaina's troubled heart did a happy dance. "I can't imagine not having you with us."

"You could replace me with Persimmon," Tawny joking swiped at Elaina.

"She's no Tawny Pia Westerfield."

Tawny's voice fell to a hush. "Between you and me, it's not Pia. It's Piala." She grimaced. "I'm named after my mom's mom's mom's mom's mom."

"Your great-great-great grandmother was Piala?"

Tawny counted on her fingers. "Something like that. I'm sure she was a strong, beautiful woman just like her great-great-great granddaughter but her mother must've been in a foul mood the day she gave birth. There's no other reason to stick a child with the name Piala."

They shared a laugh.

"If you tell Steph and Grace, you'll rue the day."

Elaina twisted her lips with her fingers to lock away the information. She reached for her coffee and slanted a grin at Tawny. "I might've been too hasty putting the secret in the vault. I should've used it as a bargaining chip to get the facts."

Tawny's forehead creased with confusion.

"You haven't told me how you're sort of leaving."

"Oh that."

* * *

Chad topped off Elaina's wine glass. "Did you know Maine is the birthplace of Prohibition?"

"Is there a hidden message there, Chaddy-boy?" Grace asked.

"Absolutely not. It just popped in my head." He drew his blue-eyed gaze from Grace and set it on Elaina. "I didn't mean anything by it."

Elaina brought her goblet to her lips and made eyes at Chad through the refraction of the glass. "No worries."

"Did you know most of Stephen King's books are set in Maine?" Philip put his feet up on the coffee table and Grace shoved them off.

"Ert."

"You say that a lot."

"It's my go-to word. Instead of saying duh, I say ert. Is that going to be a problem? Because if it is..."

Philip successfully disarmed Grace's tough stance with a wicked smile and a question that made everyone pay attention. "Or what? You won't pose nude for me?"

Elaina choked on her wine. Chad tapped her back, as if that would help.

Steph shook a finger at Grace. "You better not take your clothes off for the sake of art."

"His name is Philip, not Art."

Bart, who was becoming less quiet the more he was around them, spoke up. "The name of your bed and breakfast fits. I've never met four sassier chicks."

Nicholas had been taking it all in. His eyes ricocheted back and forth from Philip to Grace. "I get that you're a free spirit, Philip, but be careful what you say. We know you're kidding with that nude painting thing; the public doesn't."

Elaina expected Grace to mouth off that Philip wasn't kidding. She was surprised when Grace pressed her lips together, allowing her date to defend himself.

Philip pealed with laughter. "I'm not out to defile anyone's name or ruin their business. My teasing is just that and it won't leave this room. Rest assured that when I paint Grace...and I will someday...it will be tasteful."

"Thank you. This is an incredible group. I'd like to see it stay that way. I enjoy your company." Nicholas kissed Steph's hand. "I especially enjoy yours, Stephanie."

Persimmon had been sitting in front of the 'fake' fireplace, running her fingers over the leaves of a poinsettia that sat on the hearth. "All this lovely-dovey stuff is making me nauseous." She stood and targeted a smile at Elaina. "Christmas is the season of hope. I *hope* to be a better person from now on. Thanks to you. By letting me stay here for the past few weeks, I've learned a lot about myself and how to channel my angst – for lack of a better word – into something positive. The time has come for me to go. Husband number four wants me back. He's actually ex number four, but he wants to get married again. Can you believe it?"

Elaina wasn't sure Persimmon had made enough progress. She seemed happier though. Remarrying her ex might stall or undo the strides she'd made toward realizing her self-worth. "You can't leave."

"Why not?"

"Uh, because...Tawny's sort of leaving."

Steph shouted "Nooooo" loud enough to make Lula leave the protection of her hideout under the sofa and head for the upstairs.

Grace ran to the front door and splayed her body across it. "I refuse to let you go, Tawn'. You're staying right here."

Stony loped over to Grace.

"No I'm not."

Grace ran a hand the length of Stone-man. "You're not taking this precious dog from us. I won't let it happen."

Bart eyed Tawny. "We just met and things are going well; at least I thought they were. Did I do something wrong?"

Grace locked the door. "Seriously. You're not leaving."

"Tawn', you'd better come clean or you're going to give the poor girl a heart attack. I think Bart might be having palpitations too."

"Killjoy."

"And then some."

"No freaking out, people. I'm staying in Maine. Bart, you and I are good." Tawny kissed the tip of his nose. She directed her finger to the spot on the sofa vacated by Grace. "Unlock the door and have a seat. My discussion with Elaina earlier involved me doing PRN work, which will limit my ability to help out around here."

Persimmon's face contorted in bewilderment. "What's PRN work?"

Bart answered before Tawny had a chance. "Pro re nata."

Persimmon snapped her fingers. "English please."

"She'll work as an on-call nurse."

"Bartholomew Simpson, I'm impressed."

It must've been the ultimate compliment because he hugged Tawny to him.

Steph nudged Tawny with her toe. "You don't know how close I came to binding you with duct tape and shoving a dirty sock in your mouth."

"Touché."

Nicholas leaned away from Steph. "Is there a dark side to you I should know about?"

Steph lifted a sexy eyebrow. "There's a dark side to all of us, Nicholas."

Tawny put Nicholas's mind at ease. "I threatened Steph a while back with duct tape and a dirty sock when we thought she was going to reunite with the snake who broke her heart, and now she's tossed the threat back."

Persimmon rallied their attention with a clap. She pointed at Elaina. "You're awesome." She did and said the same thing to Tawny, Grace, and Steph. "But I draw the line at duct tape and dirty socks. I'm outta here, you lovable psychos."

* * *

Steph was up to her elbows in rigatoni when Elaina walked into the kitchen.

"That looks like enough to feed the entire city of Portland."

"It's better to have too much than not enough."

"Good thinking. If we run out of anything, Grace will be a basket case." Elaina took a spoon from the silverware drawer to taste the spaghetti sauce simmering on a back burner. "This is delicious. It may be the best sauce I've ever tasted."

Steph's expression filled with pride. "Spaghetti sauce from scratch is better than jar sauce any day of the week."

Tawny guided Grace into the kitchen. "Will you tell her to breathe?"

"Breathe, Grace."

"I could've done that. Give her some words of wisdom, ole wise one."

"Such as?" Elaina got another spoon from the drawer and handed it to Grace. "Try this. It's delizioso! Your son, daughter-in-law, and granddaughter will think they're still in Italy."

Grace sampled the sauce. "Hai ragione."

"No. It's rigatoni," Steph explained."

Grace rinsed her spoon and put it in the dishwasher. "Hai ragione means 'you're right' in Italian. It is delizioso. I've been brushing up on the language for the past hour. I'm afraid I won't retain any of it."

"Do you really think Cody or Isabella gives a rat's patootie that you aren't fluent in Italian? No they do not. Now calm the heck down or I'm not driving you to the airport to pick them up."

Grace frowned at Tawny. "I'm capable of driving the van."

Tawny jangled the keys. Grace made a swipe for them.

Perspiration dotted Steph's upper lip. "Out of my kitchen. I have homemade bread baking in the oven. If it falls, I'll knock some heads together."

"Clowning around doesn't make bread fall."

"Out!"

Tawny saluted Steph. "The queen of the kitchen has spoken."

Steph aimed a serrated knife at Tawny.

Elaina sang *Jingle Bells* to lighten the mood.

"Your vocal chords need tweaking."

"Your brain needs tweaking." Elaina kicked Tawny and Grace on their butts. "Get moving. Cody's plane is scheduled to touch down in an hour."

"It takes fifteen minutes to get to the airport."

Steph handed the serrated knife to Elaina. "Don't be afraid to use it."

Chapter Seventeen

~ *Joy to last a lifetime!* ~

Elaina got goose bumps when Cody walked through the door carrying his mom in his arms. The natural impulse was to rush to them out of fear she'd gotten hurt. Given their calm manner, she decided to leave a little space. "Did you fall, Grace?"

Cody beamed a familiar grin. According to pictures she'd seen of Brince, he was his dad through and through. But when he smiled, he was all Grace. "Nothing as drastic as that, thank goodness." His smile expanded. "Do you want to tell her, Mom? Or do you want me to?" He eased his mother to a standing position and wrenched an arm around her waist to hold her steady.

"I got lightheaded."

Elaina couldn't stay planted in place. She was at Grace's side in a blink. "I told you to eat something earlier." To Cody, she explained that his mom had been a nervous wreck in anticipation of his visit.

"Same here. For different reasons. Good reasons."

Tawny pushed through the door with luggage,

followed by Isabella and Karina.

Steph came into the living room with a ladle in one hand, a hot pad in the other, and a smear of spaghetti sauce on her chin. "Benvenuto. That's it. That's all I know."

"Thank you for the welcome." With his free hand, Cody drew Isabella and Karina close. "Steph, right?"

Steph winked at Cody. "You're getting extra dessert." She chastised Grace. "I made turkey loaf for lunch. You took maybe two bites. And now you're dizzy. See what happens when you turn down my cooking?"

"Cody, help Isabella with Karina." Grace placed her hands on the back of the sofa for support. "Your cooking is eccezionale, Steph."

"Yeah, I don't know what that means. I'm taking it as a compliment."

Grace snickered. "Ert!"

"She said your cooking is awesome."

"How do I say she's awesome, too?"

Elaina answered the question. "With your mouth."

Cody broke into hearty laughter. "Izzie, remember when I said everything they say is off-the-cuff? That's what I meant. They're sarcastic-funny without trying. We're going to love living here."

"Did I hear right?" Elaina's eyes zipped to Grace.

Grace waggled her eyebrows. "It's ecc...eccezi... It's awesome!"

Steph made a joyful noise. Tawny used Josie's word, "Boom!"

"Now do you see why I had to carry her? She got so excited and her legs went out from under her."

Elaina congratulated Grace with a kiss on the side of the head. "What a wonderful Christmas present." She extended a hand to Cody. Instead of a handshake, he drew her into a hug. "You've been a good friend to Mom. You changed her life in so many ways, especially with the move here. In the process, you changed ours. We'll be forever grateful."

"Your mom changed our lives. If she hadn't been in that jewelry store..." Elaina smiled. "You've heard the story. Anyway, moving to Maine was a joint decision."

"I give you ladies a lot of credit. You weren't afraid to take a chance. Along that same line, we're also taking a chance. Eventually, we'll call Portland home." Cody snuggled against his wife and daughter. "Not only us. Niccolo and Francesca are preparing to relocate as well."

Grace was taken by surprise by the additional information. "Niccolo and Francesca are pulling up stakes?" She put a hand on her mouth. "I should've been the one to move there. Not the other way around." A sob tore from her chest. "I can't stop blubbering."

"It's okay, Mom. Blubber away."

Isabella squeezed Grace's hand. "This was an easy choice for my parents. They're excited to move to the U.S. More importantly, they didn't want an ocean to keep us apart, including you. It will take a while for them to get everything in order, but they're thrilled to be given the opportunity. And so am I." She sat Karina in a recliner and gave her a fuzzy blankie decorated with hippopotamuses. "Karina will have the best of both worlds."

Grace could barely speak through her tears. "I'm so

blessed. I know your father is making this happen for us, Cody." She looked up. "Thank you so much, Brince."

"He's up there orchestrating everything, Mom, including putting a new man in your life."

Elaina pulled a wad of tissues from the box on the end table and handed them to Grace.

Grace blew her nose and asked if that serrated knife was still handy. "Tawny couldn't keep her yapper shut on the ride home. She spilled the beans about Philip."

"When I asked if you were seeing anyone, you made a left turn with your answer. I asked Tawny. She gave it to me straight. When do I get to meet him?"

Tawny butted into the tender moment. "Tomorrow. He's coming for Christmas Eve. I should warn you, Philip is a bit of a hippie."

Grace went into defensive-mode. "Don't listen to her. Philip is a warm, caring man who has long hair."

"And a tattoo of a peace-sign on his arm."

"That doesn't make him a hippie." Grace lifted her pant leg to reveal the infinity tattoo on her ankle. "The four of us have tattoos. That doesn't make us hippies."

"She gets riled so easily."

Grace made a fist but hid it from Karina. "You're lucky there's a child present."

Cody removed his jacket and lifted the sleeve of his t-shirt. On his upper arm was a red heart tattoo with 'Mom' written in blue ink.

Emotion ran amok. There were so many happy tears spilling around the room that if they didn't shut off soon, they'd soon need a canoe. Poor Cody was hugged so much he finally straight-armed them so he could breathe.

In that five-minute span of affection, Isabella's sense of humor emerged. "Ladiessss." She sported an eye patch.

Rich belly laughter replaced the tears.

Grace sniffed and laughed, blew her nose, and laughed some more.

Tawny fell onto the purple beast of a loveseat, snorting.

Elaina slung an arm around Steph. "Happy days."

Isabella gave the thumbs-up.

"Grace." Elaina nodded toward Karina.

Warmth emanated from Grace when she saw Karina wearing an eye patch, too.

Out from under the sofa, came Lula. She ducked her head and surveyed the scene. With an unexpected lunge she landed in Karina's lap; startling her at first, then making her giggle.

Grace traipsed to her granddaughter, knelt down, and pecked her forehead with a kiss. "I love you, sweetie." She looked over her shoulder. "I love you guys, too. Every last one of you. Even you, Tawn'." She cupped her face with her hands. "This is more than any woman could hope for."

"Persimmon said it best – it's the season for hope."

Cody crinkled his brows. "Who's Persimmon?"

* * *

Christmas Eve came and went fast, like someone tampered with the hands on the clock. They sang carols, drank egg nog, ate a scrumptious meal prepared by

Nicholas and Steph, watched *Home Alone* and listened to Karina giggle over Macaulay Culkin's antics with the would-be-thieves, and then drove around Portland to look at Christmas lights. Cody repeatedly commented how wonderful it was to have a white Christmas. Around eight o'clock, they did a FaceTime session with Niccolo and Francesca. An hour later, they did the same thing with Bo and Quentin.

Elaina reflected on how well the evening had gone. Cody approved of Philip. While the girls cleared the table of dirty dishes and cleaned up the mess in the kitchen, Philip had drawn a charcoal portrait of Grace, Cody, Isabella, and Karina. It now graced the fireplace mantel. Because of the time difference between Italy and the U.S., the Italian family of three were tuckered out by eleven and retreated to their third-floor bedroom, leaving the couples alone for a while.

The party of six sat in the living room with the lights dimmed and watched *It's A Wonderful Life.*

Shortly after one in the morning, Chad put his forehead on Elaina's. "Is there any chance in the coming days you and I could go out on a date? We've been together as a group a few times. It would be nice to have you to myself for a night."

"I thought you'd never ask. How does the day after Christmas sound?"

"Perfect."

Elaina dragged him to the archway of the dining room where a sprig of mistletoe beckoned. "Kiss me, Officer C. Ferguson."

"With pleasure."

Involuntary tremors of delight quaked through Elaina when their lips touched. It was a soft meeting of mouths that lasted no more than a few seconds due to having an audience, but it had a mind-boggling impact. By the sparkle in Chad's eyes, it affected him the same. "You're quite the kisser, officer."

"Right back at you, Miss Samuels."

"Get a room," Tawny teased.

"Someday perhaps," Elaina promised with a wink.

Steph yawned. "I had a great time and I hate to send you away, Nicholas, but my butt is dragging."

"I hear ya, doll. The Christmas parties at the restaurant have been great for business but they've taken a toll. I may sleep for days."

Steph led him to the door and stepped on her tiptoes to give him a special goodbye with her lips. When they broke the kiss, she gave him another quick peck on the mouth. "I don't want it to be days before I see you again."

"Philip, they're planning intimate rendezvous'. We should too."

"Mai Tais. My place." Philip gathered Grace is a bear hug. "You have a lot of loving to dole out to your son and his family. So there's no hurry. When you're ready, you know where to find me."

The ever-quiet Bart suggested they do New Year's Eve together. He added, "We have to start the year off right."

Tawny pushed her chest into Bart's. "That's a yes from me."

It took a good fifteen minutes to dispense more kisses,

hugs, and wishes for a Merry Christmas.

When the house was quiet again, Elaina took a bottle of Merlot from the wine rack. Drilling the corkscrew into the cork, she looked at the tired faces of her friends. "I have a lot of sweet memories from Christmas, mostly from when I was a kid, but this one is right up there."

Steph sat wine glasses etched with holly leaves on the counter for Elaina to fill. "We don't have to let it breathe for an hour, do we? I'm not sure I'll hold up that long." She let out a lengthy yawn.

"Hazel said it best – screw that." Tawny chuckled. "I miss those wisecrackers."

Grace handed out the glasses of wine. "All I have to do is look at you guys and they're here."

Elaina lifted her glass. "This has been an incredible journey so far. We've shaken things up with a move to the far corner of the continental U.S." She looked around the kitchen. "This place has taken us out of our comfort zones and from what I've been told we've not yet experienced the full effect. They say the summer months will get a little crazy. I'm up for a little crazy. How about you?"

Glasses clinked in agreement.

"I thrive on crazy. Ask my sons." Instead of melancholy, Tawny beamed with joy. "I expect them to pay us a visit in the middle of the summer nuttiness."

Grace leaned against the counter, with a reflective expression. "I can see Cody, Bo, and Quentin hitting it off. Wouldn't it be great if he talked them into joining us permanently on the east coast? He has subtle influence, ya know. He got his wife and daughter and in-laws to reposition to a snowy place across the big, blue pond."

"I won't hold my breath. For now, I'm content knowing they love me."

"My cookbook is half finished. I decided tonight that it's going to be co-authored. I haven't told Nicholas yet. He'll be tickled. I'm glad to have met someone who has as much enthusiasm for food as I do."

"Isn't it amazing how far we've come, and I'm not talking distance from Ohio. Grace, you said you hated change yet you've done well." Elaina chuckled. "Tawny, the day we left Cherry Ridge you mouthed off to Arden and said dog wardens make great lovers. You're dating a dog warden. None of us could've seen that coming. It just goes to show you anything is possible." She sat her glass down. "I'm the one dating a cop, not Grace as we presumed." She sighed happily. "We've all met someone special. Where these romances go, remains to be seen."

"I'm going to take things slow with Bart. He's quiet. I'm vocal. We couldn't be more different."

"There are similarities, Tawn'. You love animals. He loves animals. You're trying to kick cigarettes. He occasionally smells like tobacco."

Tawny smirked. "Just like me, he's tried to quit. Neither of us has conquered the beast."

"The purple loveseat? Or cigs?"

"Ha. You're a riot, Steph."

"I try."

"Philip and I click. In many ways he's like Brince, which means I have to be extra-careful. If I eventually give Philip my heart, it has to be for the right reasons, not because he reminds me of my late husband."

Elaina enjoyed another sip of wine and pondered Grace's situation. "You've decided to err on the side of caution to be fair to Philip. That says a lot about your character."

"What about you and Chad? Are there handcuffs in your future?"

"You're the one with the handcuff fetish, not me." Elaina jiggled with a laugh, although she was serious when she said, "He's a great guy with a lot to offer a girl. There's some chemistry on the burner. Thankfully, it's just simmering. I'm not ready for it to boil."

"Are you chicken?"

"I don't know. Maybe. There's only one thing I'm fully certain of – my life would be empty without you ladies. And there's nothing I'd rather be doing right now than drinking Merlot with you in Maine."

~ The End ~

** It's been a joy to write this book. Truthfully, I thought this would be the last one in the *Wine and Sweat Pants* series. Now I'm certain there will be a fourth book. Stay tuned. **

Books by Jan Romes

Wine and Sweat Pants Series:
No Sweat Pants Allowed – Wine Club – Book #1
Sipping Sangria – Book #2
Merlot in Maine – Book #3

Texas Boys Falling Fast Series:
Married to Maggie – Book #1
Keeping Kylee – Book #2
Taming Tori – Book #3
Not Without Nancy – Book #4

One Small Fib
Lucky Ducks
Kiss Me
The Gift of Gray
Stay Close, Novac!
Stella in Stilettos
Three Wise Men
The Christmas Contract
Mr. August
Three Days with Molly
Big on Christmas
Wild Goose Chase
Loving Lindy

About the Author

Jan Romes grew up in northwest Ohio in the midst of eight zany siblings. Married to her high school sweetheart for more years than seems possible, she's also a mom, mother-in-law, and grandmother. Jan writes contemporary romance and women's fiction with sharp, witty characters who give as good as they get. When she's not writing, you can find Jan with her nose buried in a book or finding new ways to stay fit. She loves spending time with family and friends. A hopeless romantic, she enjoys sunsets, sappy movies, and sitting around a campfire. Though she doesn't claim to have a green thumb, she takes pride in growing pumpkins, flowers, and veggies. She loves to interact with her readers.

You can follow or communicate with Jan here:
www.authorjanromes.com
www.jantheromancewriter.blogspot.com
www.twitter.com/JanRomes or @janromes
www.facebook.com/jan.romes5
www.goodreads.com/author/show/5240156.Jan_Romes

Made in the USA
Monee, IL
26 June 2022

98643135R00157